The Cola Smile

by

Earl
Underwood

A Detective Jack Storm Mystery

Shoppe Foreman Publishing
Oklahoma City, Oklahoma, USA

Cover image by Luann M. Cox
LMC Photography – www.LuannMCoxPhoto.com

Published by
Shoppe Foreman Publishing
Oklahoma City, Oklahoma, USA
www.ShoppeForeman.com

See last page for place and date of printing.

ISBN-13: 978-1977949134
ISBN-10: 1977949134

Dedication

To my wife Sue,
with all the love God will allow.

Acknowledgements

I give special thanks and acknowledgement to the following:

My wife Sue for her encouragement, support and love that
 keeps me focused.
Shaunie Underwood Shaw, my daughter.
My close friend Earl Dedrick – enjoy your character pal.
My brother-in-law John Paradis – you make a great Captain.
My son-in-law Rolando Corimanya – enjoy your character.
Linda Ward Green, good friend and former co-worker with
 the Lake County Sheriff's Office.
Adria Underwood, my wonderful daughter-in-law who tells
 it like it is.
Wayne Foresman – rest in peace my friend.
Luann M. Cox – thanks for the great cover.
Larry Foreman, my editor and publisher who makes it all
 happen for me.
Finally, to Dakota, you know who you are.

Chapter 1

HURRICANE ALICE, THE FIRST STORM of the season, had made its turn northeast from the southern tip of the Gulf of Mexico and was now on a path that would take it across the southernmost part of Florida. Richard Snyder, a prosecutor for the Dade County State Attorney's office, was working late into the night, finishing up closing arguments for a trial that was to wrap up the following day. It all depended on the hurricane as to whether or not the proceedings would start on time. Luckily, Alice had not had the time to build into a major hurricane and was considered mostly a rain-laden storm, with winds of only eighty-four miles per hour near the center – a minimal hurricane. Still, it was not a storm to be taken lightly. With its lingering bands of showers and wind squalls, Alice was predicted to prevail throughout most of the day as it passed through the Miami area. Still, Richard was now prepared for closing arguments and pleased he had made the decision to stay and finish his work.

It was ten o'clock, dark, rainy and windy when he exited the State Attorney's office and headed for the parking lot. When he stepped outside the wind was already picking up, with gusts of at least forty to fifty miles per hour.

Maybe I should have left earlier, he thought to himself. He had his umbrella out but declined to open it since the wind would immediately turn it inside out or wrench it completely from his hand. He gripped his briefcase tightly in one hand, and with the umbrella and car key in the other he headed for the parking lot, leaning into the wind.

As he neared his car he pressed the button on his key fob and was rewarded with the interior car lights coming on and the doors unlocking. Quickly opening the door he tossed his briefcase and umbrella onto the passenger's seat and climbed in. Staying true to a habit he had picked up many years ago, he felt under the edge of his seat, placing his hand around the grip of his semi-automatic .380 Beretta handgun. At the same time he glanced in the rearview mirror. Satisfied he was alone in his car, he locked the doors and started the engine. Years ago he had been advised by an old detective friend to always check his rear seat before getting into the car, especially when alone at night. It was a habit he had adhered to religiously but tonight it was so windy and rainy he changed his ritual and checked *after* he had gotten in the car.

Pulling out of the parking lot he turned east on Northeast 1st Street and upon reaching North Miami Avenue he turned south, heading to Brickell Avenue. It was only a few miles to his townhouse on Southwest 14th Terrace but it would take him a little longer than usual because of the stormy conditions. There was hardly any traffic on the road, but he still maintained a safe speed. He could see a lot of palm fronds in the road, but no trees were down so far. Now and then he saw a trash can someone forgot to put away blowing down the street. The traffic signals, violently swaying in the wind, were still functioning but probably would lose power before too long. He hoped he could get home and inside his house before the power went out, if it were going to.

At least he didn't have to worry about his wife, Sharon. She had left the day before to visit her ailing mother in Tallahassee. He would have to rough it as far as dinner went, but he didn't feel like cooking anything on this night. Besides, with his luck the power would go out in the middle of cooking.

Just before he reached Southwest 8th Street he saw a Steak n' Shake, still open. *Unbelievable!* he thought. Quickly he turned into the parking lot. With only two cars there he was able to park near the front door. Dashing inside he ordered three burgers to go. After paying his bill he was soon on his way home again, albeit a little wetter now. He thought about eating one of the burgers in the car but decided to wait until he got home where he could wash it down with a nice cold beer.

Richard pulled into his driveway, and the garage door automatically began opening. As he waited for it to open fully he checked the yard and noticed his trees were holding up well. He didn't see any palm fronds in the yard, and his outdoor furniture was still secured. What he didn't see was the man dressed in all black, standing in the dark hugging the wall of the house.

When his car had completely entered the garage, the door began closing. At the last possible second the man in black squatted and slipped into the garage, hiding behind the car. At that angle Richard wouldn't have seen him in the side-view mirrors, even if he had been looking. Once the door had fully closed Richard used his key and entered the house through the kitchen door. He placed the bag of burgers on the counter and proceeded to the living room where he set his briefcase on the floor next to the sofa. He turned on the television to get an update on the hurricane. While he stood for a second watching the weather forecaster, relishing his extended airtime, he failed to hear the kitchen door, which he had neglected to lock, slowly open and quietly close.

All of a sudden his body went into shock. His knees buckled, and, unable to stand, he fell to the floor. Before he could turn to see what had happened, he was struck in the back of the head. Blackness engulfed him before his confused mind could determine what had happened.

When he finally regained consciousness he realized he was bound to one of the dining room chairs. He now knew that he had been shot with a high-powered taser gun, possibly one of those that put out over 50,000 volts. His wrists were strapped to the arms of the chair with plastic ties, and his ankles were secured in the same manner to the lower rungs of the chair. Frantically turning his head, he saw a figure in black standing in the doorway to the kitchen, eating one of the burgers, the wrapper folded back. His hair was plastered from the rain, and he was studying Richard intently.

"I don't think you'll need any food for awhile, and it would be a shame to let these go to waste," the intruder said while slowly chewing.

"Who are you and what do you want?" Richard asked, unable to suppress the tremor in his voice.

"Oh, you'll know soon enough," the intruder said.

"If it's money you want just take it and go. My wallet is in my briefcase by the sofa," Richard said.

"I don't want your money," he said.

"Then what do you want?" Richard asked.

"I want you to look at a picture," said the intruder.

"You had to knock me out and tie me up just to look at a picture?" Richard asked incredulously.

"I didn't *have* to, but it will serve my purpose for now," said the intruder.

Finishing the last bite of the burger the intruder crumpled the wrapper and stuffed it in his pocket, not intending to leave anything behind. He failed to notice that it was half hanging out of his pocket. He walked over and stood in front of Richard, staring hard at him, not saying anything for a few seconds. Then he unzipped his running suit from the top and pulled out a manila folder. It was at this point Richard noticed the intruder was wearing rubber gloves, obviously not wanting to leave any fingerprints in the house. Opening the folder, he pulled a photograph out and held it up for Richard to look at.

"Do you know who this is?" asked the intruder, his voice so soft it almost seemed he was whispering.

Looking at the photograph, Richard immediately recognized who it was, but instead he shook his head.

"I've never seen that person before. Who is he?" he asked with obvious nervousness.

"I know you recognized the person in the picture. So cut the crap," the intruder said in a cold voice.

"NO, I don't know who he is. What is this about?" he asked, the rising fear evident in his voice.

The intruder said nothing for a few seconds, staring at

Richard coldly. Then he reached into his pocket and pulled out a roll of duct tape. Unraveling a piece about ten inches long he tore the piece off and stepping behind Richard he suddenly reached over his head and affixed the tape to his mouth. Richard started struggling, but the intruder slapped him hard in the back of the head. Richard ceased his struggling. The intruder walked back around and faced Richard.

"I'm going to tell you a story, and the tape will ensure that you'll listen without interrupting me," said the intruder. "Do you understand?"

Richard nodded his head slowly, trying to appease the man.

He began by telling Richard who the person in the photograph was, even though he knew that Richard knew. After about ten minutes he stopped talking and smiled, a really cold smile, no warmth in his eyes.

"Now you know why you have to die," he said.

Richard was frantic now, squirming and struggling to get free of his bonds, the plastic slicing into his skin with each effort, the blood beginning to flow freely from his skin-torn wrists. No matter how hard he tried he couldn't free himself from the plastic ties. Tears were beginning to fill his eyes as he silently begged for mercy, but he could see none would be forthcoming. Resigning himself to his fate, Richard was glad that Sharon wasn't home to witness this and become a victim also. His one thought now was relief that she wouldn't be the one to find his body. His son was at a club partying with some college friends, but he didn't expect him home until early morning, if then.

Suddenly the intruder stepped behind Richard and ripped off another strip of duct tape, the tearing noise echoing in the silence of the room. He once again reached over Richard's head and placed the tape over his nose, cutting off his air supply completely. Richard knew it was not going to be long before he suffocated. He began violently struggling, almost turning the chair over. The intruder sat down on the couch and watched in stony silence as the life slowly drained from his victim. Tiny blood vessels began popping in Richard's eyes as he tried to breathe, but no air was available. Soon his eyes rolled back in his head as his oxygen-deprived brain shut down. His head suddenly dropped down onto his chest. The intruder sat there quietly and observed Richard for a few minutes, the cold smile still present on his face.

The wind was picking up, and debris was pelting the windows. He decided he needed to finish his mission and leave before it became worse. Quickly he went into the kitchen and retrieved a steak knife from one of the drawers. Returning to the now deceased body in the chair he began his final task. When he had finished, he stepped back and looked closely at the results. Carved into Richard's forehead were the numbers *241*. Trickles of blood trailed down like scarlet ribbons onto Richard's face. He returned to the kitchen and washed the knife off and placed it back into the drawer.

Taking one last look around to make sure he had left no incriminating evidence, he turned the lights off and left the house. Standing outside in the rain, he held up his hands, allowing the rain to wash the blood from the rubber gloves. He took the gloves off and stuffed them in his front pocket. He would dispose of them later, far away from the scene. Fighting the gusting wind and sheets of blowing rain he walked quickly two blocks away to where he had parked his car.

Once inside, he flicked on a penlight and took a marker from the console. He crossed off the first name on the sheet of paper he had retrieved from the passenger's seat. Wearing the same cold smile he had exhibited in the house, he started the car, made a u-turn and headed north, taking the same route his victim had driven an hour earlier on his way home.

Chapter 2

JACK STORM, HOMICIDE DETECTIVE for the Hialeah Police Department going on fourteen years now, made a mad dash to his car. He was trying to keep from getting drenched by the rain squall that had moved in about fifteen minutes earlier. It looked as if Hurricane Alice was going to reach the area mid-morning. The forecasters said that it had lost some of its punch. The winds had died down to sixty miles per hour near the small center with gusts up to seventy miles per hour in some bands. It could still do some damage but probably not too severe, if it spawned no tornadoes. Mostly it would dump a lot of rain, and the area sure could use it. The summer had been a scorcher, and conditions were drier than normal.

After getting into his city-issued car, a new 2013 Dodge Charger, steel-gray in color, which he loved, he keyed his radio and told dispatch he was now on duty. The dispatcher came back and advised him he was to report directly to Captain Paradis in the Criminal Investigations Division, commonly referred to as "C.I.D.," once he arrived at the station.

"10-4," he replied. "It may take a little longer this morning with the weather conditions."

He started the car, loving the throaty roar of the police interceptor engine when he revved it. Backing out of the driveway of his house, he could see that some neighbors had failed to heed the advice from the Weather Service about securing garbage cans. He could see several cans blowing down the street and onto the sidewalks. Maneuvering around the ones in the street, he headed for the station.

He wondered what the Captain wanted. It was seven-thirty in the morning and usually Captain Paradis was not in until around nine. Probably, as it happened with most hurricanes that hit the area, all of the detectives would forego their investigations and simply drive around the city, assisting where needed. But the Captain wouldn't want to see him for that – the Lieutenant in road patrol made that decision. The extra manpower would help deter a lot of crime with so much police visibility. It was a measure that made sense because the criminal element didn't care if a hurricane was in the area or not. In fact, they would take advantage of it to cover up their criminal activity. A lot of businesses would be closed until the storm passed, and that made easy targets for the burglars, especially if the power was off. That would eliminate the worry of most alarms.

Jack, or "Stormy," as most of his fellow detectives called him, headed for East 8th Avenue where the station was located. As he drove, the wind buffeted his car, at times almost blowing him off the road. He began thinking of the cases he needed to follow up on but more than likely would not get to on this day.

He was to be assigned a new partner today. Gil Torres, his old partner for the last fourteen years, had taken retirement. His wife wanted to travel and at fifty-nine years of age, he was more than ready to take it easy. It had been hard to say good-by, but they promised to keep in touch. He intended to do just that. Gil had been like a father figure to him and had taught him the basics of investigations when they had paired up all those years ago. He had also given him insight to some investigative techniques that didn't come in a manual. They were old school but very effective, and he was never afraid to use them.

Now, he hoped that his new partner would be a good fit for him. A lot of detectives never got comfortable with new partners, probably because they didn't have the patience to teach them. Jack didn't really know if he had the necessary patience himself since he had always been with the same partner. He would soon find out though and would deal with it the best he could.

The drive to C.I.D. was uneventful, other than some tree limbs on the road and fast moving rain squalls at times. As he pulled into the parking lot, the rain slackened just enough for him to get into the building without getting drenched. Upon entering the squad room, he saw several other detectives standing around laughing, drinking coffee and chatting about God knows what.

"Hey, Stormy, shoot anybody this morning!" laughed Ben Harper.

During his fourteen years in C.I.D. Stormy had been involved in five shootings, all justified by Florida Department of Law Enforcement. Ben was considered the jokester of C.I.D. and never meant any real harm, but sometimes he could be so crude.

"No, but thought about it a few times on the way here," Stormy replied, with a tolerant grin.

"What are you doing here so early?" asked Parsons.

"Got a call the Captain wanted to see me," said Stormy.

"Probably wants to give you a medal for not shooting anyone this week," Ben chuckled.

"You're a funny man, Ben," said Stormy, shaking his head.

Stormy walked down the hall leaving the chuckles behind and lightly rapped on the Captains door.

"Come on in, Stormy," called out the Captain, looking through the office window.

Entering the office he was told to take a seat. Now his curiosity was piqued because normally when in the Captain's office you didn't sit unless you were in trouble. His mind raced to determine what he had done recently to warrant this summons.

"What I'm about to tell you is strictly confidential, at this point," began the Captain.

"Last night between eleven and midnight, Richard Snyder, a prosecutor for the State Attorney's office, was found murdered in his home. At this time the Miami homicide investigators don't have a single lead, and the media only knows that Miami is investigating the death of a prosecutor. There are some things about the body that have not been released, but you'll be brought up to speed once you get there. Snyder was alone in the house because his wife was out of town. She was contacted this morning using Snyder's phone and was asked to return home. She'll be driven back by a Tallahassee police officer for obvious reasons.

"Now, I know what you're thinking, why am I telling you about a homicide out of our jurisdiction? It's because you were requested by Major Aramas, who is in charge of C.I.D. at the Miami Police Department. He knows about the deep-cover confidential informant you have and how for the last few years you've gleaned so much vital information from him. He needs you to contact your informant later and see if there's any word on the street about this murder. In addition, you'll be attached to Miami C.I.D. indefinitely. To assist in the investigation, at the Major's request of course. Do you have any questions?"

"Is that all the information you have?"

"What I told you is everything I was told," replied the Captain.

"Then I best be getting to Miami C.I.D. and find out more," said Stormy.

"Before you leave I need to introduce you to your new partner."

"Oh, yeah, Captain, about that. Are you sure I need a new partner right now, I mean, couldn't it wait until next week?" asked Stormy.

"Now is as good a time as any Stormy. I know it'll take some getting used to since Gil retired. We all know how well you both worked together, but you know departmental policy, each detective *will* be paired with a partner. Besides, this will be a good time for your new partner to get his feet wet."

"Okay, Captain, bring him in," Stormy sighed.

Captain Paradis picked up his phone and told the receptionist, Adria, to send in the new detective. As Stormy waited he wondered if he would know the new guy when he came in. At one time or another he had either worked with most of the officers on the road or met them in some other manner. When the new guy walked in Stormy knew he had never seen him before. He was probably in his mid-twenties, around six feet in height and had an athletic build. He had dark hair and deep brown eyes. *Not a bad looking dude,* he thought. Standing, he stuck out his hand and was rewarded with a firm handshake.

"Detective Jack Storm, meet your new partner, Rolando Fuentes."

"Pleased to meet you, Rolando," replied Jack.

"Likewise, and may I call you Stormy?"

"No problem, that's what most everyone calls me," he said.

"Okay, Stormy will brief you on the way out," said the Captain, dismissing them.

Stormy stood and left the office, Rolando following. When they passed through the squad room, they received a few curious looks, but no comments were made this time. Stopping at his desk, Stormy motioned for Rolando to take a seat at the desk opposite his.

"That will be yours, for now," he said.

"For now?" asked Rolando.

"Well, not every new detective works out. Some are cut out for it, and some decide they want to get back on the road," said Jack.

"I'll work out. This has been my dream for a long time," said Rolando.

"We'll see," said Jack. "We'll see."

As Rolando began organizing the desk Jack got on his private cell phone to contact his C.I., or confidential informant. He never used the office phone in case Pablo was with someone who could see the caller I.D. and would know he was talking with the police. While the phone was ringing, he looked at the desk Rolando was now occupying, Gil's old desk. He felt a twinge of guilt that someone else would be using it now, but then he reminded himself, it was a piece of furniture and Gil was gone, not coming back.

****

The Mariel Boatlift was a mass emigration of Cubans who departed from Cuba's Mariel Harbor for the United States between April and October, 1980. The event was precipitated by a sharp downturn in the Cuban economy which led to internal tensions on the island and a bid by up to 10,000 Cubans to gain asylum in the Peruvian embassy. The Cuban Government subsequently announced that anyone who wanted to leave could do so, and an exodus by boat started shortly afterward. It was soon discovered that a number of the exiles had been released from Cuban jails and mental health facilities. The exodus started to have negative political implications for U.S. President Jimmy Carter. The Mariel boatlift was ended by mutual agreement between the two governments involved in October 1980. By that point, as many as 125,000 Cubans had made the journey to Florida.

Pablo Gondar was a young man when he was released from a Cuban prison and allowed to join the Boatlift. He ended up in the Miami area after being processed in Key West, where the boat he was on came ashore. For a few years he kept his nose clean, taking menial jobs and avoiding trouble.

But getting by from small paycheck to paycheck wasn't cutting it for him. He wanted more so in the mid-eighties he walked into the Hialeah Police Department and asked to speak with a detective. Gil Torres had the good fortune to be the one to talk with him. He told Gil how he had been friends with most of the criminals that came over on the boatlift and was willing, for money of course, to become an informant. Gil could see the opportunity that had presented itself and took full advantage of it.

After the influx of exiles from the Boatlift, criminal activity had soared all over Dade County. It wasn't long before Gil was making arrest after arrest. He was recovering massive amounts of stolen property and solving homicides, both in Hialeah and Miami. The Hialeah Police Detective Bureau had a slush fund that was set aside strictly for informants. There was a considerable amount of money in it since it was continuously being replenished with confiscated drug money, of which there was no shortage.

Shortly after Jack became Gil's partner around 2000, he was introduced to Pablo, and the game was on from there. They made police officer of the month more times than they could count. They also made a name for themselves in the greater Miami area with their exemplary investigative skills. It was rumored that a contract had been put out on both of them at one time by the so-called

"Cuban Mafia," so they had been extra careful, even changing cars. More than once they were called upon to help other agencies with an investigation.

But they never gave up the name or location of their informant, Pablo. Gil even served a day in jail once for contempt of court when he had refused a judge's order to divulge his informants name for the defense. He told the judge, "If I do that he'll be dead before I walk out of this courtroom!" He stuck to his guns and gained a lot of respect from within the law enforcement community.

Pablo was now in his early fifties and still a valuable informant for Jack. Sitting in his room in downtown Miami on Southwest 8th Street, he was looking out the window from the second floor, watching the old men play dominoes in front of a Cuban cafe. The storm was no deterrent to them as it was a ritual they would never give up. Besides, they were under the overhang of a balcony. Now and then they would pause when a gust of wind blew rain in on them. Still they played on!

Pablo smiled and thought of the home he had left so many, many years ago in Cuba. The one thing the Cubans in Miami did do was turn Southwest 8th Street into an area that reminded them of home in Cuba. Not many Anglos worked or came to this area now.

Suddenly he was jolted from his thoughts when his cell phone began to ring. He looked at the caller I.D. and saw that it was Jack's private phone. He quickly answered it, hoping he was going to get a chance to make some money. He was tapped out and hadn't been called on for a couple of weeks now.

"*Hola*, he said, *Que Pasa?*"

"*Hola,* Pablo, how goes it," asked Stormy.

"Slow my friend, very slow. I hope you have something for me," replied Pablo.

"It's possible, Pablo, depending on what you know about the murder of a prosecutor in Miami last night."

"I haven't heard anything, but I'll get right on it," said Pablo.

"As soon as you find out anything, and I mean anything, Pablo, call me," said Stormy.

"You know I will, *amigo.*"

"Okay, go work your magic, and I'll talk with you later," said Stormy, breaking the connection.

"Who was that?" asked Rolando.

"Maybe you'll get to meet him someday," Stormy said. "But not right now. Grab whatever gear you need and let's go."

They left the office and dashed to Jack's car. The rain was really coming down now, and they were almost soaked by the time they got inside the vehicle. The storm was upon them as the forecasters had predicted, but the winds had diminished to much less than hurricane force. Still, it made for a nasty mess. The highest winds were on the east side of the storm, and that allowed the heaviest rain and wind to be directed well into the Homestead area and the Keys.

Stormy drove down LeJuene Road to 103rd Street and took a left. He decided to drive to I-95 and take it down to Miami P.D. instead of the usual route. He figured it would take the same amount of time, and he was in no hurry. Once he made the turn onto 103rd Street, he started talking to Rolando.

"First, let me say welcome to C.I.D.," he began. "As you know I had a partner for many years, and we were a great team. We could anticipate each other's moves, finish each other's sentences and took our job seriously. I will admit to you that I didn't want a new partner but departmental policy dictates that we have to have one. Now that you're here, there are some rules that you *will* follow, to a T, or you will be back on the road. Some of these rules are the department's rules and some are unspoken rules. Also, some are *my* rules. Tell me now if you don't think you can follow *my* rules, which will seem a little unorthodox."

"I've been a rule follower all my life, and now will be no different," replied Rolando. "I personally feel that a great partnership develops when two people understand and trust each other unconditionally. If you have personal rules, and they won't someday land me in jail, I don't care how unorthodox they are. I'll follow them the best as I can."

"Well said," answered Stormy. "I'll give you the department rules regarding investigations first."

For fifteen minutes Stormy recited the rules, pausing for a question now and then. When he had finished, he didn't stop, but just went into some unspoken rules, such as detectives' perks and their authority on crime scenes, and so forth. Then he said, "Now I'll give you the rules that you cannot break or you're out."

"As senior partner on this team, whatever I say goes, without question, of course unless you think it's illegal. Any input you have on a case that we work on together will be evaluated and used if pertinent. You will do all the paperwork unless I say otherwise. And lastly, never *ever* try to go around me to find out something or get something done. *I mean never*! We work as a team and in order to be effective we have to be on the same page. Do you have any questions?"

"None whatsoever," responded Rolando.

"Good, now I'll tell you why we're going to Miami C.I.D."

Stormy brought Rolando up to speed with everything he knew about the murder last night. He told him they would be attached to the Miami C.I.D. until further notice.

"That's all I have for now, but I'm sure we'll learn more once we get there," said Stormy.

Rolando wanted to ask why they were being attached to Miami C.I.D. but didn't dare after he had just been given the "Stormy" rules. He would find out soon enough.

They pulled into the Miami Police Department parking lot, showed the guard their identification and were allowed to park in the rear. They exited the car and went into the building. At the front desk Stormy showed his badge to the officer on duty and asked to see Major Aramas. When the officer, in a holier-than-thou voice asked the nature of his business, Stormy's eyes turned a dangerous gray and he replied, "Why don't you ask him, *he* sent for *me*?" Looking into Stormy's eyes the officer could see no humor and meekly picked up the phone. When he had the Major on the line and told him who was there he was told to send him up immediately. The desk officer raised his eyebrows and with a little more respect gave directions to the Major's office. All of this was not lost on

Rolando. He was starting to see things a little differently now. Evidently Stormy had a reputation and a lot of respect with the brass, not only at Hialeah but in Miami, also.

Stormy and Rolando exited the elevator on the third floor. They were directed by the receptionist to Major Aramas' office, near the end of the large open room. There were at least a dozen detectives in the room, all either on the phone or working their computers. Stormy assumed they all were working on the murder, and his assumptions were correct. Stormy knocked on the Major's door, and a voice inside called out for them to come in.

"Stormy, good to see you," the Major said, rising from his chair, extending his hand.

"Good to see you too, Bob….I mean, Major," Stormy said, catching the slip in front of Rolando. He and Major Roberto Aramas had been on other cases together and even socialized occasionally. They were first name friends, off the job of course, and had a genuine respect for each other. No one in Hialeah knew about their friendship, not even Captain Paradis, and Stormy wanted to keep it that way. Of course, the little slip in front of Rolando would have to be addressed later.

"Major, this is my new partner, Rolando Fuentes."

"Pleased to meet you, Detective Fuentes. Please, both of you have a seat, and I'll fill you in on where we are in the investigation. By the way, Stormy, did you get a chance to talk with your C.I.?"

"I did, but he's heard nothing yet. He's on the street now putting his ear to the ground," said Stormy.

"I know Captain Paradis told you some of what this is

21

about and the name of who was murdered. What he was not told is the state the body was in when it was found. The media is not aware of it either. They only think it was a murder, home invasion or something.

"Who found the body?" asked Stormy.

"It was the son who came home early this morning after a night of partying. It was quite a shock to him, and we're getting him counseling now."

"I was told the wife was out of town," said Stormy.

"Yes, she was visiting her mother in Tallahassee."

"Tell me about the state of the body," asked Stormy.

"He was suffocated," said the Major.

"What's' so unusual about that?"

Stormy glanced over at Rolando and saw that he was taking notes on a small pad.

"Put the pad away, Rolando," he said.

Without a word the pad was put back into his pocket. He was learning the rules fast. Do as you were told until you had proven yourself an equal.

"Again, Major, what's' so unusual about a strangling?"

"It's how he was strangled, and there are other unusual details," said the Major.

"Please, go on," Stormy apologized.

"He was bound by his wrists and legs to a chair with plastic ties, the kind used in wrapping wiring harnesses. Then duct tape was placed around his mouth and nose, cutting off his air supply. It must have been horrible. It was evident he struggled to break the plastic ties because of the deep cuts in his wrists. And the real kicker, there was a set of numbers carved into his forehead with a kitchen knife."

"What numbers?"

"241," said the Major.

"Any idea what they mean?" asked Stormy.

"Not a clue yet," said the Major, "but, we think it may or *may not* mean something."

"No prints? No evidence of any kind?" Stormy asked, already knowing the answer.

"Nothing at all, not even one fingerprint. Whoever it was they were very careful, even washing off the knife used to carve the numbers. We sprayed all the kitchen knives with Luminol and, bingo, found one that had been washed off but still had a trace of blood, which matched the victim's, around the edge of the wooden handle. Luckily for us the perpetrator didn't use bleach to wash it."

"My interest is the numbers and what they mean," said Stormy. "It may be random and mean nothing, but I'm not so sure. I have a funny feeling about this."

"I would like to see the pictures of the crime scene and talk with the lead detective if you don't mind," Stormy said.

"No problem, I've told my investigators to work with you and give you access to anything you need," replied the Major.

The Major walked into the squad room and called out to Detective Leo Sharp.

"Leo, this is Detective Storm from Hialeah. He's the one I talked with you about, and this is his partner Detective Fuentes. They'll be working with you, but you're still the lead on this case. He needs to see the crime scene photos and ask you some questions."

"Storm, heard a lot about you," said Leo.

"Yeah, I get around," smiled Stormy.

"Follow me to my desk, and we'll get those photos for you," Leo said.

The photos of the victim were gruesome but Stormy had seen worse, much worse. He and Gil had worked a mass murder where all five of the victims were given a "Columbian necktie" – their throats cut and their tongues pulled down and out of the cut below the chin. As Stormy looked at each photo he passed it on to Rolando. *At least Rolando doesn't seem squeamish looking at dead bodies,* thought Stormy. In fact, it seemed as if he had been that route before. He would have to ask him about that later.

"I'll need copies of these," said Stormy.

"Keep those, we have duplicates," replied Leo.

"Leo, anything else unusual you can tell me about the scene?" asked Stormy.

"Just that it was so clean, almost sterile you would say. Smudges indicate gloves were worn. Wet footprints on the floor, but nothing back on those yet. So we have nothing. I'm going back to the scene later to double-check," said Leo.

"I'll be out on my own for awhile following up something, so give me a call if you find anything," said Stormy, giving him his cell number.

"I will, and you do the same," said Leo.

Stormy and Rolando left the building. As they passed through the lobby the desk officer turned his head, avoiding eye contact with Stormy.

In the car as they were pulling out, Rolando asked,

"What are we doing now?"

"I want to scout out the victim's house and see if anything was missed on the outside," replied Stormy.

"By the way, I noticed you weren't bothered by the photos." Stormy said.

"I did a tour in Iraq, saw plenty of dead bodies," Rolando responded.

They drove in silence the remainder of the way to Richard's home. Stormy had seen the address on Leo's report. The rain was mostly gone, and the wind only came in small gusts now. Clearly the storm was on its way out to sea.

When they arrived at the house, yellow crime scene tape was stretched across the driveway and up to the walls of the house. One solitary officer was stuck with the task of securing the scene. He was sitting in his car in front of the driveway. He got out as Stormy and Rolando walked up to his car.

"Sorry guys, this is a crime scene, and you'll have to leave," said the officer, thinking they were reporters.

Stormy pulled his badge out and told the officer, "Major Aramas has given me authorization to go over the crime scene," said Stormy.

"I'm sorry, sir, I haven't received any orders allowing anyone other than our detectives on the scene," said the officer.

At that moment Leo pulled up in front of the squad car, got out and told the officer, "Its okay, they're working with us on this case." Turning to Stormy he said, "You know, we *could* have ridden together."

"We could have, but I'll be going in another direction

when we leave and you wouldn't have wanted to walk back to your office, would you? Look, Leo, I'm not trying to be difficult, but I have my own style of investigating, and it doesn't include hanging around an office or being a chauffeur."

"I understand, but I want you to understand something too. I'm not some rookie detective. This is my case and when it's solved, it'll be through teamwork. So, let's try to work together, shall we?" stated Leo.

"Understood," said Stormy.

Leo lifted the crime scene tape and held it for Stormy and Rolando to pass under. He proceeded to the house and went inside while Stormy walked around outside. Rolando asked if there was anything he should be looking for, but Stormy asked him to go inside and observe Leo and to let him know what was found.

Stormy walked slowly, scanning the ground, not knowing what he was looking for. As he approached the house, he noticed a piece of paper the wind had blown onto a hedge. It seemed out of place, so he stepped onto the grass and walked up to the hedge. It was a wrapper similar to what fast food places use to wrap their sandwiches. He slipped on a pair of rubber gloves – he always carried a pair in his back pocket – and retrieved the paper. The wrapper had a logo faintly imprinted in a continuous pattern on it. It was from Steak n' Shake! Suddenly a bell went off in his head. He had seen in the crime scene photos a Steak n' Shake bag sitting on the kitchen counter. *Why would the wrapper be out here? Did Richard eat a burger on the way home and just throw the wrapper down in his own yard? It seems highly unlikely since the yard is so immaculate.*

He walked back to the patrol car and asked the officer if he had an evidence bag. The officer opened his trunk and found one, which he gave to Stormy. Stormy put the wrapper in the bag and tagged it. He heard voices and observed Leo and Rolando laughing as they came out of the house. So far Rolando hadn't done anything wrong, like asking stupid questions a lot of rookies asked. He seemed to have bonded with Leo fairly quickly, too. It didn't bother Stormy – after all, Rolando seemed to be a personable guy.

"Find anything?" asked Leo.

"As a matter-of-fact I did," answered Stormy.

Holding up the evidence bag he showed it to Leo.

"Wasn't there a Steak n' Shake bag on the kitchen counter when you were doing your investigation this morning?" asked Stormy.

"Yeah, there were two burgers in it. I guess the poor fellow didn't get a chance to eat them," said Leo.

For the first time Rolando spoke up, "What's the importance of the wrapper if you don't mind me asking?" he said.

"I think that either Richard ate a burger on the way home and threw the wrapper down when he got out of the car, or the intruder ate one and threw it down when he left. The first scenario is highly unlikely if you notice the condition of the yard. He took too much pride in his care of the yard to just throw trash on it. That would leave the second option, but that wouldn't make sense either since the intruder took such care inside to not leave prints or evidence. So that leaves only one thing to do and that is to send it for DNA testing. As for prints, you said gloves were worn, so I doubt there will be any. If it's Richard's, then I was wrong. If it happens to be an unknown, we'll run it through the lab to see if we can find a match."

"I have to give a deposition when I leave here, so can you take it to Miami P.D. and enter it into evidence for me?" asked Leo.

"Sure, but it may be tomorrow as I need to go to Hialeah and follow up on something," said Stormy.

"No problem, talk with you later, and good work. I don't know how the others missed it when they swept the scene outside," said Leo.

"I guess we have to consider the weather conditions. It wouldn't have been too hard to miss," answered Stormy.

They got into their respective cars and left the scene, Leo heading to the Dade County Courthouse and Stormy for Hialeah. During the ride Rolando questioned Stormy about DNA testing.

"What will they do if they find DNA on the paper?" he asked.

"They'll run it through the system to see if there's a match," replied Stormy.

"What if they get a match? Does that tell them who it belongs to?"

"If they have been arrested for anything in the past, it's possible, according to whether or not a swab was taken during booking," said Stormy.

The rest of the drive was mostly mundane conversation, and soon they were back at C.I.D. in Hialeah. Once in the building, Stormy told Rolando to write a report on their activities of the day so far, but to not request a case number for it. Rolando nodded, not asking why. He had learned better already. If Rolando had thought about it, he would have known that it was a Miami case, not Hialeah's.

Stormy pulled out his cell phone and dialed Pablo's number. It rang several times and went to voice mail. Stormy left a message telling Pablo to give him a call when possible, without saying his name. Pablo would know who it was.

He arose from his desk and went to Captain Paradis' office. Rapping lightly he was called in, Adria passing him on the way out. The Captain motioned for him to take a seat.

"You're back early," he said.

"I just wanted to keep you in the loop," replied Stormy, "And I needed to postpone a couple of meetings I had scheduled today,"

"What have you learned that I need to know about?' asked the Captain.

"The Miami investigators think it's a random killing, possibly a home invasion or burglar caught in the act, but I have a strange feeling it is much more than that," said Stormy.

"What makes you think that?" asked Captain Paradis.

"Just a gut feeling plus the ritual that was performed on the victim," continued Stormy. "Something tells me that it was personal, very personal."

"What was the condition of the body that has you concerned?" asked the Captain.

"He was tied to a chair and duct tape placed over his mouth and nose. A horrible way to go, but there's something else. The perpetrator used a kitchen knife and carved numbers onto his forehead."

"Numbers? What numbers?"

"241."

"Do you have any idea what they mean?"

"Not a clue. I suppose they could be a date, year or anything. I just don't know yet," Stormy said.

Stormy told the Captain about the sandwich wrapper and his theory. The Captain thought about it for a minute and agreed with him.

"I'm going to leave Rolando here to do some paperwork while I go track down my C.I., if you don't mind Captain," said Stormy.

"I take it you haven't told Rolando about your C.I. yet," replied the Captain.

"He doesn't need to know yet. I have to wait and see if he works out. If he doesn't, I don't need someone knowing his name or location. One slip of the tongue in a bar or anywhere, and it could spell disaster for my C.I. And I'm not willing to take that chance yet."

"Okay, leave him here. I'll keep him busy," said Captain Paradis.

"Thanks, Captain, and, when his hours are up, let him go home. I'll pick him up here in the morning."

"Alright, just keep me informed on your progress."

Stormy spent the rest of the day making contacts on some pressing cases, clearing up his calendar so he could devote his time to the murder of the prosecutor. Before long it was time to quit for the day, and he headed home, stopping to pick up some Cuban food for dinner. After he had eaten he watched a little television. When he started seeing the back of his eyelids, he decided he needed to go to bed.

****

Judge Scott Hanson left the Lonely Wolf Bar at 9 p.m. sharp. His wife was going to throw a fit when he got home. It was the second time this week he had stayed out late after work. He worked hard and figured he deserved some time out with the "boys" – fellow judges and lawyers. The Lonely Wolf was a local hangout near the Dade County Courthouse and a lot of professionals stopped in after work for a quick drink, or as in Judge Hanson's case, not so quick.

The rain from the hurricane had all but gone now, the winds down to a light breeze, the stars beginning to dot the clearing skies. He slowly walked to his car, a little tipsy but still in control. Opening his car door he climbed in, fastened the seat belt and began to put the key in the ignition when all of a sudden he was in agonizing pain. He couldn't control his body and slumped back in the seat, almost falling over into the passenger's side, the seat belt keeping him from doing so. He could feel himself being pulled up and someone from behind binding him to the seat around the shoulders with duct tape.

As he began to regain some control, the door to the passenger side opened, and a stranger dressed in all black got in and sat beside him. He immediately fastened his wrists to the steering wheel with plastic ties. The intruder produced a photo and stuck it in front of his face, asking, "Do you know who this is?"

Judge Hanson looked at the photo, his eyes still blurry

from the jolt he had taken, not to mention the amount of alcohol he had consumed. Immediately he recognized the person in the picture. Fearfully he nodded his head in assent. The stranger flashed a smile, but not a friendly one. His eyes were like bottomless pits, no emotion whatsoever in them.

The intruder didn't say another word. He just took a strip of duct tape and placed it over the judge's mouth. Then he produced another strip and put it over his nose, cutting off his air. The judge began struggling, making animal noises, jerking and trying to breathe, but no breath was forthcoming. He couldn't even expel what little air he had left in his lungs before the tape had been slapped on. Within a minute or so he was dead. The intruder then took a knife out of his pocket, and exhibiting his cold smile, began his work.

Chapter 3

THE LOUD MUSICAL RINGTONE of his cell phone, the theme for *The Good, the Bad and the Ugly,* woke Stormy out of a sound sleep. For a second or two he fought his grogginess to focus on his caller I.D., wondering who was calling him at such an ungodly hour. The radio clock by the bed showed that it was only six in the morning. Not recognizing the number, he still answered. *It better not be a wrong number,* he thought to himself.

"WHAT?" he asked obviously irritated.

"Sorry, Stormy, but we have another one," said the caller.

"Who is this?" he asked, still shaking off the grogginess.

"It's Leo. Get your ass out of bed Stormy. We just had another murder with the same M.O., and this time it's a judge!"

"I'll be there in forty-five minutes," replied Stormy, jumping out of bed and now wide awake.

After quickly showering, he smiled to himself. He was right – it was not a random killing of the prosecutor. As he dressed he thought about his meeting earlier with Pablo, and how there was no word on the street about the murder. Pablo told him he would keep trying, and Stormy gave him two twenty-dollar bills. He would get it back from the slush fund later. He clipped his badge onto his belt, grabbed his gun and keys and headed out the door. When he got to his car parked in the driveway, he noticed right away that the driver's door was not closed completely. Knowing that he was always careful about locking his car, even though his neighborhood was a relatively crime free one, he became concerned. Carefully he looked inside the car and then got down on his knees and looked at the undercarriage. Seeing nothing out of the ordinary, he walked to the passenger's side and slowly opened the door, in case the driver's door was booby-trapped in some manner. It wouldn't be the first time that a disgruntled thug had tried to get even with him. Looking around the interior of the car he couldn't see anything out of the ordinary. Nothing seemed to be missing...W*ait, where is the evidence bag with the wrapper?* he thought.

Now he searched the car more carefully, looking under the seats and in the glove box. The evidence bag had been placed on the floorboard on the passenger's side, and now it was gone. He called the Communications Center on his cell phone and asked for the shift sergeant. After explaining what he had found he asked the shift sergeant to have C.S.I. come out and process the car, although he was sure that no prints would be lifted. He also asked the sergeant to have one of the detectives on night duty come and pick him up. He would use another car from the motor pool for the time being.

Detective Stan Coleman beat C.S.I. to Stormy's house by several minutes. From experience he knew that you didn't keep Stormy waiting too long. As they were getting ready to leave, C.S.I. pulled up and Stormy told them to tow the car to the station and work on it there. He didn't want the neighbors waking up to a virtual crime scene in the neighborhood. He got in the car with Stan, and they headed for the station. On the way he called dispatch and requested they call Rolando, telling him to be at the station as quickly as he could get there.

Arriving at the station Stormy had Stan let him out at the motor pool, where he signed out another car. It wasn't as new or as nice as his, but it would have to do for now. He drove it to the rear of the station and went inside to wait for Rolando. He was still wracking his brain trying to figure out if the car burglar had picked his car at random or if he had been targeted. It was possible the thief was looking for something of value and just took the bag for the hell of it. But that didn't seem likely. The evidence bag would be of no value to him.

His cell rang, and it was Leo, asking if he was on the way. He told him he would be leaving the station within ten minutes. He'd have to leave Rolando behind if he wasn't there by then. Just as he hung up the phone, Rolando walked in, looking fresh and ready to go. Young guys were starting to really piss him off with their abundance of energy. He was still half asleep, but then again, he wasn't as young as he used to be.

"Good morning," Rolando cheerfully piped.

"If you say so," said Stormy. "Don't sit down. We have to go, *now*."

On the way out Rolando asked what was happening and why the rush. Stormy told him about the murder of the judge hours earlier. Rolando raised his eyebrows and said, "Another one this quickly!"

"I had a feeling that the first one was not random," said Stormy.

"What do you think, maybe a serial killer?" asked Rolando.

"I don't know, but it sure has the makings of one."

They stopped at a Circle K and grabbed a cup of coffee before heading to the Miami Police Department. Sipping the scalding coffee, they maintained silence, each lost in their individual thoughts during the drive. When they arrived, parked the car and went inside, the desk officer glanced at their I.D. cards and told them they were expected. Stepping out of the elevator they saw that a flurry of activity was going on in the room. Leo looked up and motioned them to follow him into his office.

"It looks like your hunch was right," he said to Stormy.

"About it not being random?"

"Yeah, the crime scene and condition of the body was the same except the judge was in his car parked outside a bar."

"What about the numbers?"

"Yep, right on the forehead, 241!"

"I don't think we have a serial killer," said Stormy.

"Why not? Everything is the same, like he's making a statement," replied Leo.

"Exactly. He's making a statement, as if he has a vendetta against certain people. I think this is personal, and that there will be more. We need to really try to figure out what the numbers mean because I think that's the key to solving this and hopefully making an arrest. The first thing is to see if the judge and prosecutor were connected and in what way."

"Rolando, I want you to look into the possibility that *241* is maybe part of a case number that ties both of them together, you can do that by checking with the judge's secretary and at the State Attorney's Office," said Stormy.

"There won't be anyone at their offices this early," Rolando said.

"It's seven-thirty, so grab some coffee and wait for them," Stormy replied.

"Leo, can you arrange for a vehicle for Rolando to use temporarily?" asked Stormy.

"No problem. Come with me Rolando."

"I'll ride down the elevator with you. I want to see the judge's car. Is it in your compound, Leo?" asked Stormy.

"Yes, it was towed in after processing this morning. When we get to the lobby I'll direct you to the back door which leads to the compound."

When they exited the elevator, Leo walked with Stormy around the corner of the front desk. Suddenly Stormy stopped, looking around the lobby, a puzzled look on his face.

"What's wrong?" asked Leo.

"I don't know, something just caught my eye that set off bells, but I can't seem to see what it was right now. Maybe it was nothing. Which way to the back door?"

After being shown the way to the compound, Stormy went out the back door and flashed his I.D. to the officer guarding the gate. After checking with the front desk and getting the okay, he let Stormy into the compound, pointing out the judge's vehicle. Stormy opened the driver's door and looked inside, careful to not touch anything.

Closing his eyes, he visualized how it went down. The judge entered the car not realizing someone was in the back seat. He was incapacitated somehow, and his wrists were fastened to the steering wheel. Thinking about it, he realized that the killer had to go around and get into the front seat to fasten the judge's wrists to the steering wheel. *How did he render the judge helpless? Did he knock him out?* He'd have to ask Leo when he got back upstairs. While he was running the scenario through his mind, Leo walked up.

"Did Rolando get off okay?" he asked.

"Yeah, he just left. I told him if it took too long to just drive the car back to Hialeah and return it in the morning," said Leo. "By the way, I got a preliminary report from the coroner on the prosecutor.".

"What did it say?" asked Stormy.

"According to the nerve endings under the skin, there was evidence that he had been shocked, probably with a taser or stun gun of some type," replied Leo.

"That would fit in with what I was just thinking," Stormy said. "I was trying to figure out how he could incapacitate the judge from the back seat enough to go around and secure him to the steering wheel. I'll bet you a doughnut that the coroner's report on the judge will show the same thing."

"So now we know how, we just need to find out why," said Leo.

"Hopefully Rolando will come up with a case number

that will link them together, but I don't think that's the connection," said Stormy.

"Why not?" asked Leo.

"Most all agencies use case numbers with one or more letters in front of the number and besides, that number is so short it would have to be a case from fifty years ago or more."

"Yeah, I see where you're going with this. So that means we have to come up with another idea on what it means."

"Let's go back up to your office and brainstorm some," said Stormy.

"I know the answer already, but did your C.S.I. get any prints off the car or maybe off the tape?" asked Stormy.

"No, it's like you figured, he wore gloves in both instances and smudges were the only thing on the door handles and tape."

"We need to stop this guy quickly in case he has more victims in mind," Stormy muttered.

They went back upstairs and, after getting a cup of coffee, sat down at Leo's desk.

"I have some bad news for you, Leo," said Stormy, as he took a sip of the bitter coffee. It must have been made hours ago.

"What's the bad news?" Leo asked.

"I didn't get a chance to log in the evidence we found at the prosecutor's house yesterday, so I took it home with me and left it in my car, which I made sure was locked. This morning when I went out to the car, the door was ajar and the evidence bag, which I had placed on the floorboard, was gone. I had my car towed to the station for processing. I don't know if it was some local punk looking for a cell phone, money or whatever, or if it has something to do with this case. I'm sorry about that, but there's nothing we can do about it now," stormy said.

"The killer was wearing gloves, so there would have been no prints on the wrapper anyway. As far as any DNA, we'll never know now, but that's water under the bridge. What I did find out was that the prosecutor stopped at a Shake n' Shake just north of his house and bought three burgers, this was around ten-fifteen last night. The coroner said there was hardly any food in his stomach and certainly not a freshly eaten burger. That means the killer took time to eat one of the burgers after he bound the prosecutor to the chair," Leo said. "Sounds like a stone cold killer to me."

"Now, I've run those numbers through my mind over and over. If it's a date, it could be February 1941," Stormy said.

"I'll go to Tech Services and have our computer whiz play with the numbers and see if they can come up with anything," said Leo.

"While you're doing that, I'll drive back to Hialeah to see if C.S.I. came up with anything and retrieve my car. From there I want to check with my informant. Hopefully, he's heard something on the street by now, but the way things are looking I doubt it."

"What about Rolando?" Leo asked.

"When I finish talking with my C.I., I'll call him and advise him I'll pick him up here."

"Okay, see you later."

Stormy left and drove back to Hialeah. When he reached the back of the station he saw that his car was parked in the detectives' area. He went into the building and walked straight back to the office of C.S.I. where he found a crime tech.

"You guys find anything of value, like maybe prints, on my car?" he asked.

"No, sir. It was clean as a whistle, inside and out," replied the tech.

"I figured as much. This guy is extremely careful not to leave any prints or evidence," said Stormy.

Stormy went to Captain Paradis' office to keep him up to date but the Captain was out. He sat at his desk and saw that there was a message for him. It read, "Detective Storm, call me as soon as you can. It's in reference to the activity around your car this morning." The message was from a Dale Johnson and stated that he was his neighbor. Curious, he dialed the number and was rewarded with an answer after the second ring.

"Hello," said the voice on the other end.

"This is Detective Storm returning your call," replied Stormy.

"Detective Storm, glad you called. I think I may have some video footage you will want to see."

"I'm sorry, but do I know you?"

"I live across the street from you. My name is Dale Johnson, and I'm sorry I haven't had a chance to introduce myself," he said.

"What is this about?" asked Stormy.

"I have a home security system with a camera and after playing it back this morning I thought you might want to see it," Dale said.

"Is this about my car being broken into?" asked Stormy.

"It is, and my camera picked up the person who broke into your car," he said.

"Where can I meet with you and get a copy of the video?" asked Stormy, his excitement rising.

"Actually, I work for a law firm in Hialeah, only a couple of miles from the Hialeah Police Department."

After obtaining the address from Dale, Stormy quickly went to his car and headed for the law firm on 103rd Street. When he arrived he was met in the small parking lot by Dale. He had already made a copy of the video and presented it to Stormy.

"I really do appreciate this," said Stormy.

"No problem. Hope it helps you catch the creep. We don't need that kind of problem in our neighborhood," said Dale.

"Once again, thanks. Not everyone would take that extra step to help out," said Stormy.

He drove back to the station where he would have access to a CD player. When he was inside his office he put the CD in and started watching. Since it had happened early in the morning the light was not conducive to a sharp picture, but it was enough to see the subject walking briskly down the sidewalk and stopping at his house. The subject looked around the area for a few seconds, obviously to see if anyone was outside that would see him. He then quickly went to the car, took a jimmy from his clothing, and within seconds had the door unlocked. It appeared he had translucent looking surgical rubber gloves

42

on. He didn't enter the car but leaned his head in and looked around, as if he were searching for something. He then unlocked the passenger door using the electric button on the door panel and closed the driver's door. He didn't seem to notice that it didn't shut completely, and he swiftly walked around the car. Opening the passenger's door, he leaned in and retrieved something off the floorboard. Stuffing it into his pants, he closed the door and left in the direction whence he had come.

It was obvious that he knew exactly what he was looking for. The only thing was how did he know it was in the car? Stormy replayed the video again, trying to see if he recognized the subject. He appeared to be of average height, compared to the height of the car, wearing dark clothing and a baseball cap. At no angle could he clearly make out the face. There was only one shot where he could catch a glimpse of his profile. With the cap pulled low and in near darkness, it was impossible to make out his features. The one thing that did stand out was a white lightning bolt on the side of the cap, but there were probably a thousand of those around.

Stormy sat and replayed the video, over and over, still not sure what he was looking for. But he had a nagging feeling he knew the burglar somehow. He took the disc out of the player and put it into his desk drawer. He'd look at it again later, but now he had to find Pablo. He hoped that some information on the killings would be forthcoming, but in his gut he doubted it. This didn't seem to be an amateur – he was too meticulous in his actions. So far he was batting a thousand for not leaving any usable evidence at his crime scenes.

Stormy turned his car south on LeJuene Road and headed for downtown Miami. He dialed Pablo's number on his cell but got no answer. Usually that wouldn't worry him, but Pablo was seeking information that could get him killed. He would have to caution Pablo when he found him. When he was on Southwest 8th Street, he parked his car near the apartment building where Pablo lived. He had never visited Pablo on *his* turf and hadn't intended to now, but he needed to find him, and soon. He got out of the car and walked over to a Cuban restaurant that had a takeout window. He asked for two ham cro-quettes and a coke, paid for them and strolled down the street, slowly munching the croquettes.

He knew that he stood out like a sore thumb, not being Cuban, so he had strapped on an ankle holster, his .38 police detective snub secured within. He left his weapon of choice, an S&W 9-mm automatic, the one he wore almost every day, in the trunk of his car. He had on a turquoise polo pullover and black slacks, black lace up shoes and dark tinted shade glasses. He looked native, but his demeanor and carriage gave some of the old timers pause for thought. He carried himself in a confident man-ner, but without swagger. He could have been a drug dealer, lawyer or a multitude of other professions. The old timers wrongly assumed that he was a drug dealer.

As Stormy slowly walked up the street he kept sweep-ing the area, his eyes hidden behind his dark shades, not moving his head, just sipping his coke and searching for Pablo. The dark tinted sun glasses ensured that no one could see his eyes darting back and forth, seeking some-one or something. Suddenly he saw Pablo, standing in front of a small grocery store, animatedly talking with someone, gesturing with his hands as Latino's are prone to do when talking excitedly.

Stormy started to cross the street when Pablo suddenly looked up and saw him, subtly shaking his head. Stormy took the hint and turned the opposite direction and took a seat at another outdoor cafe. From there he could watch Pablo and also be seen by Pablo. He shook his head at the waiter who walked out and held up his coke. The waiter frowned and walked back inside the cafe.

Finally, after about ten minutes, Pablo finished his conversation and started walking in the direction of Stormy. The other party he was talking with walked inside the store they had been standing in front of. When Pablo reached Stormy he took a seat opposite him. The waiter came out again and Pablo ordered a Cuban coffee. When the waiter had left he said,

"You think this is a good idea you coming down here?"

"I've called you several times, but you don't answer your phone," replied Stormy.

"I put it on vibrate because I've been talking with a lot of bad people," he said. "I didn't want them to wonder why I was not answering."

"Well, have you come up with *anything*?" asked Stormy.

"I had one *hombre* that claimed he knew who it was, but he wanted a hundred dollars up front first," said Pablo.

"Do you believe him?" asked Stormy.

"Not for a minute," said Pablo. "He has a reputation

for scamming a lot of people and will say anything for a buck."

"So we're back to zero," replied Stormy.

"*Mierda,* Stormy. I'm trying, but I'm having no luck," said Pablo. "Besides, maybe he's not Cuban!"

"Yeah, I've considered that also. When you get a chance, I want you to come to my office, call first of course so I'll be there. I want you to look at a video. Maybe you'll recognize the person in it," said Stormy.

"You think he could be the one you're looking for?" asked Pablo.

"It's possible," replied Stormy.

"I'll come up tomorrow afternoon."

"Okay, and, Pablo, be very careful. I've a funny feeling that this is only the beginning, and we're dealing with someone who is starting to look like an accomplished killer. I don't want you asking the wrong person and getting yourself killed. It's not worth it."

"I will, *amigo.* See you tomorrow," said Pablo, rising and walking away.

"Pablo, make that at City Hall on Palm Avenue. I'm not ready for my new partner to meet you yet," called out Stormy.

"Okay. I'll call first," Pablo said, walking away.

Stormy sipped his coke while he called Rolando on his cell. When he answered he told him that he would pick him up at Miami C.I.D. in about thirty minutes. He left five dollars on the table for the waiter, to cover the coffee, even though he had ordered nothing. The waiter watched him walk away, smiled and thought to himself, *Gracias, amigo.*

Stormy drove back to the Miami Police Department, thoughts running rampant through his head. *Why had the burglar targeted his car. Of what value was the evidence to him. Maybe it was drugs, or maybe money. The evidence bag was clear, so he should have seen that there was only the sandwich wrapper inside. It makes no sense – unless he knew what he was after. But how was that possible.* Pulling into the Miami P.D. parking lot he pushed his thoughts aside, flashed his I.D. and parked the car.

Entering the lobby, he once again felt like he was missing something. He stood and slowly looked around the lobby, taking everything in. He saw the desk officer watching him suspiciously and smiled at him.

"Beautiful lobby," he said.

The officer just looked at him as if he had two heads, nodded and turned back to his work. Stormy continued to look around as he walked to the elevator. He looked at the murals on the walls, the glass case honoring the fallen officers and the displays of various law enforcement memorabilia. Yet, something was tugging at him, and it bothered him. He entered the elevator and rode up to C.I.D. where he found Leo.

"I met with my C.I. today," said Stormy.

"Did he have anything for you?" asked Leo.

"Nothing, and that's unusual for him," said Stormy.

"Do you think he found out who it is and is not telling you, maybe because it's a friend?" asked Leo.

"No, my C.I. is all about making money, and he knows that I will pay well for the information. Besides, I think I could tell if he were lying to me," said Stormy.

They didn't finish the conversation because about that time Rolando walked in.

"Did you come up with anything, anything at all?" asked Leo.

"No, the case file numbering system is totally different than the number we have. I hit a lot of dead ends, so I think that route is a waste of time," replied Rolando.

"Back to square one," said Leo.

"I'm heading back to Hialeah, so if you come up with anything give me a call," said Stormy.

"I'm cutting out of here myself," replied Leo. "See you tomorrow."

They all entered the elevator and rode down in silence. Entering the lobby Stormy still couldn't shake the feeling he was overlooking something. Every time he passed through the lobby something seemed to be jumping out at him. Shrugging if off, he and Rolando exited the building and drove back to Hialeah.

When they arrived and entered the building, Captain Paradis motioned for them to come to his office. "Anything new?" asked the Captain.

"Well, forensics determined that the prosecutor was hit with a stun gun or taser before being tied to the chair. We'll know tomorrow if the same thing happened to the judge," said Stormy.

"That would explain how he was able to subdue both of them," said the Captain.

"There's something else, Captain. My car was broken into in the early hours of this morning."

"Did you report it and was anything taken?" asked the Captain.

"The car was towed here for processing. The only thing missing is an evidence bag I had lying on the floorboard."

"Why did you have evidence in your car? Why wasn't it logged in?"

"It was late, and I thought it would be safe. Besides, who would know it was in the car," said Stormy.

"Was that the only thing taken?" asked Captain Paradis.

"As far as I can tell, that was the only thing."

"What was the evidentiary value of what was taken?"

"It was a food wrapper from the scene of the prosecutor's murder, and we thought it would be possible to obtain a DNA match from it," said Stormy.

"That's pretty important evidence. You know that this has to be written up, if only to cover your butt. Besides, you know policy, all evidence must be logged in," said the Captain with a stern face.

"I know, Captain, believe me I know. It was one of those things and Leo was aware that I wouldn't be turning it in until today. I put it on the floorboard, but in hindsight I should have taken it inside the house with me," said Stormy.

"Nothing can be done about it now. Any other information I need to know?"

"Yes, one other thing. I received a call this morning from a neighbor of mine. His home security system camera recorded the break-in of my car. He made me a CD, and I have it in my desk."

"Did you look at it to see if you recognized the burglar?" asked Rolando.

49

"I did and no, I couldn't identify him," said Stormy.

"How about this time you log it into the evidence room," said the Captain.

"Yes, sir, I was going to do just that," said Stormy.

"May I see the video?" asked Rolando. "Maybe two sets of eyes will be better than one."

"Sure, I don't see why not," said Stormy.

Stormy played the CD for Rolando and afterward turned to him asking if he recognized the person. He noticed the intense look on Rolando's face and asked what was wrong.

"Oh, nothing. I just thought for a minute I recognized that person from when I was on road patrol," he said.

"But you don't?" asked Stormy.

"Nope. Pretty sure I don't know him," said Rolando.

Chapter 4

THE KILLER SAT IN THE DARKNESS of his living room, alone with his thoughts. He was thinking about his next kill and was looking forward to it. He picked up the evidence bag he had taken from the unmarked police car in Miami Lakes and turned it over in his hand. It was only a food wrapper, but it could have been his downfall. He would have to be a lot more careful with the rest of the killings. There was no way he was going to get caught before he finished his mission.

Looking at his list he thought to himself, *Two down and eight more to go*. He hoped to finish the job within the next couple of weeks. The only thing slowing him down was the time it took to stake out his victims and plan for the best time and place to take them out. *It might even be possible to take out more than one in a night,* he thought. *But that would be pushing it.* He discarded that idea.

He started thinking about what had brought him to this point in his life, and tears began to well up in his eyes. He shook it off. *They all deserved to die and before they did, by God, they would know why.* He was determined to finish what he had started. He had only one predominant thought – *Vengeance is mine!*

****

Stormy and Rolando arrived at Miami C.I.D. the next morning and went directly to Leo's office. When they entered they could see a flurry of activity. Leo had a strained look on his face. Hanging the phone up, he called Stormy over. "We had another one last night," he said.

"Wow, this creep is doing one a night," said Stormy. "Who and where was it now?"

"Does the name Luis Herrera mean anything to you?" asked Leo.

"Wasn't he a drug kingpin back in the sixties and seventies?"

"That he was," said Leo.

"He was never arrested and charged with anything if I remember correctly," said Stormy.

"Nope, he always managed to keep one step ahead of the law or have someone else take the fall for him. Actually, he's been living a legit retired life for the last few years, somewhere on South Beach."

"So, is it the same M.O. as the others?" asked Rolando.

"Right down to the numbers on the forehead," said Leo.

"Where was he found?" asked Stormy.

"He was sitting on a bench seat on the pier at South Beach. According to the locals he had trouble sleeping and would go out at three to four o'clock in the morning and just sit, listening to the ocean."

"I'm surprised the media hasn't picked up on all of this by now," said Stormy.

"They have, and the questions are pouring in. We have a news conference scheduled for noon today."

"You know this is going to cause a panic, don't you?" stated Stormy.

"Don't I know it. But you're going to be at the news conference since you're no stranger to the media," said Leo.

"I would prefer you answering the questions," said Stormy.

"I'll give a short statement, and then you can answer a few questions. Just don't tell them about the numbers," said Leo.

"Alright. But if we have anymore killings, there's going to be a lot more questions forthcoming."

They spent the next couple of hours looking at the latest crime scene photos. As before, there was nothing different from the other two killings. They took a break to give their eyes a rest. Rolando asked a few questions, but there just were no answers. It was the same questions they kept pondering: who and why and above all, what was the meaning of the numbers?

"We have an hour before the news conference, so let's run out and get a bite for lunch," suggested Rolando.

Stormy had not eaten breakfast and was getting hungry. They all left the building and walked around the corner to a small restaurant, arriving before the lunch crowd rush. They ordered their meals and made small talk while they ate. When they finished, they sat and talked for a few more minutes but decided to leave when the lunch crowd started coming in. They walked back to the police department and saw that the three major channels – ABC, CBS and NBC – along with two Spanish stations were already setting up their cameras in the lobby. They quickly walked past them, but one reporter sought them out at the elevator.

"Steven Rondo with Channel 7, detectives. Could I maybe get a scoop from you?" he asked.

"You know better than that, Steve," said Leo. "Every station gets the same information at the same time!"

"Can't blame a guy for trying," the anchor grinned.

"Nope, you sure can't. Nice try," Leo responded.

They went up to the third floor where they went over just how much they were willing to release to the assembled media. It was decided that Leo would give a short statement in reference to the three killings, but he wouldn't divulge any pertinent information. As with any major crime, crucial information that only the killer would know was withheld. Soon it was time, and they headed downstairs for the news conference.

A bank of microphones was set up for Leo and Stormy. The media personnel with their television cameras waited anxiously. The chatter and noise ceased as Leo stepped up to the microphones. As one, all the cameras were turned on, the bright lights lit up the lobby, and the hand-held microphones were extended out to catch every word.

"Ladies and gentlemen of the media, I have a short statement to make, and Detective Storm will answer a few questions afterwards. Please use restraint and not yell out your questions all at once. Raise your hand, and Detective

Storm will select who may ask a question. Am I clear?" he asked.

No one objected to the rules, and the conference began with Leo starting his statement.

"Three nights ago, during the hurricanes approach, a prosecutor for the Dade County State's Attorney's Office, Richard Snyder, was found murdered in his home. It had the markings of a burglar caught in the act with a deadly outcome. Mr. Snyder had been working late and arrived home around ten-thirty that evening. We assume at this point that he walked in on a burglary in progress. He was killed in the process. The following night we had another murder, Scott Hanson, a criminal court judge for the county. He was found dead in his car near the courthouse. At this time we don't have any credible information that ties the two murders together. And last night, we were informed by the Miami Beach Police Department of another deceased person on the pier. As I said, at this time we don't have conclusive proof that any of them were connected. Now, Detective Storm will take a few questions."

Stormy stepped up to the bank of microphones and was immediately besieged with a barrage of questions. He just stood there, his eyes darkening, an annoyed look on his face. He kept staring at them without saying a word until they all settled down and looked at him.

"Evidently you forgot what Detective Sharp told you. Raise your hand, and I'll pick some of you to ask a question, and only one question each. Understood?"

The media were well acquainted with Detective Storm and knew that he could be blunt. He had been known to simply ignore a question and walk off a news conference. He and his former partner had been in the news so much in recent years they were almost in awe of him, so now they shut up and waited.

"First question?" he asked. Hands shot up all over the lobby at once.

"Steve," he pointed out. "What's your question?"

"Detective Storm, you work for the Hialeah Police Department, so why are you investigating these homicides out of your jurisdiction?" he asked.

"Because I was asked to assist," he answered. "Sally, Channel 4, your question?" he asked, cutting off the anchor before he could ask another question.

"Detective Sharp stated that he didn't know if the homicides were related, but it's obvious you think so or we wouldn't be having this conference. Do you think it's the work of a serial killer?" she asked.

"No, at this time we don't believe it is, and we still haven't confirmed whether they're related or not," he said.

As Stormy started to pick out another reporter, a voice from the rear of the gathering, from one of the Spanish stations, yelled out, "What about the numbers? I have a source that mentioned numbers at each scene!"

Without skipping a beat or looking at Leo, Stormy said, "We don't think that any of the victims were involved in the numbers racket. That's all folks, thanks for coming."

Amid the sudden clatter, all of the reporters yelling out about the numbers, Stormy turned and walked to the elevator, Leo and Rolando, grinning, fell in behind him.

When they were in the elevator, Leo burst out, "Where the hell did he get that information?"

"I think you need to question your uniformed officers that were on each scene. It's possible one of them is in cahoots with that station in some way," Stormy said.

"I'll have their badge when I find out who it was," retorted Leo, *"and I will find out!"*

"You know we're going to have to stall them about the numbers," Stormy said.

"I know, but we need to find something, anything, to point us in the right direction."

"One more murder, and we'll probably need the resources of the FBI, which is a choice I don't want to make, but one that may come to pass," Stormy said.

"You mean the FBI could get involved?" Rolando asked.

"If it turns out to be a serial killer, yeah, that's their bailiwick."

"In the meantime I'm going to go over the photos of all three crime scenes and see if we missed anything," said Leo, "One can only hope!"

"I'll go to the judge's office and see if I can turn anything up," said Stormy. "There has to be a connection."

Stormy and Rolando left Leo as he began to pour over the crime scene photos. In the parking lot Stormy asked Rolando to drive since he had already been to the judge's office earlier and knew the way. While Rolando maneuvered into traffic, Stormy pulled his smart phone out and punched play for a video. He had downloaded the one from the break-in of his car. There was something familiar about the subject, and he kept looking at it, over and over.

"You want to go out and get a beer tonight?" Rolando asked.

Stormy pushed the pause button on the phone and thought for a minute.

"Not tonight. I have a date. It's our first anniversary, and she wants to celebrate."

"Oh, I thought you were single," Rolando responded.

"I am. It's our first anniversary being together."

"What's her name?" Rolando asked.

"Marie," Stormy said, discouraging further conversation about his personal life.

"Maybe some other night," Rolando said.

"Yeah, maybe," Stormy replied.

Rolando pulled into the parking lot of the judge's office, parked the car and they went inside. The receptionist recognized Rolando from the day before and smiled at him.

"Detective Fuentes, I think I may have something for you," she gushed. It was obvious she was slightly infatuated with him. "I remember you wanting to know if the judge and prosecutor Snyder had any recent cases together, and I found one you may want to see."

She handed over a case file, and Rolando started to open it when his cell started ringing. He handed the file to Stormy, excused himself, and stepped to the other side of the office to take the call.

Stormy opened the file and began reading it, page after page, until he got to the end. He stopped and reread the last two pages.

Two years earlier Judge Hanson had presided over a

case involving the murder of a homeless man and Richard Snyder prosecuted the case. The defendant was Hector Gomez who swore to the end he was innocent. He was found guilty and sentenced to twenty-five years in the Raiford Penitentiary. Four months ago he was being transported to an appeals hearing when he suddenly overwhelmed the two guards and escaped. He was still at large and considered extremely dangerous. Stormy's heart skipped a beat. *This is our man*! he thought. All the indications were there for a grudge killing.

Calling out to Rolando, he told him they had to go. He asked the receptionist if she would make him a copy of the file. At first she hesitated, but when Rolando flashed a smile at her and said please, she agreed, blushing all the way to the printer.

With a copy of the case file in hand, they returned to Miami C.I.D. and sought out Leo. When they found him he was still going over the photos, frustrated and in a foul mood. Seeing Stormy and Rolando, and the smiles on their faces, he dropped what he was doing and walked over to them.

"*Please* tell me you found something we can use," begged Leo.

"Better than that, possibly the name of the killer," smiled Stormy.

He handed the file to Leo and waited until he had read it through. He did the same as Stormy and reread the last two pages.

"It looks as if Mr. Gomez held a grudge," smiled Leo.

"My thoughts exactly," said Stormy. "But, there's two problems"

"And that is?" asked Leo.

"We have to find the connection with Luis Herrera and how he fits in with these murders, and second, we don't know where Hector is."

"We need to do a thorough background on Gomez to see if he had any connection with Herrera say, in the last five years," Stormy said, "and see if anything pops up as to any acquaintances we can contact and question."

"If you'll run Gomez's background Leo, the three of us can quickly go over it."

Leo went downstairs to the records division to begin the process of a records search. Stormy walked over to the side and called Pablo on his cell. There was no answer, just a voice mail so he left a message, "This is your old buddy, and we won't be able to do lunch today so call me." This was a code they had worked out long ago in case someone got hold of Pablo's phone. Also, he was letting him know that he couldn't make it to City Hall with the CD at this time.

Leo came back from records in about fifteen minutes and handed Stormy a sheaf of printouts. Mr. Gomez had an extensive rap sheet, everything from traffic violations to murder. It listed an address for him in Hialeah, on West 72nd Street and 16th Avenue. That would be the first place they would begin the investigation into Gomez. They had to find out if relatives were still living there and also talk with the neighbors. It was a long shot, but sometimes long shots paid off. Stormy was thinking to himself, *His address is less than a mile from my house. He could have walked there and broke into my car, but how would he have known the evidence was in my car that night, or more importantly, where I live?*

"We're going to drive to Hialeah and check out his last known address," Stormy said.

"I'll keep going over the photos and his rap sheet, maybe something else will pop up," Leo said.

Stormy and Rolando left the building and drove to Hialeah. Rolando was asking a lot of questions which was the correct thing to do, but he seemed a little over-excited. *The newbie jitters,* thought Stormy as he answered the questions.

It took them almost forty-five minutes because of heavy traffic, normally a twenty-minute drive. They pulled up in front of a townhouse on West 72nd Street, checked the address and saw that they were at the right house. There were no cars in the driveway but that didn't mean no one was at home. They got out of the car and walked to the door. There were two doors, but one was probably an entry to the kitchen. Stormy told Rolando to stand to the side of the second door in case someone, especially Gomez, tried to run out. Stormy knocked on the door and waited. He could hear noises coming from inside, possibly from a television or radio. After waiting about thirty seconds he knocked again, a little harder this time. Within a few seconds the door opened, and a middle-aged woman with a paint brush in her hand asked, "Yes, can I help you?"

"Hello, I'm Detective Storm with the Hialeah Police Department. May I come in?" he asked.

"What is this about? I'm in the middle of painting," she said.

"I would like to ask you about Hector Gomez,"

61

Stormy said.

"Come in," she said, reluctantly.

Stormy turned to Rolando and told him, "Speak with the surrounding neighbors. See what they have to say about Hector and ask if they've seen him lately. I doubt you'll get much cooperation, but we have to try."

Entering the modestly furnished house, Stormy was invited to take a seat on the plastic covered L-shaped couch that took up much of the small living room.

"Let me put my brush away. I'll be right back," she said.

Stormy took his smart phone out, punched the record button and placed it beside his leg on the couch, out of sight. When she returned to the room she took a seat at the opposite end of the couch.

"What do you want to know about Hector?" she asked.

"First, are you related to him?" asked Stormy.

"He is my husband," she said.

"When was the last time you saw him?" he asked.

"About six months ago when I visited him in prison," she replied.

"And you haven't seen him since?" asked Stormy.

"No, sir. Why do you ask?

"Hector escaped from prison about four months ago," Stormy said.

"I did not know this," she replied, without exhibiting much emotion.

"You're sure you haven't seen or heard from him recently, Mrs. Gomez?" Stormy asked, not convinced.

"No, sir, but I will call you if I do," she said.

"Do you know of any friends he may be with?" Stormy asked.

"I don't know many of his friends. Since he went to prison, I haven't seen any of them," she said.

"Very well, I appreciate your time and here is my card. If you hear from him please give me a call."

She walked Stormy to the door and softly closed it behind him. Stormy saw Rolando walking back towards the car from two houses down. He waited for him at the rear of the car. When he approached, Stormy asked if he had any luck.

"You were right. No one knows anything," he said. "Were you able to find out anything from the woman in the house?"

"She denies knowing Hector escaped, but I think she's lying," Stormy said.

"Who is she?" asked Rolando.

"Hector's wife," Stormy said.

"And she hasn't heard from him?" Rolando asked. "Do you believe her?"

"Not for a minute," said Stormy.

"Where do we go from here?" asked Rolando.

"I'm going back to the house," Stormy said. "Wait here."

Stormy walked back to the door and knocked once again. Mrs. Gomez opened the door, a puzzled look on her face.

"Yes, sir. Did you need something else?" she asked.

"I'm so sorry to bother you again," said Stormy, flashing a big smile, "but I think my phone slipped out of my pocket when I was sitting on your couch."

"Wait please, I'll go see," she said.

In a few seconds she returned to the door, holding Stormy's phone.

"Here it is, *senor*. You dropped it where you were sitting," she said.

"Thank you so much, and once again, sorry for bothering you," he said.

Stormy walked to the car, a satisfied grin on his face, not unnoticed by Rolando. Once he got in the car and they drove away, Rolando asked what that was all about. Stormy pulled into a service station on the corner and parked out of the way. He took out his phone and punched the play button, putting it on speaker. He fast forwarded past his conversation with Mrs. Gomez, his exit from the house, and waited. They could hear the sounds of a phone being dialed then a one-sided conversation began.

"Hector?" she asked. "The police were here asking about you…I didn't tell them anything, I swear…No, they were talking about your escape and wanted to know if I had heard from you…They just left…*Si*, I'll take a taxi."

The conversation ended and there were only muffled movement noises on the speaker now.

"Can't we arrest her for obstruction or something?" asked Rolando.

"Afraid not, Rolando, I taped it illegally," Stormy replied.

"We know that she knows where he is, so what do we do now?" he asked.

"We wait for the taxi, and then we tail it," replied Stormy. "It sounded as if she was going to him."

They moved the car to the corner of the block where

they could see both exits from 72nd Street. When Mrs. Gomez had opened the door, Stormy remembered that she had not stepped out where she could have seen the car he was driving. He doubted she would think he would be tailing her.

Rolando nodded towards South 16th Avenue and Stormy saw a taxi driving in their direction. Sure enough, it turned onto 72nd Street. After waiting for only a few minutes the taxi came back to 16th Avenue and turned south, driving past them. They could see Mrs. Gomez in the rear seat. Taking a right at the light, it was obvious they were getting on the Palmetto Expressway. Stormy started the car and took the turn also, following at a distance. Once they were southbound on the expressway, he called dispatch to advise the station they were heading south on the Palmetto and would give a more precise address once they arrived.

The traffic was extremely heavy this time of day, so Stormy had to keep switching lanes to maintain a two to three-car separation and avoid possibly being spotted. So far Mrs. Gomez had never once turned her head as if she were looking to see if anyone was following her. Soon they were passing beneath the 836, the Dolphin Expressway, still maintaining a two to three-car distance between them. When they reached West Flagler Street, the taxi suddenly took the exit ramp, turning east towards Coral Gables. The taxi had ran a yellow light to make the turn, so Stormy had to run the red light to keep up, amid the blowing horns and screeching brakes of oncoming cars. Rolando looked a little pale but was impressed with the maneuver.

They followed the taxi east on West Flagler Street for several miles when two cars ahead they saw the taxi driver put on his turn signal and take a left onto 27th Avenue. Evidently they weren't going to Coral Gables, more likely to West Little Havana. After the taxi turned back east onto Northwest 3rd Street, it only went about four houses before pulling into a driveway.

Stormy pulled into the first driveway immediately and cracked his tinted window enough to see clearly. They were only three houses from where the taxi had stopped. He watched as Mrs. Gomez got out, paid her fare and went up to the door. From the angle of the house, which sat back a little further than the one they were in front of, they couldn't see who answered the door but did see her enter.

If Hector was in the house, he apparently wasn't going to come out. Now they had to decide what they were going to do. Stormy sat thinking for a minute, and then the door of the house they were parked in front of opened and a burly man came out, walking towards the car. Stormy rolled down his window and before the man could ask anything he said, "Sorry, pal, wrong house," and backed out of the driveway.

He drove down the street past the house where Mrs. Gomez had entered. Three houses past was a house in foreclosure, apparently empty. Stormy drove to the end of the block to give the man who had approached them time to get back into his house. He didn't want him to see them parking in another driveway and start getting curious. He turned the car around and returned to the empty house. He parked in the driveway up close to the garage, nearly out of sight of the suspect's house.

Switching off the car engine, he turned to Rolando and said, "Do you remember those rules I gave you?"

"For the most part, yes," replied Rolando.

"Well, this is one of *my* rules, the one where you do what I ask with no questions. Understand?"

"What do you want me to do?" asked Rolando, with one eyebrow raised.

"I want you to go to the rear of the house, stand out of sight of any windows and wait until you hear me knock on the door. When you hear the knock, I want you to say loudly, "Come in!"

Rolando started laughing, trying to control himself. "I like it," he said.

"Just be prepared in case anyone tries to run out the back door. Have your weapon ready but don't fire unless you are fired at first. Do you understand?"

"Understood. Let's go," said Rolando.

Before getting out of the car Stormy called Hialeah dispatch and advised them of their location and that they were getting out of the car to conduct an investigation. They exited the car, and Rolando walked to the rear of the houses and started strolling to the suspect's house. Stormy paced himself to give Rolando time to get in position.

Inside the house Hector was grilling his wife. Voices were raised, and he was berating her severely.

"What do you mean you didn't look to see if you were followed?" he yelled.

"I did…I mean I didn't think about it…I'm not really used to this kind of thing," she said.

"You crazy *puta*. Why do you think I'm here and not

at home. Every law enforcement agency in Florida is looking for me. Now you may have led them right to the front door."

Hector Gomez didn't know how prophetic he was at that moment.

Chapter 5

WHEN STORMY WAS SURE Rolando was in position at the rear of the house, he stepped up to the door, listening to the raised voices coming from inside. He only hoped Rolando could hear his knock above the yelling, but if he didn't, so be it. He raised his knuckles and rapped loudly on the front door. At that moment he heard Rolando yell from the rear of the house, "Come in!"

Stormy turned the door knob, his foot ready to kick in the door at the same time in case it was locked. It wasn't! The door swung in, and Stormy saw Hector standing over his wife, waving his hands wildly. He stopped, and they both looked up at Stormy standing in the doorway. Hector turned and ran to the back door, jerking it open and running outside, Stormy hot on his heels. He didn't get past the back step when he was tackled by Rolando, rolled over and his hands cuffed behind his back.

All of a sudden Stormy was attacked from behind, a shrill scream erupting in his ears. Hector's wife had run out behind him and jumped onto his back, pummeling him with her tiny fists, doing no harm whatsoever. Stormy reached back and pulled her off, gripping her hands together while he pulled his handcuffs out. He cuffed her, and they led the two of them back into the house. After seating them on opposite sides of the living room, he took his cell phone and called Leo, who answered on the first ring.

"Leo here," he said.

"Leo, we have him. Also, we have his wife. You want us to bring both of them in?"

"Great work, the Major was right in asking for you to assist us. Yes, bring both of them in, and we'll sort it out here."

Stormy conducted a cursory search of the living room for weapons. He found none in the immediate vicinity. Any search other than the "wingspan rule," without a warrant would result in the dismissal of any weapons or evidence found. He tossed the car keys to Rolando and told him to bring the car to the house. When Rolando parked in front Stormy ushered the pair out to the car, putting them both in the back seat. After fastening their seat belts, he and Rolando headed to Miami C.I.D. where they would be questioned and booked.

When they arrived at C.I.D., they parked at the rear of the station. Taking the prisoners out of the car, they took them through the sally port. Once inside, their cuffs were removed, and they were placed into individual holding cells. Neither had spoken a word during the drive, but now Hector spoke up, "Let my wife go. She has nothing to do with this."

"Your wife may be facing charges for obstruction of justice, so she's not going anywhere yet," said Stormy. "So button up and keep quiet."

Stormy and his partner headed to the elevator and

rode up to Leo's office. When they exited the elevator, Leo was waiting for them, grinning from ear to ear.

"Good work," he said.

"They're both in holding right now. Do you want to start with Hector first?" asked Stormy, brushing off the accolade.

"Yes. I'll have an officer bring him up. We can use interrogation room three – it's the only available one for now."

When Hector was brought up by the uniformed officer, he walked into the room defiantly, his eyes glaring at Stormy.

"Do you want me to remove the cuffs?" asked the officer.

"No, for now we'll leave them on and see if he behaves," said Leo.

The interrogation room was the same as in most every large police department – sparsely furnished with only a table and couple of chairs. The camera was mounted in the ceiling, directed down on the table where it would video tape every conversation. There was also the ever - present two-way glass through which other detectives could observe the interrogation, if they were so inclined. Rolando was outside the room now and standing at the glass, watching the events unfold. Hector was seated with his back to the wall where the camera could video him full face-on. Leo placed a legal pad and pen on the table in front of Hector, which he looked at it with complete disdain.

"Save your breath. I'm not saying anything," he said.

"I haven't asked you anything yet," replied Stormy.

"You plan to, otherwise why would I be in here," smiled Hector.

Stormy just sat and stared at Hector, his expression passive, without saying anything. He won the stare down after a minute, and Hector wiped the smile off his face and looked around the room.

"First, let me advise you of your Miranda rights," began Stormy.

"Skip the rights. I have nothing to say," replied Hector.

"For the record, I'm giving them to you anyway," said Stormy.

After he finished issuing the Miranda warning he had Hector sign the form, indicating he understood.

"Tell me about Luis Herrera," Stormy said.

"Luis Herrera, are you *loco* detective. He is old news, no longer in the business," spouted Hector.

"You're right. He is no longer in the business as you say, and never will be again. He was murdered," Stormy said.

"So? His past caught up with him, and someone offed him. What's that got to do with me?" asked Hector.

"Everything. Why did you kill him, Hector?"

"WHAT? Are you out of your mind? Why would I kill him?"

"Well, he did plan to let you rot in jail. I noticed that you had to use a public defender at your trial. You would think that with all his money Luis would have taken better care of you, like furnishing you with a high-powered attorney."

"And you think that was enough reason to kill him?

72

You are *loco* man!" Hector said.

"Killing is no problem for you, Hector. Remember the homeless man?"

"I didn't kill *anyone*," a defiant Hector stated.

"Well, the jury thought differently," replied Stormy.

"Enough! I want a lawyer," said Hector with finality.

"Officer, take Mr. Gomez back to holding where he can wait for processing."

"I thought you tracked me down for the escape," said Hector as he stood.

"Don't say anything else without your lawyer," smiled Stormy.

After Hector left the room, Leo signaled for the camera to be turned off.

"You believe him?" asked Leo.

"The preponderance of circumstantial evidence says he did it, but we can't get a conviction with *circumstantial* evidence," Stormy replied.

"What do you want to do with his wife?" asked Leo.

"Charge her with obstructing and make sure Hector knows," said Stormy. "Maybe that will convince him to make a deal, in exchange for her release."

"It's getting late, and I have an important date tonight," Stormy said, rising from his chair.

"Alright. See you in the morning. Maybe Hector will be ready to talk then," said Leo.

"Okay, goodnight, Leo, I'll see you in the morning."

On the ride back to Hialeah, Rolando had a plethora of questions about Gomez and the charges he faced. *It's good he's interested enough in being a detective that he wants to know everything,* thought Stormy.

"So, where are you celebrating your anniversary tonight?" asked Rolando, changing the subject.

"The Palm on Bay Harbor Island," said Stormy.

"Wow, that's sure to impress her. I ate there once, and the bill was over one hundred and fifty dollars for the two of us," replied Rolando.

"I'm not trying to impress her," said Stormy, "I just want a romantic atmosphere, but also somewhere that is kinda laid-back."

"You picked the right place. It's very laid-back and totally romantic."

They arrived at Hialeah and Stormy let Rolando out of the car in the front parking lot. He would have gone inside to bring Captain Paradis up to date but it was after five, and he knew the Captain would be gone for the day.

Stormy drove to Snow's Jewelry Store in Miami Lakes, and after finding a parking spot he went inside. Snow's had been in business for decades. The original store started in the old K-Mart plaza on 103rd Street in Hialeah. Stormy had purchased an engagement ring and was having it sized for Marie's finger. He planned to propose to her tonight at The Palm, a four-star restaurant on Bay Harbor Island. Just thinking of her made him smile. He had known she was the one for him after their very first date. Now one year later, he was ready to propose and was confident she would accept.

Shaunie Marie Kelly was born and raised in Hialeah. She attended school at Hialeah-Miami Lakes High and had graduated with honors. Her family was upper middle class and insisted that she attend college. Her parents had some college credits but no degrees, and they explained to her how the lack of a degree had denied them good jobs, or hindered promotions.

When Shaunie was a teenager she worked at Doral Country Club and saved every penny she could. All her co-workers called her Marie, and she decided to stick with it. She didn't want her parents having to bear the full burden of paying her college tuition. Of course, her parents objected, and they finally reached an agreement – she would use the money she saved for personal expenses and they would take care of the rest.

To the delight of her and her parents, Marie was awarded a full-ride scholarship to the University of Miami. She chose Computer Science as her major and never regretted it. She had conducted her research and discovered there was a need for core programming skills, algorithm skills and quantitative analysis.

During her last year at the University of Miami she developed an anti-virus program that turned out to be better than anything on the market at the time. Lacking the funds to market it, she sold it to a major software firm for a substantial amount of money. She had the foresight to also include in the contract the inclusion for a five percent royalty for each one sold.

After Marie graduated from U.M. she opened her own business with only an assistant and a secretary as employees. She became a high tech troubleshooter for major businesses around the country. She also continued to develop other software programs. Her reputation preceded her and she had no problem finding customers, in fact, they sought her out. That was how she and Stormy met. She had been hired by the City of Hialeah to ferret out an elusive bug that repeatedly renumbered system files, making it nearly impossible to conduct business as usual. Within hours she isolated and systematically destroyed it.

Stormy had been at City Hall on business when he bumped into her coming out of the elevator. After retrieving the files, he had knocked from her hands, he impulsively asked her out on a date, to which she agreed. After that they were always together, whenever their schedules allowed.

Grant Snow showed the ring to Stormy, the three-quarter caret diamond displaying brilliant flashes of red and blue under the intense florescent lights. The ring was beautiful and way over his budget, but he had fallen in love with it the first time Grant had shown it to him. He took the ring, now in a velvet box, and left the store, vowing to bring pictures of it on her hand to show Grant.

Glancing at his wrist watch, Stormy saw that he needed to speed it up – he didn't want to be late. One thing he had always hated was people that were never on time. He only had a couple of miles to go before reaching his house, but he still exceeded the speed limit, but not by much. It wouldn't do to be late because of an accident of all things.

When he arrived home, he went directly to his bedroom, shed his clothes and jumped into the shower. Finishing, he went to his closet and pulled out a pair of dress khaki pants, a pale blue Carlo De'Mont pullover and a pair of stylish Moroccan loafers. Lightly splashing on some Solarium cologne, he checked himself in the full-length mirror, smiling his approval. Making sure he had the ring, he flipped off the lights and headed for his car, excited about what he had planned for the night.

On the drive over to Marie's condo in North Miami Beach he was hoping she didn't overdress. He had told her they were going to dinner, but it was to be casual. During the drive he tried to put out of his mind the case he was working on. He didn't want any distractions on this night, especially this night!

Pulling up to the gate to her condo the night guard recognized him, opened the gate and waved him through. He had been here so many times in the past year that all the guards knew him and who he was visiting. Only once had a guard challenged him, having to call Marie to verify that it was okay for him to be there. That guard was a replacement for one of the regulars who had been injured playing touch football.

Stormy parked the car and went into the lobby of the condominium, pausing to ring her apartment. She could see him on the monitor and playfully spoke to him through the intercom above the elevator.

"Do I know you?" she asked.

"Nope, I'm just your everyday stalker," he laughingly replied.

Laughing, she hit the buzzer allowing him access to the elevator. He entered and punched the button for the fourteenth floor. Her apartment faced the Atlantic Ocean and afforded her one of the best views on the beach, unlike so many condos that were on top of each other, blocking some of the views.

Tapping lightly on her door he was rewarded with the door opening and Marie giving him a big hug and kiss. She was wearing a pair of beige slacks, a white semitransparent blouse that wasn't too fluffy or revealing and simply looked gorgeous. Stepping into the room, he asked if she was ready to go, although they still had some extra time to kill. Stormy had made a reservation for eight o'clock, and it was only a thirty-minute drive to The Palm from her apartment.

"We have time for a quick drink," she said.

"Okay, make mine neat," he said.

Marie stepped over to her bar and quickly poured the drinks, knowing he liked to sip Jack Black neat, when he drank, which was seldom.

They stood together on the balcony and looked out at the ocean as they sipped their drinks. The ships in the distance with their lights reflecting on the water like scattered diamonds, the whitecaps of the waves as they splashed on the beach, all made for a scenic view. On the horizon they could see heat lightning, and Stormy was beginning to wonder if he should propose to her now during this idyllic setting. He decided against it, and they finished their drinks. She turned off all the lights except one, and they left the apartment, taking the elevator to the lobby.

When they reached the parking lot, Stormy asked if they could drive her car, an Audi, since he had driven his unmarked police car. She handed him the keys and told him to drive. They left the parking lot and headed for Bay Harbor Island. During the drive she held his hand and made small talk. Then she asked him if he was involved in the serial killings that were all over the news.

"Yeah, I'm assisting Miami on the case, and we made an arrest today," he said.

"Wow, good work, honey. I know that people were getting worried we could have a serial killer on the loose."

"We don't think it was a serial killer, more likely someone with a grudge," he replied.

"He has a grudge with that many people?"

"May have been more, but hopefully it stops now. Let's not talk about work, honey. Tonight is our time together, and I don't want to put a damper on it," he said.

She squeezed his hand and enjoyed the ride the rest of the way. She knew that he didn't like to talk about heinous crime with her, especially the really gruesome ones.

Before they knew it they were at The Palm. The parking lot was full, so Stormy pulled into the valet parking lane. The attendant opened Marie's door, helped her out and after closing it, ran around the car to move it.

Putting his arm around her waist they walked inside the restaurant and stood behind two couples that were waiting to be seated. When he finally moved up to the Hostess, he told her his name and reservation time. She diligently checked her list and marked him off, telling him to follow her. The restaurant was crowded, but the noise level was not as high as some of the other places in town. Stormy had specifically requested the quietest seat available when he made the reservations, and he was not disappointed. She led them to the back of the restaurant, opposite the traffic area the wait staff used. His booth was partially blocked off from most of the other diners by several small palm trees, positioned in good taste.

They had been seated mere seconds when the waiter arrived and took their drink orders. He left the menus with them after explaining the various steaks available and the Maine lobsters that ran up to fifteen pounds. When he left them, they both started laughing, wondering who in the world could eat a fifteen-pound lobster. Soon the waiter returned with their drinks, Jack Black neat for Stormy and a Manhattan iced tea for Marie. Perusing the menus, they soon came to a decision of what they wanted.

When the waiter returned they were ready with their order. Marie ordered the lobster, telling the waiter that a two-pounder would be more than enough for her. She also ordered extra clarified butter for the lobster. Stormy ordered a rib-eye steak with all the trimmings. They both asked for water with lemon, and the waiter left with their order.

Stormy asked Marie about her day, and although he hated technical discussions, he listened attentively as she talked about a new computer virus making the rounds and the contract she was signing with a major company in Broward County. By the time she had finished, the waiter returned with their meal, which covered most of the table.

They settled down and enjoyed the sumptuous meal, Marie deliberately smacking her lips as she dipped a piece of meat in the clarified butter.

"You have to try this lobster, honey," she said, obviously enjoying it immensely.

Stormy reached over and took a piece on his fork, which she had just removed from the claw.

"Hey, crack your own claw," she laughed.

Stormy laughed with her and after dipping the meat in the butter, he put it in his mouth and rolled his eyes.

"You're right, that is so fresh and good," he said

Stormy was happy that Marie was having such a great time and enjoying the meal so much. Neither of them had ever eaten here before tonight, but he was sure it would be on their list to do again.

When they finished their meal, the waiter arrived punctually, almost as if he were watching to see when to return. He cleared the table and asked if they wanted coffee or dessert. They both asked for coffee but were on the verge of declining the dessert. The waiter told them the cheesecake was flown in from a bakery in Brooklyn, New York, each day. He told them they had to try it, and if they didn't like it, he would take it off the bill. They decided to give it a try and settled on the mango cheesecake. They ordered one slice to share since the waiter told them how huge the slices were.

When the waiter returned with the coffee and cheesecake, they couldn't believe how big the slice was and were happy they had decided to share one. It would have been a huge waste if they had ordered two slices. The first bite made their mouths cry out with happiness, their taste buds going crazy with delight. It was that good. They ate all of it in silence, just enjoying being together and savoring the wonderful meal. The cheesecake really topped it off!

When they were down to just sipping their refilled coffee cups Stormy made his move. He stood up and took the small box from his pocket and flipped it open. He knelt down on one knee. He hoped and prayed she would say yes. It would be so embarrassing if she didn't. It happened so fast Marie was caught off guard, thinking for a minute he had fallen. But then he spoke!

"Marie Kelly, would you do me the honor of marrying me?" he said, holding out the diamond ring, still in the open box.

Marie was stunned, her eyes wide, tears welling swiftly. Holding her hand to her chest she screamed and said, "YES, YES, a hundred times yes!"

Other patrons in the restaurant turned at the outburst and saw what was happening, Stormy still down on one knee. All at once they started applauding, and Stormy slipped the ring on her finger, the fit was perfect. Marie couldn't take her eyes off of it, taking in all its beauty, a huge smile that was marred only by the tears slowly flowing down her cheeks. Stormy stood at the same time as she did, both hugging and sharing a long, lingering kiss, the applause still echoing in the restaurant.

During the excitement of the moment Stormy failed to notice the only person not applauding them. Sitting on the far side of the restaurant, a lone man was intensely staring at Stormy but most of all, Marie. While the commotion was beginning to abate, the man arose and slipped out of the restaurant.

Stormy and Marie walked out of the restaurant, acknowledging the smiles and congratulations from other patrons. They held hands as the valet took his ticket and ran to get the car. He returned quickly. He held the door open for Marie to get in and then trotted around the car to collect the tip Stormy was holding up for him to see. Leaving the parking lot, Stormy headed for Marie's apartment, both of them smiling and basking in the glow of the moment. When he drove through the gate, he got out and walked her up to the lobby.

"Aren't you staying the night?" she asked.

"Of all nights I want to more than anything in the world, but I need to finish up the arrest and interrogation in the morning. You won't be upset, will you?" he asked.

"Of course not. We have plenty of time, but you won't get off so easy next time," Marie said with a demure smile.

Stormy gave her a warm, lingering kiss and made sure she got on the elevator. Then he left the building and got into his car, heading home.

The lone man had parked across the street and watched them pull into the parking lot, taking notice of the guard and security procedures. He made a mental note about the placement of the security cameras, at least the three he had spotted. He had followed Stormy and Marie from the restaurant, and now, he knew where *she* lived!

Chapter 6

STORMY AWOKE WITH A JOLT! Looking over at his alarm clock, he realized he forgot to set the alarm. It was 8:35 and he was late, not normal for him, but last night had been anything but normal. He was still in a euphoric mood, and nothing was going to dampen that for now, especially being a little late for work. He took a quick shower, dressed, grabbed a glass of orange juice and headed out the door. He pulled out his cell and called his office, asking if Rolando was in yet. He was told that Rolando had called and advised that he wouldn't be in until around noon, due to an unforeseen emergency. His mother had flown in from out of town and needed a ride from the airport.

Stormy arrived at his office about thirty minutes later and went in to brief Captain Paradis. Tapping on the Captain's door he was asked to enter.

"Good morning, Stormy," the Captain said. "Care for a cup of coffee?"

"Sounds great, Captain, I was running late and didn't get a chance to have any."

Captain Paradis lifted the desk phone, punched a number, and asked Adria, his administrative assistant, to bring two cups of coffee, if she didn't mind. The Captain waited for Adria to bring the coffee before he let Stormy begin his report. When she had set the cups down, the Captain asked her to close the door and hold all calls.

Stormy began with the events that had taken place the day before, not leaving out anything and finishing up with the arrest of Hector Gomez.

"Do you think he's the killer?" asked the Captain.

"Everything points to it, his connection to Luis, the escape...," Stormy said, his voice trailing off.

"What does your gut tell you?"

"To be honest, Captain, my gut says he is not the killer!"

"I've worked with you too long to ignore what *your gut* tells you, Stormy, so why don't you feel he is the killer?"

"I can't put my finger on it, but something just doesn't feel right about it," Stormy replied.

"He won't admit to any of it?" asked Captain Paradis.

"He denies any part at all, and when I look in his eyes I feel he's telling the truth."

"Do you plan to interrogate him further?"

"I planned to do that this morning, but Rolando won't be in until after noon," said Stormy.

"Then go without him, he can take a pool car and join you later," the Captain said.

"Okay, Captain. I'll head to Miami now and see what I can come up with," replied Stormy.

Stormy drove to Miami P.D. and walked into the lobby of the station, this time not having to show his I.D. to the desk officer. He had been in and out so much the last few days that they knew him by sight now. Looking around the lobby, he tried to see if he could pinpoint what it was that was bothering him earlier, something that kept standing the short hairs up on the back of his neck. Not seeing anything, he rode the elevator up to C.I.D. and went straight to Leo's desk. Leo was on the phone and held a finger up, indicating he would be through in a minute. Stormy waited patiently, scanning the crime scene photos Leo had scattered about his desk.

"I've been swamped with calls from the media since the arrest," started Leo, after hanging up the phone. "Do you feel we have enough evidence to charge him with the murders?"

"Unless we get him to talk or we can obtain some more conclusive evidence, no, I don't feel comfortable charging him at this time," Stormy said.

"He says he won't talk with us without a lawyer," replied Leo.

"I wasn't thinking about him," said Stormy. "How about his wife? Is she still here?"

"She's been booked and is waiting for a bond hearing later today," replied Leo.

"Good, I want to talk with her first, and then maybe I'll try Hector again," Stormy said.

"You want me to go with you?" asked Leo.

"Sure, if you're not too busy."

They left the office and headed to the Dade County Jail, talking about the case on the way.

"Well, we didn't have another killing last night," said Leo. "Maybe that means we have the right man in custody."

"I'm not too sure about that," replied Stormy. "Something tells me he's not the one."

"What makes you think that?" asked Leo.

"You saw him. Do you really think he has the finesse that was needed for those killings?"

"You may have a point, but we have to consider his connection to Luis and his escape. Maybe he had help, as far as the finesse thing," said Leo.

"I don't think he had help, and I really feel he's not the one. But, we still need to talk with his wife."

They arrived at the jail, parked and went inside. The desk Sergeant made arrangements for them to have a room to interrogate Mrs. Gomez. While they waited Stormy told Leo, "We're going to have to cut her loose, you know?"

"What are you talking about?" asked Leo.

"I taped her conversation without her knowledge or consent, heard her talking with Hector and then followed her to his hideout," said Stormy.

"She still obstructed your investigation. Can't we charge her with that?"

"A good attorney, or heck, even a good Public Defender will know to ask how I knew to follow her and why!" said Stormy. "It may be better to let her think she's going to be charged. That way she would be more inclined to make a deal."

"I heard you were unorthodox in your methods, but we'll do it your way," said Leo.

When she was led into the room, she looked harried and scared. She probably had never been in a jail cell before and most likely didn't sleep at all last night.

"Mrs. Gomez, you know who I am. This is Detective Sharp. We want to ask you some questions," started Stormy.

"I don't know anything, Why am I here?" she started, tears in her eyes.

"Before we start I need to inform you of your rights under the Miranda warning."

Leo read her the rights and had her sign and put her initials at the bottom of the form.

"You are going to be charged with obstruction of justice. Do you understand what that is?" asked Stormy.

"Not really. Does it mean I have to stay in jail?" she asked.

"It means that you interfered with a criminal investigation by either hiding or covering up knowledge of Hectors whereabouts. It also means that if you are found guilty you could spend some time in jail. Do you understand?" Leo asked.

"But I didn't know where he was. I told you, I last saw him six months ago in prison," she replied, tearfully.

"How did you know where to tell the taxi to go?" asked Stormy.

"Hector told me on the phone," she replied.

"Then how did you get the phone number if you haven't seen him?" asked Leo.

"He called me last week and told me he was hiding out and would send for me later," she said.

After asking several more questions Stormy called an end to the session.

"Mrs. Gomez, I believe you, and I'm going to try to get you out of here," said Stormy.

"Oh, would you please. I hate it here. I really don't know anything more than I've told you," she said, hope showing on her face.

After the guard took her back to her cell, Stormy asked the desk sergeant to have them bring out Hector, indicating they would use the same room. In a few minutes Hector was led into the interrogation room. After Hector took a seat, Stormy quietly observed that some of the defiance he exhibited earlier was absent.

"Hector," he began, "this is your last chance to talk with us. Do you want your attorney here now?"

"I've told you I didn't have anything to do with Luis's murder, and I have nothing else to say," he replied.

"Okay, but be forewarned, if you are connected, all deals are off the table," said Stormy.

Motioning to the guard that the interview was over, Stormy stood and walked out of the room. Leo followed. They didn't say anything until they were out of the jail and in their car heading back to the station.

"I don't know," Leo said, shaking his head.

"Nor do I," Stormy replied. "But, the killings seemed to have stopped, so I guess we'll have to wait and see for now."

Within thirty seconds after Stormy's comment the dispatcher for Miami called Leo on his portable. He was advised to respond to 221 Northeast 2nd Street regarding a homicide. Leo had dispatch switch to a private channel.

"Dispatch, we're working an active investigation. Don't you have any other available detectives?" he asked.

"Detective Sharp, you're going to want to take this one. It may be related to what you're working," she replied.

"10-4, on our way to the 10-20," Leo said.

Looking at Stormy he shook his head again, this time in disbelief.

"I honestly hope she's wrong," he said.

"I have a funny feeling she's not," Stormy replied.

With blues flashing from the grill of the car they increased their speed, weaving in and out of traffic. They soon arrived at the address they were given. Patrol units were already present, parked in front of the house, blues flashing. They were met at the front door by the road sergeant.

"Detective Sharp, we received a call from the daughter of the victim. She returned home from shopping and found her mother dead in the bedroom. She's pretty shook up by what she saw. From what I observed it fits the other murders from the last few nights," he said.

"Is there anyone else in the house?" asked Leo.

"No sir. I closed the door and haven't allowed anyone in, was waiting for you to get here," he said.

"Thank you, Sergeant, and if you will, set up a perimeter around the house and, for God's sake, keep the press at a distance," Stormy said.

Just as Stormy and Leo were starting to enter the house, a car pulled up to a screeching halt. Stormy looked over his shoulder and saw that Rolando had pulled up. He turned and walked back to him, meeting him as he stepped into the driveway.

"Sorry, Stormy, the plane was late, and when I got to C.I.D., they told me you had been dispatched to this address. I hurried here as fast as I could. What's the story? Is it another one?"

"We just got here and haven't been inside yet. I want you to check the exterior of the house and see if you can come up with anything."

"I guess this puts Hector in the clear," Rolando said.

"Yeah, for the murders, if the one here is the same as the others. But he's still going away for the escape, not to mention the rest of the sentence he was serving."

Stormy went into the house, his shoes clacking on the terrazzo floor. He saw Leo standing at the bedroom door, shaking his head sadly.

"Such a shame," he said.

Stormy stepped into the room and observed the woman lying supine on the bed. Her wrists were fastened in front with plastic ties, duct tape on her nose and mouth, her eyes still open in death. He saw the numbers on her forehead, and that was all it took to convince him that they had not caught the killer yet.

"Do we know her name or anything about her?" Stormy asked.

"She's Sylvia Connery, a retired school teacher, according to her daughter," Leo replied.

"Why on earth would someone want to kill an elderly school teacher?" Stormy asked, speaking to no one in particular.

"All we can do now is to wait for C.S.I. to process the scene," Leo said.

"The other murders were committed at night. Why did this one happen during daylight?" Stormy said, talking to no one in particular.

"Do you think it's a copycat killing?" asked Leo.

"No one knows about the numbers," replied Stormy.

"Except that Spanish television station reporter," Leo said with disgust.

"Did you find out how they were able to get that information?" asked Stormy.

"I did, and that particular officer is on administrative leave until Internal Affairs finishes with him. Then we'll see what happens to him. If I have my way, he'll work a desk the rest of his career if IA doesn't recommend termination."

While Leo and Stormy were double-checking the room for evidence, Rolando walked in.

"I couldn't find anything of evidentiary value in the front or back yard," he said.

"I didn't think you would. This guy is too careful," Stormy responded.

They left the room just as Miami C.S.I. Tech Millie Simmons walked in, dusting kit in hand and a grim look on her face.

"Why the long face, Millie?" asked Leo.

"I'm just disgusted. Are we ever going to catch this creep?" she asked.

"We're working on it, Millie. We're trying really hard. Sooner or later he's going to slip up, and then we'll have him!"

"The judge was black, the prosecutor white and the last one Spanish. Now a woman. What's next, a kid?" she asked.

"Don't even think that," Stormy said. "We'll leave you to your work. If you find *anything,* call us at once, and I mean anything. We have to get this guy!"

They left the house and headed for C.I.D. Rolando followed in his car. When they arrived and parked the car, they went in through the front door. Upon entering the lobby Stormy had that feeling again, and this time he was determined to scour the lobby until he figured out what it was that was nagging him.

Slowly walking around the lobby, he stopped and looked at everything, not sure what he was looking for. Then he stood in front of the memorial for fallen officers, and it hit him. Light bulbs went off in his head, and a big smile spread across his face.

Leo noticed the transformation and asked, "What is it? You got something?"

"I think I may have the answer for the numbers," Stormy said, confidently.

He pointed out the photos of the officers that had died in the line of duty and asked Leo if he noticed anything common to them all. Leo stood and looked intently, not seeing what Stormy had seen.

"I don't see anything," he said.

"Badge numbers, Leo. Badge numbers!"

Looking at the photos, Leo suddenly saw that a small number of them had three digit badge numbers. He slapped Stormy on the back, exclaiming, "I think you just solved the meaning of the numbers, Stormy!"

"Let's not count our chickens just yet," Stormy said.

"I'll go to Human Resources and have all the three-digit badge numbers pulled for the last, let's say ten years," Leo said.

Leo rode the elevator to the top floor where Human Resources was located. He told the clerk behind the counter what he was looking for, and within ten minutes she had pulled up and printed out the results. Leo took the small sheaf of printouts and headed for his office.

When he walked in, Stormy and Rolando were anxiously waiting for him at his desk. Spreading the sheets out on his desk, they began to scour the pages, looking for the badge number 241.

"It's not here," said a disappointed Leo. "I thought we really had it."

"How far back did you go?" Stormy asked.

"Ten years," he replied.

"Go back and request ten or fifteen years prior to these," Stormy said.

"Okay, maybe I didn't go back far enough," he said.

"Better yet, call and ask the clerk if she can just put in the number and see if it will pull up anything," Stormy said.

"Good idea. That may save time *and* paper."

Leo made the call to the clerk and asked her to call him back if she came up with anything.

"Where did Rolando go?" Stormy asked

"I don't know, he was here a minute ago," Leo replied. "He probably went to the restroom."

About that time Rolando walked out of the restroom. Leo looked at Stormy as if to say I told you so.

"Get anything back yet?" Rolando asked as he walked up to the two detectives.

Before either could respond, the phone on Leo's desk rang. Leo answered and listened for a minute.

"Yes, I understand, but make it as quick as possible," he said, hanging up the phone.

"That was Records, the information we want is on microfilm now. Anything past ten years involving personnel files is now put on microfilm and stored at another building. She's calling over for them to do a hand search and will forward the results to us as soon as possible," Leo said.

"I'll head back to Hialeah. Rolando, you can drive the pool car back, and I'll pick you up there," Stormy said.

While driving back to Hialeah, Stormy dialed Pablo on his cell phone. Pablo picked up on the first ring.

"*Hola*, Stormy my friend."

"Pablo, have you found out anything yet?" asked Stormy

"Not a thing. I can't believe no one knows anything," he said.

"Where are you now?" asked Stormy

"I'm in Hialeah visiting a friend," he replied.

"Meet me at Hialeah City Hall. I'll be there in twenty minutes," Stormy said.

"Okay, my friend. See you there."

Stormy called Rolando and told him to continue on to the station and that he would be there in about an hour. He was still not ready for him to meet Pablo. He checked his glove box to make sure the copy of the CD was still there – it was.

He pulled into the front parking lot twenty-five minutes later and saw Pablo's car, a ten-year-old Toyota, parked in front. Pablo was sitting in the driver's seat. He exited his car and walked over to Pablo, who was getting out of his car at the same time. They shook hands, made some small talk and walked into City Hall. Stormy knew that the City Council Chambers had a CD player, so they took the elevator to the second floor. When he and Pablo entered the Chambers he didn't see the player at first, but then looked behind the huge curved desk the Councilmen sat at and saw it sitting on a shelf, out of sight.

At that moment a man walked in and asked what they were doing there. Stormy showed him his badge and told him he was going to use the CD player for a minute. The man told him he didn't have authorization to use it and that he would have to leave. Stormy, exhibiting a frown, stared at the man and said,

"Why don't you go ask Tom if it's okay for Jack Storm to use the machine?"

"Tom? You mean the Mayor, Tom Boyce?" asked the man.

"Yes, that's the Tom," replied Stormy.

"I'll do just that," the man said, leaving the room in a hurry.

Stormy didn't wait and walked around the desk, turning on the CD player and inserting the disc. As the image came up, Pablo stared at it intently. He asked Stormy to play it again and to pause it when the profile of the man in the image came up. He stared at the image for a minute and then exclaimed wide-eyed to Stormy, "I know him. He's a *cop!*"

Chapter 7

L EO SAT BACK IN HIS CHAIR, giving his eyes a rest. He had scanned the crime scene photos for all of the murders for hours, trying to make a connection. If Stormy was correct in his assumption that the badge numbers could play a role then they would definitely be a step closer to solving this case. Thinking of Stormy he couldn't help but smile a little.

Stormy was well known in the law enforcement community and had achieved almost legendary status with his investigative techniques and the closing of hundreds of cases. He had a reputation for fairness but would not tolerate ignorance. A lot of his cases were high profile, but mostly he was known for his ability to make quick arrests. Leo knew about Stormy's C.I., but like everyone else, didn't have a clue as to who the C.I. was. As far as he knew, no one other than Stormy's commanding officer and his former partner, Gil, had ever met the informant. All he knew was that an abundance of valuable information was gleaned from that informant. Leo respected and liked Stormy despite his unorthodox style and lone wolf mentality,.

Leo was jolted out of his thoughts when his desk

phone started ringing. Reaching over and lifting the receiver, he straightened up and answered.

"Detective Sharp?" asked the caller.

"Speaking," replied Leo.

"This is Candice in Records."

"Hello, Candice. I hope you have something for me," said Leo.

"I do. I searched the microfilm records back twenty-five years and came up with two officers issued the badge number 241 during that span of time. I also had a friend of mine at Metro-Dade check their records, and he came up with only one badge issued with that number."

"Do you have a printout of their personnel files ready for me?" asked Leo.

"Yes, and my friend faxed his over to me as well. You can pick them up anytime," she said.

"I'll be right down, and, Candice, great work. I really owe you one," said Leo.

Leo bounded from his chair and headed for Records to pick up the printouts. When he reached Candice's desk she smiled at him and said, "That was fast. You must have run all the way!"

"Actually, I took the elevator and even that seemed too slow for me," laughed Leo.

"Here are the printouts, including the one from Metro-Dade," she said, holding out the paperwork.

"Thanks again, Candice. Great work," said Leo, taking the printouts and heading back to the elevator.

When he reached his desk, Leo sat down and took the first printout and started reading. It was the one from Metro-Dade. When he had finished, he knew that this wouldn't be of any use to him. The badge had been issued to Humberto Alvarez in 1970 when he was fresh out of the academy. He had been twenty-four at the time and that would now make him sixty-seven years old...besides, he had been retired for eight years and had moved to Costa Rica with his native-born wife soon after retiring.

Putting that file aside he began reading the next one in line. He didn't have to read very far before he discovered that the officer had been killed in an automobile accident while responding to a call one night in 2001. He set that printout on top of the one from Metro-Dade and picked up the last one. If this one didn't pan out, they would be right back where they started – with nothing!

As he perused the first page his heart skipped a beat. At the top right-hand corner of the page was a red stamp, *Security Clearance Eyes Only*! The stamp had been dated by Internal Affairs in June of 1993. Leo was puzzled at first, but after reading further he soon found out the whole story.

Jose Miguel Acosta had started his career with the Miami Police Department in November 1984 at the age of twenty-two. He had an average police career until he was selected for an undercover assignment by the Vice Section of the Department. This happened in 1990, and all of a sudden he was deeply entrenched in his undercover role. His information for the next couple of years resulted in numerous arrests ranging from loan sharking to major drug busts.

In January of 1992 he began an investigation into the business empire of one Luis Herrera, a vicious drug kingpin in the greater Miami area. Herrera was said to be untouchable, but Jose was able to work his way up through the organization with access near the top of the heap. He was in the process of delivering overwhelming evidence that would put Herrera away for a long time. Before he could turn over the evidence, an anonymous tip called in to the police department resulted in him being stopped and his car searched. Two kilos of cocaine and twenty thousand dollars were found in the trunk of his car. He was arrested and taken to jail, vigorously denying any knowledge of the contraband in his car. He claimed that he had evidence recorded in a small black book hidden in the door panel of the passenger side of the car, but when it was searched the black book was not there.

Jose was put on trial and convicted, based solely on the evidence found in his car. He repeatedly told his lawyers and visiting police detectives that he had been set up. He claimed that somehow Herrera found out he was undercover and arranged for the call, planting the contraband in his car. His pleas fell on deaf ears, and he was subsequently sentenced to twenty-five years in prison.

Three months after he began serving his time he was found stabbed to death in a shower in the prison. That prompted the Miami investigators to open the case and investigate further. Their findings a year later pointed to an inmate who had ties to Herrera had stabbed Jose to death. Jose was cleared of the charges, but it was too late for his family. His death and wrongful conviction cast a long shadow on the Department for years.

To try to compensate for the gross miscarriage of justice he was put in the Hall of Fame in the lobby of the Miami Police Department. The Internal Affairs Division stamped the file with a security block to keep the media from digging into the case and jeopardizing further ongoing investigations into Luis Herrera. Herrera was never charged with any crime, and in 2004 he dropped from sight. Later it was determined that he had turned over his empire to his only son and had retired to South Beach. It was assumed that he still had a hand in the operation, although the link couldn't be proven.

Jose had two sons – one four years of age and the other six – when he was killed in prison. His wife, Lourdes, died in 2005, never fully recovering from the death of her husband. When she died, her sister, Bella Diaz, and her husband took in the two boys, Lonnie and Eduardo, and finished raising them. An address was listed for Bella and that would be the first place he and Stormy would start.

Leo quickly dialed Stormy's cell number, silently urging him to answer. The phone went to voice mail, so Leo left an urgent message for Stormy to call him as quickly as possible.

****

Stormy glanced down at his phone which he had set on vibrate and saw that Leo was calling. He would call him back in a few minutes he decided. First he had to make sure he had heard Pablo correctly, that the person who had broken into his car was a cop.

"Pablo, are you sure?" he asked, incredulously.

"Well, he sure looks like the one that stopped me and my friend a couple of months ago," replied Pablo.

"Was it in Hialeah?" Stormy asked.

"Yeah, my friend lives on West 29th Street, and we

cruised through a red light. The cop was coming from the opposite direction and fell in behind us, and then he put on his lights and pulled us over."

"When exactly was this?"

"I dunno, maybe two, three months ago."

"Look at the CD again and make sure," said Stormy "It's important.

They played the CD again, stopping it on the area where the subjects profile stood out the most. The picture looked very grainy to Stormy, but Pablo was adamant that it was the cop who stopped them. As Stormy ejected the CD, the unknown man stepped in the Chamber room and apologized to Stormy. He said he had checked with the Mayor and had been given approval for Stormy to use the machine.

"No harm. You were just doing your job," said Stormy.

Stormy and Pablo started to leave the Council Chambers as the man said, "Aren't you going to use the machine?"

"Maybe later, we have to go now," replied Stormy, smiling.

They left the building, the man still standing in the doorway to the Council Chambers, scratching his head, wondering what had just happened.

Stormy told Pablo to wait by his car and walked away a few feet to dial Leo's cell.

Leo answered on the first ring, "Stormy, you need to get here right away."

"Hold on. What's going on? Why the urgency?" asked Stormy

"I just got the personnel files on three badge numbers, all 241. One is from Metro-Dade, and there is one you need to read, right now," Leo said, the excitement evident in his voice.

"I'll be there in about thirty minutes, and I have some news for you too," Stormy said.

"What news?"

"I'll tell you when I get there," said Stormy.

Walking over to Pablo, who was standing by his car smoking a cigarette, Stormy said to him, "I have to go to Miami P.D. now, but I'll need you to come to my office tomorrow morning. I want to show you some police photos and see if you recognize any of them to be the one on the CD.

"What time?" Pablo asked.

"Make it around nine. I need time to pull the photos," replied Stormy.

"I'll be there," Pablo said.

As Pablo got into his car Stormy reached in and handed him two one hundred-dollar bills.

"If what you say is true about the cop, there'll be more money for you," Stormy said.

During the drive to Miami P.D. Stormy let his thoughts run wild. *I won't tell Captain Paradis about what Pablo said until I have concrete evidence tomorrow. Maybe Pablo is guessing, or maybe the image only resembles the cop that stopped him. I have to be sure before my next move. Oh crap, Rolando is waiting for me back at the station!*

He quickly called Rolando on his cell and told him to start a report on the day's activities, that he had something to take care of and would be there in an hour or so. Twenty-five minutes later he pulled into the parking lot at Miami P.D. and quickly parked the car. He walked at a fast pace into the building and patiently waited for the elevator to arrive at the ground floor. When he exited on the third floor, Leo was pacing back and forth, his adrenalin obviously high.

"Hey, Leo, you look like you're going to have a heart attack. Slow down," Stormy said.

"Wait until you read this," he replied, holding out a file.

Stormy took a seat at Leo's desk and began reading the file, his eyebrows arching higher the more he read. Just to make sure he had all the facts he re-read it. Then he looked at Leo and smiled.

"It seems to have all the elements for someone to hold a grudge," he said.

"My thoughts exactly," Leo said.

"Well, what are we waiting for? Let's go see if Bella Diaz has any information we can use."

Grabbing the file, he and Leo headed for the elevator. Once they were in Stormy's car, Leo gave him the address again, and they headed out of the parking lot. Bella's home was in Broward County, so Stormy maneuvered his way through the side streets until he reached I-95, which he took northbound. It was a good forty-minute drive, so they had plenty of time to talk about the case.

Leo started by asking, "What was the news you had for me?"

"Remember the CD that my neighbor recorded, the one when my car was broken into?" Stormy asked.

"Yeah, did you ever come up with anything on identifying the person?"

"That's the news. My C.I. viewed the CD today and is positive that the person is a cop, one that stopped him and a friend a couple of months ago," Stormy said.

"Wow, now that would be something. Do you think it's possible he's correct, or do you think he's just guessing?"

"He sure seemed awful positive about it. I'm having him come into the station tomorrow to look at some of the officers' pictures, unless I run into a snag getting them from Human Resources. When we get back from Broward, I'll go by City Hall and make the arrangements."

"Something that sensitive may require you to go through your Captain," Leo said.

"I thought about that, too. But if Pablo is wrong, it'll not look good for him or me," Stormy said. "So I thought I'd wait until Pablo has a chance to look at the photos."

"Good point, but you may get some resistance from Human Resources. Just be prepared for it," said Leo.

"If that becomes a problem I'll have no choice but to let the Captain know. He'll have to use his position to secure the release for me," Stormy said.

"What's your take on Jose Acosta after reading his file?" asked Leo.

"First, it was some very sloppy investigating to try to clear him, no offense to Miami P.D., and second, a real miscarriage of justice. He should have been put into a more secure facility or cell when he was incarcerated. Most cops put in jail are in danger and to avoid a publicity nightmare for the prison they're usually protected from the general population. Why wasn't Acosta?"

"That call is usually made by the warden, so I guess we would have to ask him," replied Leo.

Stormy continued driving northbound on I-95 until he reached Ives Dairy Road, where he exited. He took a left under the overpass and only had to drive a few blocks to reach Northeast 15th Avenue. Turning south on 15th Avenue, he drove slowly until he spotted the address on the left side of the street. There was a work van in the driveway and an old Chevy Caprice. The house looked well kept on the outside, the proverbial white fence present in front and the exterior seemed newly painted, a slight peach color, a favorite of many of the older Spanish people. Stormy pulled in the driveway behind the Chevy and switched off the engine. They sat for a minute to see if anyone would come out. When no one did, they exited the car and walked to the front door.

After ringing the doorbell, they heard someone's shoes clicking on the floor, approaching the door. Stormy knew immediately, another terrazzo floor, something not many Floridians had anymore.

The door opened partially and an older woman appeared, asking,

"*Si*, can I help you?"

"Are you Bella Diaz?" asked Stormy.

"*Si*, what can I do for you?" she asked.

"I'm Detective Jack Storm, and this is Detective Sharp. We would like to come in and ask you a few questions. That is, if you don't mind of course," Stormy said.

"Have I done something wrong?" she asked, wringing

her hands.

"No ma'am. We're just following up a case, and your name came up. Do you know Jose Acosta?"

"Yes, please, come in," the woman said, holding the door open.

The house was immaculate, clean beyond belief. And Stormy was right – the floors were of terrazzo and highly polished. Bella directed them to take a seat. They sat on a plastic covered ornate couch that had probably never had the plastic off. Bella asked them if they would like something to drink, and they both declined.

"So, Detective Storm, what would you like to know about Jose?" she asked.

"We know about the false charge that put him in prison and also about his death. Please accept our condolences. In his personnel file it stated he had two children, both boys, and that you took them into your family and raised them after their mother died. We're interested in the boys and where they are now. We would very much like to talk with them," Stormy said.

Before she could respond, Stormy's cell phone began to vibrate. Glancing at the screen he saw that Rolando was calling him. Excusing himself, he arose and walked to the front of the living room.

"Hello, Rolando," he answered.

"Stormy, I had a question to ask about the report I'm doing," Rolando replied.

"What is it?" asked Stormy, slightly irritated.

"Do you want me to include the details about the CD your neighbor gave you and do I wait for you when I'm finished, or go home?"

"Include the CD in the report, and I may be awhile. I'm in Broward County right now," Stormy said.

"What's going on in Broward, another lead?" asked Rolando.

"Leo found a name to match the numbers, and we're checking it out now."

There was a silence on Rolando's end of the line.

"Rolando, you still there?" asked Stormy.

"I'm still here, just thinking about how I would like to be there with you," he replied. "What's the lead you're working?" he asked.

"There was a police officer in Miami that was framed and later died in prison. His badge number was 241. We're talking with the woman, Bella Diaz, who raised his kids after his wife died. I was just asking her about the two sons of the officer when you called, so I need to get back," Stormy said.

"Okay, I'll see you tomorrow," Rolando replied.

Hanging up the phone Stormy walked back to the couch and sat down, apologizing for the interruption.

"Where can we find Lonnie and Eduardo, Mrs. Diaz?" asked Stormy.

"I don't know what they could tell you about their father that would be of any interest to you. They were four and six years old when he died," Bella said. "They wouldn't remember anything about it."

"Where can we find them, Mrs. Diaz?" Stormy asked again, softly.

"Eduardo is living in Orlando with his wife and child. Lonnie…I don't know where he is. He joined the Army when he turned eighteen, and we haven't heard from him since."

"I'll need an address for Eduardo, if you don't mind. Maybe he's heard from Lonnie," Stormy said.

"I don't mind. Wait and I'll get it for you," she said.

Stormy and Leo looked at each other, thinking the same thing. Now they had to take a four-hour trip to Orlando. There was no other way around it.

"Here's the address," Bella said, holding out a piece of paper to Stormy.

"Thank you very much," Stormy said, taking the paper from her hand.

"Can you tell us anything about the boys, how they handled their father and mother's death in later years. Was there any hostility towards anyone? Did they have issues that weren't normal for a kid?" asked Leo.

"Eduardo was a typical kid. He didn't understand why his father died, but when his mother died he seemed to withdraw from his friends, and us, for awhile. It was understandable, and we were patient with him until he recovered from his sadness," she began. "Lonnie, well he was a different story."

"What was different with Lonnie?" asked Stormy.

"He was six when his father died and was able to understand and feel the loss, more than his younger brother. He wasn't told the circumstances of how his father died until he was a teenager, and that was after his continued insistence. After that revelation he became a different person, not talking with family and friends, staying in his room alone for hours on end, and lashing out when he was pressed for answers to his behavior," Bella said, sadly shaking her head. "Actually, we were so happy he joined the Army as we felt it would help him grow up and forget his awful past."

"Did he ever resort to physical violence when pressured?" asked Stormy.

"No, but you could see that he was on the verge of it and probably would have if pressed much further, so we just let him be," she said.

"I know this is hard, bringing up his past, but was he ever on drugs that could explain his behavior?" asked Leo, gently.

"My husband and I considered that possibility, but we were never able to find any in his room. Eduardo swore he never saw him taking anything, so I really don't think so," she said.

"Speaking of your husband, where is he if I may ask?"

"He went to a poker game with some friends this morning. He should be home in a few hours," she said.

"We want to thank you for your time and all your help, Mrs. Diaz. Are there any questions you would like to ask of us?"

"I still don't know what this is about, but I pray that my boys are not in trouble," she replied.

"Well, thank you again. We'll be on our way," Stormy said, without answering her question.

Stormy and Leo stood and left the house. Bella watched from the doorway, a worried look on her face. They gave her a slight wave goodbye and backed out of the driveway. As they drove back towards Ives Dairy Road she watched them until they were out of sight.

Once they were on I-95 southbound they started to encounter the beginnings of rush hour traffic. The congestion seemed to get worse with each passing year. They rode in silence for a few miles, maneuvering in and out of traffic until they were pretty much ahead of the heaviest traffic.

"What now?" Leo asked.

"I'm going to drop you off, and then I need to get to Hialeah City Hall before they close for the day," replied Stormy.

"When are we going to Orlando?" Leo asked.

"I guess we can plan on going tomorrow afternoon, and we'll probably have to spend the night. I can't leave until Pablo looks at the photos, assuming I don't hit any snags obtaining them," Stormy said. "At any rate, I'll know tonight, and if there's a problem we can leave for Orlando in the morning and *not* have to spend the night."

"Either way, it's going to be a long day for us," Leo said.

Chapter 8

S TORMY DROPPED OFF LEO at Miami P.D. and drove to Hialeah City Hall. He would be pushing it to make it before they closed for the day. He pulled up in front of City Hall with ten minutes to spare. He rushed to the elevator and when he got out on the second floor he swiftly walked to the office of Helen Wentworth, the supervisor of Human Resources. Tapping on her door he heard her tell him to come in. Entering the office, he could see that she was wrapping up for the day and appeared anxious to be on her way. He could tell from her expression that she was thinking, *I hope this doesn't take long*!

"Ms. Wentworth, I'm Detective Storm, and I have a problem that only you can help me with," he started.

"And what would that be, Detective Storm?" she asked.

"I need photographs of all of the police officers in the city," he said.

"You have got to be kidding me," she said. "That would take an hour, and we close in ten minutes."

"I wouldn't ask, but it's urgent. I have to have them for an investigation I'm working on. I only need the photos, not any personal information on the officers themselves," he begged.

"You know I could deny your request and make you get the proper paperwork," she responded.

"I know, and I hope it won't come to that," Stormy said, smiling as sweetly as he could.

"What is so important about the photos that you have to have them today?" she asked.

"I can't release anything about the case, but I will tell you that it may be a matter of life and death, if that makes a difference."

"I suppose I can approve it on those grounds, but I hope this won't become a habit," she snorted.

"I'll get one of my assistants to start pulling them for you. But be advised, I expect them to be returned, tomorrow, promptly!"

"Yes ma'am, they definitely will be, and thank you so much. I really mean it," Stormy replied, knowing full well that he was going to Orlando and couldn't bring them back tomorrow. Maybe he could get one of the other detectives to bring them back for him. He would ask.

He waited for forty-five minutes, patiently, until the assistant came out with a large box full of loose photos.

"There are 445 photos in here, including the Chief. You'll have to sign for them before I can release them to you," she said.

"No problem," Stormy said, signing the form she held out.

He took the box and headed down to the parking lot, putting the box in his trunk. He was taking no chances on another car burglary. He would take them into his house when he arrived home. Also, he would make arrangements for another detective to return them to City Hall after Pablo had reviewed them. He called Leo and advised him they would be leaving for Orlando around noon the next day, barring any unexpected events. Figuring Rolando had already left the station he headed for his house, stopping at a Chinese takeout on the way for some dinner, which he would eat at home.

Stormy arrived home and suddenly remembered that he was supposed to take Marie out for dinner tomorrow night. He quickly dialed her number and was rewarded with her answering on the first ring.

"I wondered if you were ever going to call me," she said.

"Sorry, honey, you wouldn't believe how busy I've been today," he replied.

"I figured you would be tied up on those killings," she said.

"I'm afraid I have some bad news for you," Stormy said.

"Uh, oh, now what?" she said slowly.

"Me and Detective Sharp have to go to Orlando tomorrow and may have to spend the night," Stormy said, timidly.

"Is it in reference to the case you're working on?" she asked.

"It is, and I wouldn't go if it wasn't so important to the investigation," Stormy replied.

"Well, I do understand. So go, and don't worry about me. Hurry and solve this thing, so we can spend more time together. After all, we're engaged now," she laughed.

"That's another reason I love you – you're so understanding, I'll make it up to you," Stormy promised.

"Oh, yes. That you will," she said, laughing again.

Stormy watched the news while he ate, listening to the local news anchor give a brief update on the murders. There wasn't much for him to talk about other than the news release from Miami P.D. There was a small reference to the arrest they had made, but not much more than that. At least they hadn't mentioned the murder of the female. One more and the news would be screaming for information and the public demanding action. Maybe the trip to Orlando would yield some viable information, but he'd have to wait and see. He flipped the channels and found his favorite program, *Person of Interest*, and watched it to the end. When it was over, he decided to hit the sack, even though it was a little early for him. But first he had to pack an overnight bag for the trip to Orlando tomorrow.

As Stormy was preparing for bed he suddenly realized he had forgotten to bring the box of photos in from the car. Slipping on his robe he went outside, opened the trunk and retrieved the box, bringing it into the house. He was tempted to go through the photos himself to see if he recognized anyone similar to the image on the CD. He decided to wait until tomorrow. He was tired and needed rest for the drive to Orlando. His last thoughts before he fell asleep were about whether or not to take Rolando with them to Orlando.

****

The figure dressed in a black running suit stood outside the townhouse on Golden Beach. He made sure he blended into the shadows even though there were no people on the street. It was eleven o'clock at night and most of the residents on the street were preparing for bed, or had already retired for the night.

When he saw the upstairs light go out in the townhouse he had been intently watching, he slowly inched his way into the yard, avoiding the streetlight's glow. He had studied the house earlier and knew that the occupant was divorced and lived alone.

He made his way to the side door of the garage, where he had earlier jimmied the door and placed a small piece of tape over the hole that the bolt slid into. When he got to the door, hoping his tampering hadn't been discovered and the door locked, he gently pulled on the door knob. The door opened quietly and he entered the dark garage, careful to not bump into anything that would bring the occupant down to investigate. Taking a small flathead screwdriver from his pocket, he gently inserted it between the door jamb and the locking mechanism and carefully forced the bolt to slide back, allowing him to pull the kitchen door open. There was no squeaking of dry hinges, which he was thankful for. He entered the kitchen and quietly pushed the door shut.

There was a glow coming from what appeared to be the dining room, so he carefully peered around the corner. He saw that there was some type of nightlight plugged into an outlet behind the dining room table. Looking around the room he saw the downstairs rooms all had the lights turned off. That meant his victim had retired to his

116

bedroom for the night. Since he had seen the upstairs light go out, he assumed his victim was in bed and maybe asleep.

Charles "Chuck" Knight had spent almost thirty years as Warden of Raiford Penitentiary in Stark, Florida. It had caused him his marriage, his wife not able to cope with the many nights she spent alone. He had spent many of those nights out with friends drinking and not coming home until after midnight. Three years ago she decided she'd had enough – the marriage was not working – so she filed for divorce. They had no children. Their only pet, a toy poodle, she took with her.

Chuck had retired with his State pension in 2009, quit drinking for health reasons and taken up painting. He was better than average and gave away most of his paintings to friends. The past few months he and his wife were on the verge of getting back together, and he was looking forward to it. He never realized how much he missed her until she was gone. That's the way it is most of the time.

Chuck had taken his shower, and after climbing into his four-poster bed, he turned on the television. He almost always fell asleep with it on. Tonight was no different. He was soon fast asleep, the television still on, the volume turned low, the soft glow emanating from the screen dimly illuminating the room.

The figure in black softly nudged the bedroom door open, the glow from the television allowing him to see that his victim was sound asleep. He stepped into the bedroom and paused by the side of the bed, staring at his victim. Chuck was a heavy sleeper and most always slept on his back, prone to lightly snoring. The intruder took four plastic ties from his pocket along with a taser.

Aiming at the sleeping man he fired the taser at his chest, which immediately caused him to awaken in pain. While he was incapacitated the intruder fastened his wrists to the two posts at the head of the bed. Chuck was still in shock but could now see the intruder, his eyes widening in fear. Once the man had his ankles secured with plastic ties to the posts at the foot of the bed, he stepped back and waited for Chuck to recover from the 50,000-volt shock.

Struggling to get free of the restraints, Chuck knew he was in deep trouble. He looked at the intruder and said, "If it's money you want, just take it and go!"

"I don't want your money," the intruder said coldly.

"Then what do you want?" he asked.

The intruder pulled out the same photo he had shown all of his victims and held it in front of Chuck's face.

"Do you recognize this man?" he asked.

"No, should I?" Chuck asked in puzzlement.

Shaking his head slowly, the stranger tore off a strip of duct tape. In one step he was by the bed, placing it on the mouth of his victim.

"I'm going to tell you a story, and now you have no choice but to listen began the intruder…"

Chapter 9

STORMY SLEPT SOUNDLY throughout the night, jolted out of his sleep with the buzzing of the alarm clock. Reaching over to the night stand, he pressed the off button, rolled over and almost dozed off again. He got out of bed and took a shower. After dressing he went into the kitchen and turned on the coffee pot, took out a box of frosted flakes from the cabinet and poured himself a bowl of cereal. While waiting for the coffee to brew he stepped outside and picked up the morning paper, the *Miami Herald*, glanced at his car to see if it had been disturbed during the night and went back into the kitchen.

He scanned through the local section first and seeing nothing of interest he flipped through the rest of the paper. At least there were no murders last night. Maybe the killer had run his course, but a funny feeling in his gut told him that was unlikely. Draining the last of his coffee, he placed the bowl and cup in the dishwasher, noting that it wasn't full enough to turn on at this time. He went to the bedroom and grabbed his weapon, badge and the box of photos along with the small overnight bag he had packed. He left the house, putting the box of photos on the front passenger's seat, and headed for the station.

When he arrived at the station he grabbed the box of photos and went directly to his office. Placing them under his desk he then went to Captain Paradis's office to bring him up to speed on the investigation.

"Good morning, Stormy," Captain Paradis said, sipping his cup of coffee. "You want a cup. It's fresh?"

"No thank you. I just finished one before leaving home," replied Stormy.

"How is the case going?" asked the Captain.

Stormy proceeded to fill the Captain in on the latest findings, watching his reactions as he explained about the badge numbers.

"Do you think the badge numbers may be the key to solving this case?" he asked.

"That's the other thing. I have to go to Orlando today with Detective Sharp. We plan to talk with the son, Eduardo, and see if he has anything of value for us," Stormy said.

"What could he possibly have of value for you. He was only a child when his dad died."

"We have to cover all the bases, talk to everyone. You never know what small insignificant bit of information could surface," replied Stormy.

"There is one other thing," Stormy said, deciding to tell the Captain now.

"Pablo looked at the CD my neighbor gave me, and he swears that the person breaking into my car is a cop – one of ours," Stormy said.

Captain Paradis sat with his cup suspended in mid-air, digesting what he had just been told. Slowly he sat the cup down on his desk, leaned forward and looking intensely at Stormy he said, "That's a serious accusation. Do you believe him?"

"He has no reason to make it up, Captain, but there is another thing I need to tell you," said Stormy.

"Not as outrageous as what you just told me I hope," said Captain Paradis, sitting back in his chair.

"I went to City Hall and had the Human Resources people pull photos of all of our sworn personnel. I have Pablo coming in at nine this morning to see if he can pick out who he thinks it is," Stormy said.

"Did you tell Human Resources why you needed those photos?" asked the Captain.

"Of course not. I told them it was an urgent matter and that I would have the photos back this afternoon, which I hope you can arrange for me," replied Stormy.

"I want you to have Pablo go through the photos in an interview room. I don't want any other detectives to see what he's doing. You understand?"

"Yes sir. I had already thought about that."

"Good. Make sure you let me know as soon as he has finished," Captain Paradis said.

Stormy left the Captain's office and retrieved the box of photos. He took them into interview room two, turned the sign around on the door that read, "*Interview in progress, keep out*," and began preparing for Pablo's arrival.

Pablo always donned some type of disguise when he visited Stormy at the station, which was rare. It was for his protection and to keep other detectives and police officers from getting a good look at him. Stormy had no idea what Pablo would look like this morning, but he was sure that he would go to the same extreme he usually did and completely alter his look.

This morning, Pablo was wearing a bushy paste on beard, looking like one of the characters on the *Duck Dynasty* television show that was so popular now. He had on a baseball cap with a long bill pulled low over his face, and he sported dark sunglasses. Even if you knew him you would never have recognized him in that disguise. Stormy met him at the front of the squad room and led him directly back to the interview room.

Stormy emptied the photos out of the box and placed them into several stacks on the table in the interview room. He told Pablo he would be at his desk and would check on him periodically. When he left the room Pablo had taken off his cap and sunglasses and started sifting through the first stack of photos.

Stormy took his cell and called Leo, drumming his fingers on the desk as it rang several times. After about eight rings, Leo answered.

"Good morning, Leo," Stormy said.

"Hey. Stormy. I was in the Major's office when you called. I stepped out to take it," Leo said.

"I just wanted to let you know I'm tied up here in Hialeah, and I'll call as soon as I'm leaving to pick you up," Stormy said.

"No problem. I have to catch up on some paperwork, but I'll be ready to leave when you get here."

"At least we didn't have another murder last night," Stormy said.

"Yeah, at least there's that," Leo replied. "Call me when you're leaving."

"Will do. Talk with you later."

Stormy arose from his desk and went into the interview room to check on Pablo's progress. He took a seat across from the table, noticing that Pablo had already gone through one of the stacks of photos.

"Any luck yet, Pablo?" asked Stormy.

"Still looking. Found one that I'm setting aside that looks close," Pablo replied.

Pablo kept flipping through the photos as Stormy watched. Most he discarded immediately. Some he took a closer look at before tossing it on the discard pile. Suddenly he came to one that he peered at more intently, soon putting it on top of the other one that he thought looked familiar.

Stormy left the room to follow up on some calls, suddenly realizing that Rolando hadn't arrived for work yet. It was almost ten o'clock. So he approached the secretary, Adria, and asked if Rolando had called. She told him that he had called and said he wouldn't be in today, something about a personal problem. Stormy nodded his head and walked back to the interview room, thinking, *Rolando sure is taking a lot of time off, and he just got assigned here. Maybe I need to speak with the Captain about it.*

When he went back into the interview room he saw that Pablo had almost gone through all the stacks of photos. The pile he had started with that he felt was worthy of a second look had grown to maybe a dozen or more. He was now turning his attention to that pile, briefly glancing up as Stormy entered the room.

"Most of these will be discarded, but I wanted to take a second look," Pablo said, as Stormy took a seat.

When Pablo had gone through the dozen or so photos

he had laid aside he ended up with three that he kept looking at, over and over. Finally, he narrowed it down to two photos, telling Stormy that he was positive it was one of the two who had stopped him and his friend. He just wasn't sure which one.

"We need to be one hundred percent sure before any action can be taken," Stormy said. "Look at them again and again until you're sure."

Pablo took the two photos and laid them side by side on the table, intensely looking at them.

Finally, Stormy took the two photos and looked at them, recognizing both officers. One was a young-looking officer that had been terminated during his probation period. He had met the officer once when he was on a case and the officer had secured the crime scene. He had been terminated because he had attempted to have his girlfriend's traffic citation voided. He had been so insistent that a verbal argument had erupted, and the sergeant on duty had to break it up. Stormy noticed that he did resemble the person on the CD, but he was unable to positively identify him as the one.

The second one caused Stormy to do a double-take. It was Rolando Fuentes! Taking the photo, he left Pablo in the room, telling him to stay there until he got back. He went to his office and retrieved the CD from his desk drawer. He went to the Captains office and knocked on the door. The Captain told him to come in, noticing the look of concern on Stormy's face.

"What's the matter Stormy?" he asked.

"I think we've identified the person who broke into my car," Stormy said. "Can I use your CD player for a minute?"

The Captain turned on the CD player and took the CD from Stormy, inserting it into the player. When the image came up Stormy told the Captain to freeze it on the profile of the car burglar. When he did, Stormy took the photo of Rolando that Pablo had chosen and gave it to the Captain.

Captain John Paradis was a dedicated police officer. In fact, police officers went back as far as his grandfather in his family. He was proud of his profession and was a by-the-book officer. His reputation had never been blemished or sullied, and he intended to keep it that way. His retirement was only a year away, and he didn't need anything to mar his tenure of over thirty years. When he saw the photo he was shocked but didn't exhibit any outward expression to Stormy. Instead he held the photo up to the image on the screen and looked at it for several minutes. Finally, he turned to Stormy and said, "It looks awful close but not enough to draw any definite conclusions yet."

"Captain, it's *too* close to not look into further," Stormy said.

"I agree, but quietly, Stormy, quietly. Until you're sure," Captain Paradis replied.

"I have a friend at the regional FBI office, and I'd like your permission to take the photo and CD to them. They have the Facial Recognition Program. That would be the best bet now," Stormy said.

"Good idea. I never thought of that. Can you drop it off before you leave for Orlando?" asked Captain Paradis.

"No problem. Their office is just down the street from Miami P.D. Besides, my friend owes me one. So I'll put the pressure on him to speed it up. Hopefully he'll have it ready for me when I return," Stormy said.

"Also, I just remembered," Stormy continued "Rolando was with me when I put the evidence bag in the car, but why would *he* want to take it?"

"Maybe there's the remote possibility he knows who is doing the killing and is trying to help him," Captain Paradis said.

"That would put him on the same level as the killer, covering up a murder and destroying evidence," Stormy said.

"Another thing, Captain. Rolando has been late a few times and taken off a couple of days from work since he's been here, and he hasn't been here that long," Stormy said.

"I'll look into it and have a word with him," said the Captain.

"When you return from Orlando, you need to follow this up, discreetly, until you're sure," the Captain said.

Stormy went into the interview room and told Pablo he could go. He slipped him another hundred dollars – now the fund owed him three hundred. He would get it before he left since he would be needing cash for the trip to Orlando.

He took the two photos and packed the rest back in the box. Taking the box into the Captain's office, he also ejected the CD from the player and put it with the photo of Rolando in a manila envelope. After going to Adria and getting his three hundred dollars back, he headed to his car with the manila envelope. When he reached 103rd Street, he called Leo, advising him he was on the way but had to make one stop first. He told him he should be there within an hour and to be ready to go. He wasn't looking forward to the four-hour drive at all, but he had a feeling it was now a trip they needed to take.

Just before he arrived at the FBI office, he called Marie and told her he was leaving for Orlando and would call her from there. He entered the FBI building and asked the receptionist at the front desk to speak with Agent Lawrence Foresman. The receptionist smiled and pointed behind him. Lawrence had just walked in behind him on his way to his office.

"Larry, good timing. I'm heading out to Orlando and kind of in a hurry," Stormy said, shaking his hand.

"Going to Disney, Stormy?" asked Larry.

"Nope, unfortunately it's business," laughed Stormy.

"What did you need to see me about?" asked Larry.

"I need a really big favor. I need you to take a couple of photos and run a Facial Recognition on them, comparing them to an image on a CD I have," Stormy said.

"Well, I do owe you one after that tip your informant gave us on the counterfeit ring in Kendall," replied Larry. "How soon do you need them."

"I would really appreciate it if you could have them ready when I return from Orlando tomorrow," said Stormy.

"I don't know if I can get the technician to do it *that* quickly," replied Larry.

"It's really important, and time is of the essence," Stormy said. "And, it involves one of our guys."

"You got something going on that I need to know about?" asked Larry.

"I'll fill you in when I return, but if the faces don't match, it won't matter. Just something my Captain wants to do as a final solution to a possible problem."

"I'll pull a little weight and get it done for you. Have a good trip," replied Larry.

Stormy gave him the manila envelope and left the building, rushing to his car. He needed to pick up Leo and get on the road. He wanted to be there before dark and make contact with Eduardo. If they could do the interview tonight, they'd be able to be back in Miami by noon tomorrow.

Leo was waiting for him in the parking lot when he arrived. He had a small overnight bag sitting on the ground next to his feet. He threw it in the back seat of Stormy's car when he pulled up. He climbed into the front seat.

"Let's *hit the road, Jack*," laughed Leo. "I always wanted to say that."

"Very funny Leo," replied Stormy, knowing it was a song by Ray Charles.

Once they were on I-95, Stormy maintained a speed of between seventy-five and eighty miles per hour, slowing for traffic when they reached the West Palm Beach area. It was always congested in that area for some reason, even during off rush hour. He exited I-95 and drove the short distance to the Florida Turnpike. He had checked the address and discovered it was in Clermont, a small town just west of Orlando. There was an exit from the Turnpike on State Road 50 that would put them within a mile of the address for Eduardo.

After they had driven for around two hours, they

stopped at a rest stop. They both used the rest room, and Stormy asked Leo to drive some. Leo didn't drive quite as fast as Stormy but still maintained a good speed. They made shop-talk about the case, and soon Stormy was dozing. He felt he had barely dozed off when Leo lightly punched him on the shoulder, letting him know they were close to the exit for State Road 50. They had made good time and were only about five minutes from Clermont.

Leo took the exit, and they stopped at a convenience store on SR 50 to buy a soft drink and candy bar. They hadn't stopped for lunch, and it was too late in the day to eat a meal because dinner hour would be upon them before long. They would get a decent dinner after they had spoken with Eduardo, assuming he was home. It was five-thirty and probably too early for Eduardo and his family to be having dinner, so the timing should be perfect for everybody. They ask the clerk for directions to the Greater Hills subdivision, and she said it was only a couple of miles from the store.

They got into the car and headed west towards Clermont. They soon saw the sign for Greater Hills. They turned in and saw that it was a sprawling development – hundreds of houses built on small rolling hills. *A nice community*, thought Stormy. They drove through the winding streets until they spotted the street they were looking for. After turning right they looked at the house numbers until they found the house.

Two cars were parked in the driveway – a Lexus and a mini-van. The house was quite nice, and the landscaping well maintained. Leo wondered what kind of business Eduardo was in to afford the house and car, but that was none of his business. They pulled into the driveway and parked behind the Lexus.

While they were walking up to the door. it opened. A man in his twenties stood there, waiting as they walked up.

"Hi, are you Eduardo Acosta?" asked Stormy.

"Yes, may I help you?" he asked.

"I'm Detective Jack Storm, and this is Detective Leo Sharp. We just drove up from Miami to talk with you, if you don't mind."

"I don't mind, but what in the world could I know that would bring you all the way from Miami?" he asked.

"Do you mind if we come in. We'll explain everything?" Leo asked.

"Please, come on in. Can I get you something to drink, tea or water?" asked Eduardo.

"No, thank you. We just finished a drink a few minutes ago," replied Stormy.

The house was beautifully furnished, clean and spacious. It had to be about three thousand feet of living space. The floors were a white veined marble, and the furniture looked to be fairly expensive. When they entered the living room Eduardo introduced them to his wife, Gloria. No children were present and nothing in the visible area showed toys or any sign of kids living there.

After they were seated, Stormy explained to them that they were looking into his father's death and had a few questions for them.

"My father? He was exonerated years ago. Why are you looking into his case again?" Eduardo asked.

"He is still exonerated, and we're not reopening the

case. It's just that our Captain wanted to clear up a few things that came up," Leo replied.

"What sort of things?"

"First, when was the last time you were in Miami?" Stormy asked.

"I haven't been back to Miami in almost three years," replied Eduardo. "Why do you ask, and how did you know where I lived?"

"We spoke with your Aunt Bella yesterday, and she gave us your address. You're not in any kind of trouble, but we need to ask you a few questions," Leo said.

"What else do you want to know?"

Stormy and Leo asked a few more questions and were satisfied with the answers. Eduardo didn't seem agitated that they were there and asking questions, only concerned and puzzled.

"One last question, if you don't mind," Stormy said. "Do you know where we can find your brother Lonnie. Your aunt didn't know and said she hasn't heard from him in years."

"I haven't heard from Rolando in years myself," replied Eduardo.

"Rolando? I thought his name was Lonnie," Stormy said, a surprised look on his face.

"When he was in middle school he wanted to be called Lonnie so that he would fit in with the American kids. From then on, that's what we all called him. But as I said, I haven't heard from him since he joined the Army."

"We won't bother you any longer, but could I have your phone number, just in case I remember something I forgot to ask?" Stormy asked.

"Sure, no problem," said Eduardo, pulling out a business card and handing it to Stormy.

"Thank you for your time and patience, Mr. Acosta. We'll be going now," Leo said, shaking Eduardo's hand, "and here is my card in case you do hear from Lonnie...Rolando."

When they backed out of the driveway and were on their way out of Greater Hills, Leo took the card from Stormy and looked at it.

"Eduardo is a sales rep for Pfizer pharmaceuticals," Leo said. "I hear those guys make a ton of money."

Stormy didn't reply. He just kept driving, working his way back to SR 50. He took a right on 50 and headed towards Clermont, looking for a motel to spend the night. Just before they reached the overpass of Highway 27, they spotted one on the left side of the road.

"That one look okay to you Leo?" asked Stormy.

"Yeah, it looks fairly new, and it's close to the turnpike so let's check in."

Stormy made a U-turn just before the light and drove back to the motel. They took their bags and went inside to register, each getting their own room. Thankfully the rooms were on the ground floor and adjacent to each other. They entered their respective rooms to take showers and change clothes, agreeing to meet in the lobby in thirty minutes. It was getting dark and they needed to find somewhere to eat dinner. Thirty-five minutes later they met in the lobby and asked the clerk where they could find a good restaurant to eat. He told them there were several up and down SR 50, it all depended on what they liked.

"You like Thai food?" Stormy asked Leo.

"Sure, sounds good to me," he said.

They left after getting directions from the desk clerk and headed to Clermont. They found the restaurant just past the overpass, just as the clerk had directed them. They parked and went inside, were seated and placed their orders. Stormy ordered his favorite, beef ginger with extra white rice, with water to drink. Leo ordered the same but chicken instead of beef, and he ordered a beer to go with his meal. In fifteen minutes the meal came out, steaming hot, with the flavor of ginger permeating their air space. They were famished and were almost finished with their meals before they started talking about Eduardo.

"Do you believe Eduardo hasn't been to Miami recently?" asked Leo.

"I do. I didn't detect any sign that he was lying about anything we asked him."

"I also thought it was weird that his brother's name was Rolando, the same as your partner," Leo said.

"Yeah, that caught me by surprise," replied Stormy, "but my partners last name is Fuentes, not Acosta."

"We better get back to the motel. I'm kinda tired and would like to leave no later than eight in the morning," Leo said.

"I'm with you on that. I'm beat also," Stormy replied.

They paid the check and headed back to the motel, said goodnight and went into their respective rooms. Stormy undressed and turned on the television, watching a little of the *Big Bang Theory*, before turning off the set and pounding his pillow flat – he hated big pillows. Just before he fell asleep he was thinking about the Facial

Recognition Program and wondering if he was in for a surprise when he returned home. He hoped not, nothing worse than a *cop* committing a crime, getting caught and tarnishing the image of his department.

Chapter 10

THE TRIP BACK TO MIAMI was uneventful, long and boring. Leo slept most of the way, so Stormy drove the entire trip. He didn't mind because his head was full of thoughts, puzzles that needed solving, bits of information to piece together. So far he had nothing!

He dropped Leo off at the parking lot of Miami P.D. and made his way to the FBI building. It was twelve-thirty in the afternoon. He hoped that Larry would be there and not out on a case or having a late lunch. He parked and went inside the building where he asked the receptionist if Agent Foresman was in. He was told yes, given a visitor's pass, and directed to the agent's office. Stormy rode the elevator up to the second floor and turned left following the corridor until he came to an office with Foresman's name on the door.

Larry was sitting at his desk, on the phone. When he saw Stormy, he motioned him in, pointing to a vacant seat. Stormy half listened to the one-sided conversation, hearing mostly yes's and no's. Soon Larry hung up the phone and turned to Stormy while taking a manila envelope from the center drawer of his desk. He tossed it across the desk to Stormy, saying, "I got lucky and caught the tech guy in a good mood. He ran your photos, and the results are in the envelope."

"I really appreciate your help, Larry. Now I owe *you* one."

"My pleasure, Stormy. Tell Marie hi for me, and by the way, when is the wedding?" asked Larry.

"We haven't set a date yet, but you'll be one of the first to know," Stormy replied, rising from his chair.

Shaking hands with Larry and thanking him once again, he left the building, hands trembling, not knowing what he would find in the envelope. When he was seated in his car he opened the envelope and pulled out the two sheets of paper. At first there was a lot of mumbo jumbo, but then he got to the results. His eyes widened, and his heart began pounding when he read there was a 98.9 percent probability that the photo and the image on the CD were the same person. *The Captain is not going to be a happy camper*, thought Stormy. His thoughts were interrupted by the vibration of his phone. Looking at the screen he saw that it was Leo calling. He quickly answered.

"Stormy, you back in Hialeah yet?" Leo asked.

"No, I'm still in Miami, but I was just starting to head there. Why?"

"We have another one. You need to come to my office, and you're not going to believe who it is this time!" Leo said.

Stormy hung up and headed for Miami P.D., wondering who the victim was this time. He called Hialeah C.I.D. and asked for Captain Paradis. He was told that he was in a meeting, but Adria said she would leave a message for him to return the call. He arrived at Miami P.D., parked the car and hurriedly entered the building, getting lucky with the elevator being on the ground floor this time and the door standing open. He stepped in, punched the button and rode to the third floor where he exited and made a beeline to Leo's desk.

"What do we have this time?" Stormy asked Leo.

"I received a call from the Golden Beach Police Department thirty minutes ago. Our victim is none other than the former warden of Raiford Penitentiary. He had retired a few years ago and was to have lunch with his ex-wife today. They were in the process of getting back together, and she knew something was wrong – he was too excited about the lunch date with her to have missed it. She called several times and never got an answer, so she called the police. They went to the townhouse and found the garage side door open. They went in, and getting no answer when they knocked on the kitchen door, they forced their way in. They found him in his bed on the second floor. The same M.O. as all the other victims, numbers on the forehead, duct tape, etcetera."

"Prosecutor, judge, warden…how far does this grudge go?" asked Stormy.

"I don't know but, it sure seems as if the killer has an agenda. He must have a long list of people. I just wonder how many more will die before we stop him?" Leo pondered.

"What about the female victim? Did you talk with the daughter?" asked Stormy.

"I had one of the other detectives talk with her, but she had no idea who would have killed her mom, nor why," Leo replied.

"So far, all the victims are connected through various parts of the justice system – prosecutor, judge and warden. But where does Luis, a common criminal, and the elderly woman fit in?" Stormy said, thinking out loud.

Stormy's cell phone began to vibrate again. He held it up and saw that the call was from Captain Paradis. Excusing himself, he walked to the end of the corridor and answered.

"Hello, Captain, thanks for returning my call," Stormy said.

"When did you get back in town?" the Captain asked.

"A little over an hour ago. We made decent time. I was on the way when Leo called me and told me we had another victim. He was a retired warden from Raiford. This case gets stranger and stranger all the time," Stormy said.

"That it does. Have you made any connections with the victims yet?" he asked.

"So far that most of them had ties to the judicial system."

"Well, call me if come up with anything new," the Captain said.

"There is one thing," Stormy said.

"What's that?" asked the Captain.

"I stopped by the FBI office and picked up the results of the Facial Recognition agent Foresman ran for me. You're not going to like the results," Stormy said.

"Who is it?" asked the Captain.

"Rolando, with almost a 99 percent certainty," replied Stormy.

"Damn. I was hoping Pablo was wrong," said the Captain.

"Did he show up for work today?" Stormy asked.

"No, I had planned to speak to him about his absences, but he did call again, asking if you were back."

"I'm on my way back. I'll take someone with me to his house and bring him in for questioning," Stormy said. "I'll need you to have Adria pull his address."

"I'll ask her now. See you when you get here," Captain Paradis said, breaking the connection.

"Leo, I'm going to tell you something, but keep it under your hat for the time being," Stormy said.

"You got the results on the Facial Recognition, didn't you?"

"Yeah, it's almost 99 percent that it is my partner, Rolando," Stormy said.

"Wow, that's a bummer. What are you going to do?"

"I have to get with my Captain and see where we go from here. I can't understand why he broke into my car unless he is in cahoots with the killer," Stormy replied.

"Have you considered the possibility that he may be the killer?" Leo said quietly.

"I have, but I didn't want to believe he could be so cold. He just doesn't seem the type."

"Usually they never do," Leo replied, "Ted Bundy for example."

"Let's not count our chickens just yet," Stormy said. "Maybe he's just a common thief. As soon as I get back to Hialeah I'm taking a couple of detectives and heading to his house. We'll take him into custody and charge him with the car burglary, for now. I'll keep you up to date."

****

Upon arrival at Hialeah P.D. Stormy, went into the squad room and saw that there was only one detective available. Dakota Summers was a quiet detective, usually out of the office following up on cases with her partner, Marty Reynolds.

"Dakota, where is Marty today?" asked Stormy.

"He took the day off, something about closing on his new house," she replied.

"Don't go anywhere. I need you to go with me in a few minutes," Stormy said.

"Where's *your* partner?" she asked.

"Not here, but I'll explain in a few," he replied.

Stormy went into the Captain's office and advised him he was taking Dakota with him to pick up Rolando. The Captain nodded his head, handed Stormy Rolando's home address and told him to be careful. Returning to the squad room, Stormy motioned for Dakota to follow him, and they left the building.

Once in his car he explained to her where they were going and why. To her credit she didn't ask any questions, just shook her head in disgust as she fastened her seat belt. She was a strictly by-the-book detective, followed the law to a T and had no use for officers that broke the law, no matter how minor it was. This wasn't a minor infraction. It was criminal, and it made her sick to her stomach.

The address the Captain gave him was an apartment in Miami Springs, just across the canal from South Hialeah. When they reached the apartment building where Rolando lived, Stormy parked a few units down. Exiting the car, he told Dakota to stand at the end of the only stairwell on the second floor in case Rolando decided to make a run for it. When they had climbed to the second floor, Dakota stopped, her hand on the butt of her weapon, and waited while Stormy continued on to the apartment.

Stormy stood outside the apartment, waiting to see if he could hear any sounds coming from inside. After a few seconds he heard nothing and knocked on the door. Nothing! He knocked again, a little louder this time and waited. When he concluded that no one was home, he walked to Dakota and told her to get the building manager and have him bring a key.

Dakota walked into the rental office and asked the girl at the front desk for the manager. Donald Swartz, the manager, came out of his office, looking down his nose at Dakota.

"What can I do for you, missy?" he asked.

"First of all, it's Detective Summers, not *missy*," she coldly replied. "I need a key to one of your apartments. It involves a criminal matter," she continued.

"Do you have a warrant?" the chastised manager asked.

"No, I thought you might be willing to forgo one since we're going to overlook some of the violations we observed here," she said, with a forced smile on her face.

"What violations?" Swartz asked.

"Do you really want me to list them for you, because once I do that I have no choice but to write them up and have Code Enforcement come down and check them out," she said.

141

Donald stood there for a minute, his mind racing as what to do. He made up his mind quickly – he didn't need Code Enforcement nitpicking his building. Even though he didn't know of any violations, he didn't want to take a chance that some could be found. So he decided to give her the key. After taking the key Dakota went back up the stairs and handed the key to Stormy.

"You mean he didn't insist on a warrant?" he asked, smiling.

"I kind of talked him out of it," she replied, no expression on her face.

"You can come with me. I don't think he's home," Stormy said, walking back to the apartment.

When he inserted the key into the door, he slowly pushed it opened with his foot, his hand on his gun. Seeing no one in the front room he cautiously entered. The place was sparsely furnished and looked barely lived in. While Dakota backed him up, following behind at a safe distance, they searched the apartment, finding no one in the bedroom or bathroom. In fact the bedroom looked as if no one had slept there in awhile, or Rolando was a very meticulous housekeeper.

Stormy asked Dakota to stand by the front door in case anyone showed up. He checked the dresser drawers and under the bed. There was barely a change of underwear and socks in the six drawers. In the closet he found a couple of jogging suits, black, and a pair of sneakers. Looking up to the shelf above the hanging jogging suits he saw something that brought a smile to his face, a baseball cap with a lightning bolt on the side. He now knew he had the person who had broken into his car. Calling out to

Dakota, he asked her to go to the car and get him a small evidence bag. He called the station to advise the dispatcher he needed CSI for processing. When Dakota returned with the bag, he labeled it and put the ball cap inside. Looking around the apartment, he couldn't find anything else, so they sat and waited for CSI to arrive.

When Linda Ward arrived, he showed her the jogging suits and sneakers in the closet, telling her to bag them for evidence. He gave her the bagged ball cap and asked her to log it in with the rest of the evidence. He also asked her to pull prints in the apartment. He wanted to make sure that Rolando had been living there, although it didn't look like it. Any other prints obtained could possibly be of value also.

As he was leaving the apartment, his cell phone rang. Looking at the screen he saw that it was Rolando calling. *Was he watching us while we were in the apartment*? he thought. He had no way of knowing, so he answered the call.

"Hello, Rolando. Where are you?" he asked.

"Taking care of a little business. How did it go in Orlando?" Rolando asked.

"It looks like a dead end," Stormy replied.

"Really? I thought you had a good lead on that end," Rolando said.

"Me too, but it looks like it was a wasted trip," replied Stormy. "When can we get together and go over the case?" he asked.

There was a slight pause at the end of the line, and then Rolando said, "I'll see you tomorrow morning at the office."

"Okay, see you there," Stormy said, breaking the connection.

Dakota had listened to the exchange between Rolando and Stormy.

"Trying not to alarm him and scare him into running," she said, astutely.

"Something like that," Stormy said.

As they walked down the stairs, leaving Linda to her work, his cell rang again. Looking at the screen he saw it was an unknown number, but he answered it anyway.

"Hello," he answered.

"Detective Storm?" asked the caller.

"Speaking. Who is this?" he asked.

"This is Eduardo Acosta, you were just up here talking with me earlier," the caller replied.

"Oh, hi, Eduardo. What can I do for you?"

"I remembered something that might help you find Lonnie, if you still need to talk with him," replied Eduardo.

"Okay, what do you have for me?" asked Stormy.

"I remembered that Lonnie changed his last name just before he joined the Army," Eduardo said.

"Okay, I'm listening."

"He, for reasons I never understood, changed his last name to our mother's maiden name. He goes by Rolando Fuentes now," Eduardo said.

Stormy stopped so quickly that Dakota almost knocked him down the rest of the stairs. Standing in stunned silence, he barely heard Eduardo on the other end ask if he had heard him.

"Yes, yes, I got that Eduardo. Are you sure? It's important," said Stormy, his blood racing.

"Yes, sir, I just thought you would want to know," replied Eduardo.

"Thank you very much. You've been a great help," Stormy said.

"You're welcome, and would you do me a favor in return?" he asked

"Sure, if I can. What would you like me to do?" asked Stormy.

"If you find him, tell him to contact me. We haven't spoken in so long and used to be so very close. Anyway, tell him I love him and would like to see him again."

"I'll do that, Eduardo," Stormy said, hanging up the phone.

"What was that about?" asked Dakota.

"Brotherly love, but we have a bigger problem than a car burglary now, a much bigger problem," Stormy solemnly said.

On the drive back to the station Stormy told Dakota all about the murders he was working on with Leo, including the badge numbers and up to the point that Eduardo had just called. Dakota felt as if she were going to throw up but took a couple of deep breaths and asked Stormy, "What are you going to do now?"

"First I have to get to the station and lay out everything to the Captain. Then we'll go from there," Stormy said.

****

Rolando was inside his houseboat on the Miami River, not far from the Miami Police Department. He was thinking of the conversation he had just had with Stormy. Something was up – he could feel it. *Stormy isn't telling me the truth about the trip to Orlando. He found out something, and it can't be good for me.*

He had rented the apartment in Miami Springs as a dummy living space. He knew that sooner or later the police would find out something and would be showing up there. The first mistake was not looking for cameras when he broke into Stormy's car. But, with the weather conditions, he hadn't taken the time. It was a big mistake on his part. Somehow he had the feeling that Stormy had identified him from the CD his neighbor had given him, even as grainy as it was. He knew now that he couldn't return to the station. He was done! He had to finish his mission, one that he had meticulously planned for so long and there was no way he was going to let a hotshot detective stop him. He had an ace in the hole, and he would play it if he had to.

His father had been framed and sent to prison when he was only six years old. He was subsequently murdered by an inmate. Rolando blamed the justice system. The Warden had failed to isolate his father for his safety, knowing that he was a former police officer.

He had spent many months searching the Internet, police reports and other methods, finding out the names and addresses of his victims. He only had four more jurors to go, since one had passed away over a year ago.

The judge, prosecutor, warden, drug kingpin and even the female juror had been easy prey. Killing the warden had given him the most satisfaction so far. He had deserved to die for his pompous attitude and lack of concern for the safety and well being of the prisoners he had been placed in charge of. The extensive homework he had undertaken paid off handsomely. It had enabled him to determine the most opportune times to approach his victims and dispatching them.

He hadn't expected Stormy to connect the numbers, his father's badge number, so soon. But no matter, he would continue until he had finished. He felt secure knowing that he had rented the houseboat under the name of Lonnie Fuentes. But was he really secure? There was no way that Stormy could know he had another place to live, but to ease his mind he would look for another place tomorrow.

For a few minutes he entertained the thought of waiting a few days before he took out his next victim, but he quickly dismissed that idea. He needed to finish what he had started. Stormy was too good at his job, and he needed to complete his mission so he could leave the area and disappear forever. Taking the list off the coffee table, he looked at it carefully, deciding who would be his next target. After making a decision, he began planning his next move, which hopefully would only be a few hours from now.

Chapter 11

A s STORMY AND DAKOTA ARRIVED at the station, his cell rang again, and he saw that Leo was calling. He answered his phone and Leo blurted out, "Stormy, I found the connection between our last victim – the elderly woman – and the rest of our victims," Leo said excitedly.

"So there is a connection," Stormy said.

"Yes, she was a juror during the Jose Acosta trial," Leo replied.

"It's all making sense now," replied Stormy. "The killer, and I'm pretty sure I know who he is now, is going after anyone involved with Acosta's arrest and death in prison."

"What do you mean, you *know* who he is?" asked Leo.

"When I get to your office, I'll tell you the whole story, but first, I have to stop by my office," Stormy said.

"Okay, but hurry. We need to find out who the other jurors were, and fast. I'll start working on that and hopefully have their names and addresses by the time you arrive."

"I'll be there soon," Stormy said, hanging up the phone.

Entering the office Stormy was told that Captain Paradis was in a staff meeting and couldn't be disturbed. Stormy turned and walked down the hallway to the conference room. Dakota followed him. There was a do-not-disturb sign on the door, but that didn't stop Stormy. He politely tapped on the door, hearing the voices within cease. The door opened, and Lieutenant Kirts from road patrol looked at Stormy, raising his eyebrows, pointing to the sign.

"Sorry, Lieutenant, but it's of the utmost importance that I speak with Captain Paradis immediately!" Stormy said.

Lieutenant Kirts turned to Captain Paradis, who was already walking to the door. He told the Lieutenant it was okay and stepped out of the room, closing the door behind him.

"What's so important Stormy?" asked the Captain.

"We have a big problem, and you may want to take a break from your meeting Captain," Stormy said. "It involves Rolando, and it's much more serious than the car burglary."

Captain Paradis nodded his head, stepped back into the room and told his staff to take a fifteen-minute break. When they had all left the room, he beckoned Stormy and Dakota to follow him to his office. When they had seated themselves, Stormy brought the Captain up to date, including the connections between the victims. Captain Paradis leaned back in his chair, consternation written all over his face, not saying anything for a minute, while he digested what he had just been told.

"Are you certain about this?" Captain Paradis asked,

"The car burglary I can see, but is there enough evidence to arrest him on the murders?"

"Right now he is the number one suspect in the murders, but I need more evidence. I can bring him in on the burglary charge, and we can question him about the murders and go from there," Stormy said.

"You know he'll clam up as soon as you arrest him. He's an officer and knows better than to admit anything without an attorney present," Captain Paradis said.

"I've considered that, so I want to try something else before we issue a warrant for his arrest on the burglary charge," Stormy said.

"What do you want to try?" asked Paradis.

"I'm heading to Miami P.D., and hopefully Leo and I can find out the names of the remaining jurors and where they are now. We'll put surveillance on their homes, and if Rolando shows up we'll have him."

"That's an awful risky chance to take. What if he gets into a home without the surveillance team spotting him and kills the juror?" asked the Captain.

"That would certainly be unfortunate, but it's the best shot we have right now. I don't think Rolando will show up here anymore. I could tell from his voice that he suspects we are on to him."

"I'm not comfortable with what you're proposing, and you still have to find out where the other jurors are before you can set up the surveillance," Captain Paradis said. "It just seems too risky."

"I'll head to Miami and see if Leo and I can track down the jurors. I'll call you as soon as we do, and we can decide then if we'll do the surveillance or not,"

Stormy said.

"Okay, but call me as soon as you know."

"There's one other thing, Captain," Stormy said. "I want Detective Dakota Summers assigned to me for the rest of this investigation. Her partner is out on a personal matter, and she *is* available."

"I'll handle it, head to Miami," Captain Paradis responded.

As Stormy and Dakota were driving to Miami P.D., his cell rang again, and he saw it was CSI calling. He answered, and Linda Ward was on the line.

"Stormy, I found something in one of the jogging suits that you should know about," she began.

"What did you find?" he asked.

"A partial roll of duct tape, and there was a fingerprint on the outside of it, which I ran for you," She replied.

"Let me guess, the print belongs to none other than one of our officers. Correct?" Stormy said.

"Yes, Rolando Fuentes to be specific," she replied. "How did you know?"

"An educated guess. It's something I'm working on," Stormy said.

"You want to fill me in?" she asked.

"Later, I can't right now but make sure you document everything you found in the apartment, Linda, especially the tape and fingerprint," Stormy said.

"What about the apartment. Do you want to keep it as a crime scene?" she asked.

"Yes, for the time being, although I don't think he'll be coming back to the apartment."

The Captain wants concrete evidence. He'll be getting

it now, Stormy thought. *Another nail in the coffin!*

Leo was patiently waiting when they arrived. After Stormy introduced him to Dakota, he asked if there was an available office where they could talk in private, undisturbed. Leo checked the three interview rooms and seeing they were occupied noticed that the conference room was empty. They all filed into the empty room and took seats around the massive conference table. Leo picked up the phone, hit a number and asked someone, probably one of the secretaries, if she would mind bringing in a pitcher of water and some glasses. He had correctly made the assumption that they were going to be there awhile. Once the water was placed on the desk and the secretary had left, Stormy began by bringing Leo up to date.

"That sure makes Rolando our prime suspect," Leo said.

"The fingerprint on the duct tape is damning at the very least, enough to make an arrest," Stormy said.

"Do we know where he is?" asked Leo.

"No, but I have a feeling he knows something is up, and I really don't expect him to show up for work from this point on," Stormy replied.

"Why do you think he knows we're on to him?"

"I spoke with him on the phone while we were at his apartment, and he wanted to know what we had learned from our trip to Orlando. When I tried to convince him we didn't learn anything pertinent to the case, his tone of voice changed, as if he knew I was lying," Stormy said.

"Are we going to put out an APB or BOLO on him?"

"I think we need to hold up on that for the time being. If he happens to find out, he *will* go underground and make it that much harder for us to find him. He could possibly leave the state, heck, even the country for all we know," Stormy said, "He's no dummy and probably has a fake passport and other credentials."

"Were you able to find out the locations and addresses of the remaining jurors?" asked Stormy

"I certainly did. Here is what we have," replied Leo, handing Stormy a sheet of paper.

Reading the short list Stormy saw that one of the jurors was deceased and that three of the remaining four were scattered around Dade County. The exception was one who lived in California – they would leave that one for last. More than likely Rolando would go after the three in Dade County and then head for California to finish up his killing spree, unless there were more they didn't know about. That was something they hadn't considered.

"So far we know about the prosecutor, judge, one of the jurors, Luis and the warden. That leaves the four jurors. Any thoughts as to who else we may be leaving out?" asked Stormy

"What about the inmate that killed his father?" Dakota asked.

"I checked that out earlier and found that they still don't know who killed him," Leo said. "Besides, if Rolando did know there would be no way he could get into Raiford and kill him."

"Luis is the only one that could have answered that for us, and he's dead now," Stormy replied.

"Back to the remaining jurors," Leo said. "Are we setting up surveillance tonight?"

"We have to. Their lives are at stake, and Rolando could strike at any time. We can't afford to lose another one now that we know who they are. We'd be crucified by the press if another one was to die, and they found out we could have protected them," Stormy said, "not to mention the liability."

"I agree. We need to get the surveillance teams set up as quickly as possible," Leo said.

Looking at the list, Stormy saw that one of the jurors lived in Hialeah, the other two in Miami. It was decided that Leo would take one of his detectives, and they would sit on the house in North Miami. He would pick another two-man team for the house in West Miami. Stormy and Dakota would take the house in Hialeah. After considering warning the jurors they dismissed that idea – there wasn't enough time to carry it out tonight. Tomorrow they would make arrangements for all of the jurors to stay someplace else and continue with the stakeouts. For now they had to hope that Rolando didn't manage to slip past them and carry out another murder.

"I'm going to call Rolando and come up with an excuse for him to come into the office tonight," Stormy said. "I'll be surprised if he agrees."

Stormy took out his cell phone and dialed Rolando's number, listening to it ring a dozen times before he hung up.

"He's not answering, that only re-enforces my opinion that he knows we're on to him," Stormy said.

Stormy called Captain Paradis and advised him about the stakeouts, and that he and Dakota would be on the one in Hialeah. After assuring the Captain he would call if anything happened, he cut the connection.

****

Rolando looked at the phone and saw that the call was from Stormy's number. Laying the phone back on the table, he continued to dress in his black running suit while it rang, making sure he had duct tape in the pocket. When his phone stopped ringing, he smiled, knowing that Stormy was trying to get him on the line to possibly trace the call or trick him into revealing where he was. Trace the call! Rolando picked up the phone and took out the SIM card, crushing it beneath his shoes on the tiled floor. He would have to pick up a burn phone or two, one that couldn't be traced.

Now that he was dressed, he sat down on the sofa and turned on the television. He watched the news absent-mindedly, waiting for darkness to fall, for it was in the darkness that he operated best. He had decided to kill the juror that lived in North Miami, and he wanted to make sure it was completely dark outside before he left the houseboat.

Chapter 12

STORMY AND DAKOTA left Leo's office and headed for Hialeah, preparing for a long night. Stakeouts were boring, tedious and most of all, exhausting. They were nothing like the stakeouts portrayed on television where the bad guy almost always showed up. Most of the time a stakeout would last all night without success. Staying awake was a major concern for a lot of detectives therefore the reason for two-man teams. If one got sleepy he could take a short nap while the other stayed awake. Usually both stayed awake, not wanting to show a weakness to their partner. But working a full shift and then trying to stay awake all night took its toll on some.

Stormy turned onto East 41st Street and, with the sun almost below the horizon, found the house they were looking for. As luck would have it, there was a house directly across from the juror's home that had piles of newspapers in the driveway. *The occupants must be on vacation*, Stormy thought. It was the perfect place to park and have an unobstructed view of the house. Hopefully some nosy neighbor wouldn't see them parked in the driveway and call the police, knowing they weren't supposed to be there. Stormy called the station and advised dispatch as to what they were doing and not to send any marked units to the area if a call came in. As soon as they had parked, Stormy's phone rang. Seeing that Leo was calling he answered.

"Both houses in Miami are under surveillance now," Leo said.

"We just arrived at ours," Stormy replied. "If anyone shows up, call me immediately!"

"You do the same," Leo responded.

Stormy and Dakota pushed their seats back and prepared for a long night. They noticed that lights were on in the house they were watching, but they couldn't see anyone inside as the blinds were closed. Occasionally a shadow passed by one of the windows, but as the hours passed the lights began to go out. Evidently the occupants were retiring for the night.

The street lights were several houses apart, and thankfully the juror's house was dead center between two lights. Very little light spilled into the area where Stormy had parked, making it a little harder to get a clear view of the house, but at the same time not illuminating him and Dakota sitting in the car. Midnight approached and all was quiet on the street. Only a few houses had a light on, the occupants probably watching a late movie on television.

"Do we know the name of the juror?" asked Dakota.

"Ester Gonzalez, but I don't know if she is alone or not," he replied.

"I hope this creep shows up," she said. "He needs to be taken down before anyone else is murdered."

"With only three jurors in Dade, you just may get

your wish," Stormy replied.

"What about the back door. We can't see it from here. He could come in that way," she said.

"I noticed a chain-link fence and two pit bulls in the back yard, so if he's stupid enough, and I don't think he is, the barking will let us know."

For the next hour· they made small talk and soon lapsed into silence, intently watching the house.

****

Rolando parked his car a block away at a closed grocery store. He noticed that there were two other cars parked in the lot, so he felt secure that his car wouldn't stand out. Exiting his car, he carefully scanned the area and didn't see anyone. He started walking to the house a block away, ever observant and hoping that his victim was alone. He had checked days before and knew that she lived alone, but you never knew if anyone would be visiting.

He had noticed before that there was a side door to the house, and that was the entry point he was planning to use. He decided to walk between the two houses next to the victim's house and approach from the rear, thereby avoiding the streetlight in front. When he arrived at the rear of the victim's house, he stood still and listened, slowly swiveling his head to see if anyone was outside any of the houses.

He heard a low growl coming from the back yard. He waited, holding his breath, but since he was not entering the back yard the dog evidently lost interest and stopped growling. Seeing no one around, he stealthily crept to the side door.

****

Leo and his partner were looking at the house but also softly making small talk. In mid-sentence Leo held up his hand up for his partner to stop talking. He had seen something moving along the side of the house they were watching, or were his eyes playing tricks on him. He had been on enough stakeouts to know that sometimes you saw things that weren't there. Squinting into the darkness he could barely make out what appeared to be a person standing at the side of the house. Suddenly his adrenaline began to pump, his heart racing. Telling his partner to carefully go to the house next door in case a chase would ensue, they both opened the car doors. The interior lights came on, silhouetting them as they got out. *Damn, I forgot about the lights,* Leo thought. The shadowy figure by the side of the house suddenly looked up and saw the lights come on inside the car. Quickly he turned and sprinted to the rear of the house.

"YOU HEAD UP THE STREET AND TRY TO CUT HIM OFF," Leo shouted to his partner. "I'll follow him from here."

Leo ran across the street and down the side of the house where he had seen the subject. When he got to the side door, he couldn't see anyone, so he continued on to the back yard. A dog started barking from the back yard. Not knowing which direction the intruder had ran he stood for a second, listening over the barking for the sound of running feet.

****

Rolando had just glanced up from trying to pop the lock on the side door when he saw interior lights come on in a car parked across the street. He saw two men exiting the car. He recognized Leo getting out of the driver's side in the light. *What the hell?* he thought. *How could they know I was going to be here tonight?*

He had to get away and quickly. He began running down the back of the houses towards the lot where he had parked his car. As he reached the third house down, he saw a man emerge from the side of the house. They were so close together a collision was inevitable. Rolando slammed into the detective, knocking the wind out of him and putting him on the ground. Knowing that the detective would get up and chase him, he looked for something, anything to incapacitate the man. Seeing a short piece of two-by-four on the ground, he snatched it up, at the same time the detective was getting to his feet. He swung the piece of wood hard, hitting the detective in the back of his head. The detective immediately dropped to the ground, knocked out cold, or dead. Rolando couldn't care less at this time. He knew that Leo wouldn't be far behind.

****

Leo heard a loud thud and a cry of pain. He turned and ran towards the sound, seeing a light come on at the rear of a house. He almost stumbled over the body of his partner, lying unconscious on the ground. An elderly man opened his back door and yelled out, "WHAT'S GOING

ON OUT THERE?"

"POLICE OFFICER, PLEASE GO BACK INTO YOUR HOUSE," Leo yelled.

Kneeling next to his partner's body, he could see a pool of blood spreading on the ground around his head. Carefully he checked to make sure the man was breathing then he saw the piece of wood lying next to the body, hair and blood covering a portion of it. Quickly he pulled out his portable radio and called dispatch.

"I need EMS to respond to East 41st Street, and make it fast. My partner is down and unconscious. Also dispatch all available units to this location. Have them watch for a man running from this area wearing dark clothing. He should be armed and considered dangerous."

Grabbing his cell phone he quickly dialed Stormy's number, rewarded with an answer on the first ring.

"Stormy, he was here!" Leo said.

"Did you get him?" asked Stormy.

"No, he spotted us getting out of the car and ran behind the houses. My partner ran down the street to try to cut him off. Evidently there was a struggle, and my partner was hit with a two-by-four in the back of his head. He's down, unconscious and based on the amount of blood on the ground, severely injured. EMS is on the way and I have units responding to the area to try to catch him."

"I'm on my way, give me fifteen minutes," Stormy replied, breaking the connection.

Stormy started the Charger and sped down the street, the roar of the engine echoing off the houses, heading for North Miami. He began relaying to Dakota what Leo had just told him. With his blues in the grill lighting up the darkness, he tromped on the accelerator and was soon moving at eighty miles an hour. It was early enough in the morning that traffic was still very light. Most vehicles pulled to the side when they saw him coming, a few not budging, Stormy speeding around them.

In fourteen minutes flat Stormy was on the scene in North Miami. EMS was loading someone on a gurney into an ambulance, most likely Leo's partner. There were a dozen marked units with their overheads flashing all up and down the street. Most of the houses were lit up now, everyone wanting to know what was going on. Dakota pointed and Stormy saw Leo walking towards him. They exited the car and met him on the sidewalk.

"How's your partner?" asked Dakota.

"It doesn't look good. The back of his head is crushed in," Leo responded.

"I'm sorry, Leo. I hope he pulls through," said Stormy.

"God, I hope so. He has two beautiful small children."

"We have to catch that jerk now more than ever. Now *I* have a score to settle with him," Leo said.

"Any luck with your units spotting him?" asked Dakota

"So far he hasn't been spotted. But he can't get far on foot, so I have to assume he had a car parked close by."

"I don't even know what kind of car he drives," Stormy said. "I'll have dispatch run him through DMV and see what he drives."

Stormy got on his phone with dispatch, staying off the radio because he didn't want all the units to know who they were looking for at this time. One of the officers on the perimeter walked over to Leo and advised him that a unit at the end of the street called and said that the Channel 7 news van was requesting permission to drive down the street. Leo told him that under no circumstances were they to be allowed on the scene for now – He will give them a news release later.

****

Rolando's heart was pounding away, his adrenalin rushing and panic on the verge of taking over. He hadn't expected Stormy and Leo to figure out about the jurors so soon. He shuddered to think what would have happened if he had made it inside the house with Leo watching. There would have been a deadly confrontation because he would not have given up. For a split second he felt regret for hitting the detective with the piece of wood. He knew he had struck him hard and hoped that he only knocked him unconscious. The regret was fleeting as he was not going to let anyone, especially Stormy and Leo, stop him from finishing what he had set out to do.

As he sat in his car, a block from the scene, he watched for any signs of pursuit. Seeing none, he assumed that Leo was taking care of the downed detective. He started his car and kept to the side streets, ever alert for the patrol cars he knew would be coming. Finally he made it almost a mile from the scene and began to calm down. *That was close, too close!* In the distance he could hear several sirens wailing, heading in the direction from which he had just come.

Soon he was far enough out of the area to take a main street and get back to the safety of his houseboat. The remainder of his mission would take more careful planning now. He would have to leave the houseboat and ditch the car. He would find another place to stay first thing in the morning. He also needed to go to the bank and withdraw out all of his savings.

He would go to a small used car lot and pay cash for a car to get around in. I'll *park this car on the street in Over Town. It won't last long sitting there. Probably be up on blocks within a day.* He would have to use the dealer tags on the new car for as long as he could – he couldn't take a chance on getting stopped and having a tag run with his name on it.

He was sure that there would soon be, if not already, a BOLO put out on him. He had prepared for that eventuality, taking a drivers license and other I.D. from a crime scene over a year ago. It looked as if he was going to become Miguel Ruiz after today.

The sun was just beginning to peek over the horizon of the Atlantic as he pulled into the driveway of his houseboat. Seeing no one around the area, he quickly exited the car and entered the houseboat. He had a lot to do today and needed to get started. He hadn't slept all night and was tired, but now was not the time to rest.

****

Stormy, Dakota and Leo headed to the hospital to see how severe Leo's partner's injuries were. When they arrived and entered the emergency room, they flashed their badges and were led to the back where a multitude of patients were being treated. A curtain was pulled around one cubicle, and they were told to take a seat.

Leo's partner, Felix Gunter, was being x-rayed to determine the extent of his injuries. They waited in silence for thirty minutes before a doctor came to them. He told them that Felix had sustained a fractured skull and was in very critical condition. He was now in a private room and being monitored. The doctor also advised that they contact his next of kin, advise them of the situation and have them come to the hospital. He expressed concern as to whether or not Felix would make it through the day.

There was nothing to do now but wait and see if Felix survived, so they headed for Leo's office. When they exited the elevator Major Aramas was sitting in Leo's chair, sipping a cup of coffee. He stood when they entered the room and turning to them asked about Felix's condition.

"It doesn't look too good right now. We'll just have to wait and see," Leo said.

"Was he shot?" asked the Major.

"No, sir. No shots were fired. He was chasing the subject and had a confrontation with him. He was struck across the back of his head with a piece of wood. He sustained a fractured skull and is in critical condition. We also need to contact his wife and get one of our guys to take her to the hospital," Leo responded.

"I need you to fill me in on everything that has happened since you went to Orlando," Major Aramas said.

Between Stormy and Leo, the Major was soon brought up to date. He sat and thought for a few minutes before speaking.

"We have to put out a BOLO on him right now. We can't take a chance on anyone else getting hurt. Do you have enough for a warrant?" asked the Major.

"Yes, sir. Hialeah's CSI found a fingerprint on a roll of duct tape and has identified it as belonging to Rolando Fuentes. I'll make arrangements for the warrant, and once I have it in hand we'll issue a BOLO," Leo said.

"What about the stakeouts on the jurors?" the Major asked.

"Of course we'll have to continue them until we can make arrangements for the jurors to stay somewhere else until he's caught," replied Stormy.

"Stormy, I know this has to be rough on you, Rolando being one of your own. *I'll* contact Captain Paradis and advise him of the BOLO and warrant and what has transpired tonight," the Major said.

"That would be a great help and would free me up to continue looking for Rolando."

"Also, we can expect the news media to be monitoring us. Once the BOLO is out, all hell is going to break loose. I'll arrange for our P.I.O. to handle the media. You and Leo find this guy, and do it quickly!" Major Aramas said.

Obtaining an arrest warrant is often time-consuming, in fact most of the time. The paperwork has to be typed with the charges correctly itemized and probable cause established. Then there's the task of finding a judge to sign it, and that takes more time. Time was definitely not on their side now! It was still early in the morning, and there probably weren't any judges in their offices yet. That meant one had to be approached at their home, and doing that this early in the morning would be met with less than a cheery smile. Still, certain judges were on call just for the purpose of signing a warrant when needed. Leo scanned the on-call roster and found a judge within a few miles of the station.

Now they had to word the BOLO carefully, not wanting to give away too much information, due to the monitoring by the media. The law enforcement agencies in Dade and surrounding counties would bristle at the mere thought that one of their own could commit such heinous crimes. The manhunt would be furious, and the patrol presence enhanced to the max.

When the BOLO was completed, Major Aramas looked it over and gave his approval. Leo stood and proceeded to Communications where the BOLO would be broadcast to all units, but only when he gave the go-ahead. It would also be faxed to the surrounding counties at the same time.

Now they had to hurry to the judge's home and hopefully the arrest warrant would be signed. With every law enforcement officer within a hundred miles looking for him, Rolando was about to find it extremely difficult to move around the city.

Chapter 13

WITH THE WARRANT SIGNED, Leo made the phone call to Communications advising them to put out the BOLO. They drove back to Leo's office to chart the next course of action. When they arrived, there was a message for Stormy to call Captain Paradis.

"Stormy, I got the message from Major Aramas about the warrant and BOLO. I see that it's been put out already," Captain Paradis said.

"Yes sir, after what happened last night and with the available evidence, we had no choice."

"God, why us?" the Captain said.

"We're not the first department to have a rogue cop and won't be the last," Stormy replied.

"Yeah, you're right, but it still galls me to no end. What about the remaining jurors, are they being relocated? We can't take the chance of him getting to another one," the Captain said.

"We're in the process of notifying them now. All of them have relatives they can stay with for the time being."

"Is there any reason to continue the stakeouts now? I'm sure he'll soon find out, if he hasn't already, about the BOLO," Captain Paradis asked.

"We're planning to continue for a few more nights. I don't think he would know the jurors are being relocated, so he may try again," Stormy said.

"Okay, you and Dakota watch your backs. This guy is playing for keeps and is now getting desperate," the Captain said, breaking the phone connection.

Leo looked at Stormy with a puzzled look on his face. He had listened to the conversation and asked, "We're going to continue the stakeouts?"

"I have a feeling he'll strike again. He seems determined to finish what he started out to do. This time we're going to conceal our cars somehow and do the stakeout inside the homes," Stormy said.

"That may work," Leo replied. "I'll set up the ones in the city if you'll take care of the one in Hialeah."

"I want to get set up before dark, in case he's watching for surveillance teams. He's smart and won't make the same mistake again. He'll recon the area for anyone staking out the houses, but I don't think he'll figure out we're inside. At least I hope not."

"If we get lucky, we won't have to do this – that is if he gets picked up today," Leo said.

"I wouldn't count on it. He'll definitely be on his toes now that he almost got caught last night."

"We know he has another place to live, so let's check with the utility companies and see what we can find," Stormy said.

"I'll start with the phone company but I doubt very seriously he has a landline," Dakota said.

"I agree, but it won't hurt to try," Leo said. "Stormy, you have any connections with Florida Power and Light.

They are sticklers for wanting a warrant, and we don't have time for that."

"In fact I do, Bill Murphy is an ex-cop, used to work with us but got tired of the politics and took a job as head of security for FP and L. I've used him before, so I'll give him a call."

Stormy made the call and was put on hold while they transferred the call to Murphy's office. Within a couple of minutes the call was answered.

"Bill Murphy here. Can I help you," he said.

"Bill, Stormy here. How have you been, pal?" Stormy asked.

"Stormy, it's good to hear from you. How's my girl Shaunie Marie?" he responded.

"She's doing just great. We need to get together for dinner one night with you and Christine," Stormy said.

"Are you ever going to marry that girl or is she going to have to pop the question?" laughed Bill.

"As a matter of fact, *I* popped the question just the other night, and before you make a smart remark, she said yes," Stormy said, also laughing.

"When's the big day, and you know I'll be coming," Bill said.

"We haven't set the date yet but you know she'll be asking Christine to be a bridesmaid," Stormy replied.

"And...and," Bill said teasingly.

"Oh, you mean who's going to be my best man. It's between you and Donald Trump," Stormy laughed again.

"You're crazy, but if you can get him, I'll understand," Bill said with mock sadness in his voice.

"I know you, and you didn't call to just chat. So, what

can I help you with?" asked Bill

"I know you've been following the string of murders we've had in Miami these last few days, and I need a really big favor. Time is of the essence, and I don't have the time to get a warrant. I need you to run a few names and see if they are in your data bank with a power hook-up," Stormy said, all business now.

"No problem, pal. Give me the names. You want to hang on or call back?" he asked

"I'll hang on, and, Bill, thanks. I owe you one."

Stormy gave him the names Rolando Fuentes and Rolando Acosta and sat back with the phone to his ear as he was put on hold. Looking over at Dakota he could see that she had struck out. The phone company wanted a warrant, so she hung up the phone. Leo was busy setting up the stakeouts for the night with his detectives, so Stormy just sat and listened to the music playing in his ear while he was on hold.

"Stormy, I can't find anyone with those names in our data base," Bill said, coming back on line.

"Damn, I was hoping to get lucky," Stormy said.

"You want to try any other names?" Bill asked.

Stormy sat and thought for a few seconds and the name *Lonnie*, popped up in his mind.

"Yeah, try Lonnie Acosta, and while you're at it also Lonnie Fuentes," Stormy said.

"Okay, hold on for a few."

The music came back on and Stormy waited impatiently, hoping against hope he would get a hit. The music was almost making him sleepy. Just as he was starting to nod off, Bill came back on the line.

"Bingo, pal. I got a hit on one Lonnie Fuentes. It's for a houseboat on the Miami River. Write down this address and remember you didn't get it from me," Bill said.

After writing down the address and thanking Bill, Stormy hung up the phone quickly. Dakota saw the look on his face and knew he had something. Calling Leo over, Stormy told both of them about the houseboat. They spent the next thirty minutes setting up SWAT and making sure the Miami patrol boat would be on the river near the houseboat when they made the bust. They were taking no chances on Rolando getting away again.

When they were in the lobby, heading for their cars, Leo's phone rang. He answered and started smiling. It seemed a patrol unit in Over Town had found Rolando's car, up on blocks and the tires missing. Stormy knew immediately that going there would be a dead end. He had figured Rolando would ditch the car sooner or later. Anyhow, Miami P.D. would tow it in for processing, and they could check it out when they got back, hopefully with Rolando in cuffs. They continued on and via radio contact on a dedicated channel, coordinated with the SWAT team, agreeing to meet up with them a block from the river.

When they arrived, they saw that the SWAT Commander had a marked unit already in place to block off the street. Lieutenant Earl Dedrick was a seasoned veteran, having been in charge of the SWAT unit for years now. He knew how to set up a bust and had already placed a sniper on the rooftop of an abandoned store nearby. With his powerful scope the sniper could count the freckles on a gnat from this short distance. He had already advised Lieutenant Dedrick that there was no movement on the houseboat so far. The doors were closed and the drapes drawn.

Stormy, Leo and Dakota donned bullet proof vests, and, as one, they followed the SWAT team as they crept single file towards the houseboat, holding their body shields in front of them. When they were within a few yards of the houseboat the SWAT team split up. Each team took up a position on either side of the door. Lieutenant Dedrick held up three fingers, silently counting them down. The SWAT officer with the battering ram stepped in front of the door and with one swing at the door had it crash open. All of the SWAT team rushed in, shouting "POLICE" as they entered the front room. Swiftly separating, they checked out each room, finding no one in the house. Stormy was disappointed but not surprised. Evidently Rolando had abandoned the houseboat earlier.

Leo called for CSI to process the scene, not expecting to find anything but you never knew. Stormy, Dakota and Leo went outside and after some discussion decided to leave it to CSI.

"He's already on the run," Leo said.

"Yep, we may as well continue with the stakeouts," Stormy replied.

"If anything goes down, call me," Leo said.

"Same here, and, Leo, watch your back. He'll be ready to fight back like a cornered rat if confronted," Stormy replied.

Stormy and Dakota got into the car and headed back to Hialeah, preparing for a long night. At least they wouldn't be confined to the front seat of a car.

****

Rolando had been busy this morning. He had gone to Over Town and parked his car on a side street, leaving the doors unlocked. He then walked several blocks. After waving the taxi down, he got in and told the driver to take him to the Bank of America on Brickell Avenue. He asked the driver to wait for him in the parking lot. He went into the bank and withdrew all of his money, around twelve thousand dollars. He couldn't take the chance of using his debit card or credit cards now, he was sure they would be flagged.

Getting back into the cab he directed the driver to take him to Quality motors on Northwest 27th Avenue. When he arrived, he paid the fare and walked onto the used car lot.

"Can I help you find a car today?" asked the salesman, who had walked out of his office to meet Rolando on the lot.

"I'd like a good used car, nothing expensive, but in good condition."

"We have several, but what are you looking for, sports car, sedan…?"

"Just transportation that won't let me down," Rolando replied.

After looking at several dusty cars, he finally pointed to a late model Chevy Impala, a dark green in color. The salesman opened the door and began telling him about how an elderly man had traded it in and how much it had been taken care of. Rolando looked at the salesman with disdain and said, "I don't need the pitch you guys all seem to have. Has every car traded in been driven by a little old man or woman?"

"Sorry sir, just doing my job, trying to make a sale," the salesman said.

"No problem, just take me for a test drive, and if it runs good, you'll have your sale," Rolando said.

Rolando got behind the wheel and noticed that it did have low miles for such an old car, but he didn't say anything, just drove off the lot, the salesman sitting beside him. He tested the brakes, the acceleration, which was quick, and the handling. He was surprised to see that it was a V-8. He drove back to the lot and asked the price. After being told how much, the salesman also told him they would finance it at the lot. Rolando asked the price if he paid cash and then agreed to the sale when fifteen hundred dollars was taken off for a cash sale. He didn't want to leave a paper trail for Stormy and Leo to find. He slipped the salesman a hundred dollars to extend the expiration date on the paper tag. After signing the necessary papers, using the stolen identification of Miguel Ruiz, he drove from the lot and began looking for a drug store.

Back at the houseboat he emptied the bag from the drug store and read the directions on the hair dye bottle. Going into the bathroom he began the process of dying his black hair to a light sandy brown, almost blond. Taking a pair of clippers he had also bought, he carefully cut his hair short, taking care to save a few long pieces. He glued the pieces on his upper lip and trimmed them down, giving him a moustache matching his hair. Looking in the mirror, he was satisfied that he had changed his appearance dramatically. He was sure a BOLO was now in effect for him, but he doubted anyone would recognize him from the picture on file.

Looking around the houseboat, he made sure he was taking everything he needed – his jogging suit, duct tape, knife and his Smith and Wesson 9-mm automatic. Standing at the front door, he turned and took one last look around, closed the door and left, with no intentions of returning.

Rolando drove to South Miami, searching for just the right place to rent a room by the month. Eventually he ended up on Southwest 8th Street. It was there he found a two-story apartment building, run down, seedy looking and perfect for him at this time. He entered the building, sought out the manager and paid cash for a month's rent. For some slum lords, cash didn't require any personal information.

Rolando had no idea he had just rented a room directly across the hall from Pablo!

Chapter 14

S TORMY KNEW THEY WOULD NEED a car, but he didn't want to park his Charger anywhere near the house. He and Dakota discussed it and decided that they would drive her personal vehicle, a two-year old Ford Explorer, and park it in the driveway. Rolando would be expecting someone to be home, so a car needed to be there. The house belonged to Johnnie and Sarah Hurst, an older, retired couple. Johnnie had been one of the jurors during the Acosta trial. When they had been told about the situation, it didn't take much coaxing to get them to spend some time with their daughter who lived in Broward County. They agreed to let Stormy use the house for the stakeout and furnished him with the keys.

Donning simple disguises, in case Rolando was watching the house, Stormy and Dakota pulled into the driveway around five o'clock. Before getting out, they glanced up and down the street. Seeing no one standing around, they exited the car, keeping their heads down, entering the house quickly.

As soon as they were inside Dakota went to the front windows and pulled the drapes. Checking the other rooms, they performed the same task, not wanting to take the chance that Rolando would look in the windows and see them before entering. That is, if he was still hellbent on killing off the rest of the jurors. There was a one-in-three chance he would pick this juror's house. Leo and his crew were performing the same actions on the two houses in Miami.

Checking in with Leo by phone, Stormy was told that Leo and his crew were already in place. Stormy and Dakota sat in the living room, waiting for darkness to fall before they would split up and take the two bedrooms. They had no intentions of letting him get the drop on both of them in the same room. By splitting up, at least one of them would be able to get the drop on Rolando, if he showed.

The minutes slowly crawled by, darkness seeming to take forever to arrive. They didn't dare turn on the television for fear they wouldn't hear anyone making an entry. Finally, it was dark outside, and they made their way to the bedrooms where they would spend the rest of the night.

Dakota had moved an easy chair into the room where she would be. She wasn't going to lie on the bed for fear of dropping off to sleep. She took two king-sized pillows and stuffed them under the covers, forming what could pass for two bodies sleeping in the bed. She moved the easy chair to the far corner of the room, facing the door, her weapon in her lap. Then she just sat and waited!

In the adjacent bedroom Stormy performed the same act with the pillows. He opened the walk-in closet and sat a chair just inside, facing the bed. It would be hard for anyone to see him sitting there in the dark. Besides,

Stormy was hoping that if Rolando did show he would be focused on the beds. He tried to not get too comfortable in the chair, willing himself to stay awake, and settled down for what could be a long night.

****

At the exact same time, Rolando was stretched out on his bed, hands clasped behind his head, thinking about his next victim. Johnnie was the foreman of the jury, and, therefore, he definitely needed to be killed. In fact he had been one of the first under consideration but had been out of town on vacation according to his neighbor. Now, tonight he would get his due. Rolando, not taking anything for granted, was planning to take a good long look around the house and on the street to make sure there wasn't any surveillance. He was hoping that they would figure he was on the run and wouldn't be coming after any more of the jurors. *How wrong they are!*

Looking at his watch, he saw it was coming up on midnight. He arose, already dressed in his black jogging suit, the tape and knife secured in its pockets. He figured it would take him about forty minutes to get to the area of the house in Hialeah, another thirty to make sure there were no stakeouts and less than five minutes to get into the house. His timing would be right on spot, around one thirty, if everything went smoothly.

He walked out of the room, closing and locking the door behind him. Downstairs he walked out onto the sidewalk and down the block to where he had parked his newly acquired car. Getting into the car, he started the engine, and pulling out into the street, he headed for Hialeah.

****

Stormy stood up to stretch his legs and let the blood flow for a minute or so. On a whim, he dialed Rolando's cell number but didn't even get a dial tone. *He's ditched the phone or taken out the SIM card,* thought Stormy.

He sat back down in the chair in the walk-in closet where he had been for the last few hours. Stakeouts were hard, especially if you had already put in a full day of work. He lightly tapped the wall connecting the bedroom with the one Dakota was in. He was immediately rewarded with a light tap back, indicating she was awake.

His thoughts turned to Dakota. She had been very astute in the way she handled herself so far and would make an excellent partner. He had heard through the grapevine that her partner, Marty Reynolds, had been given an offer to go with the Secret Service. He was seriously contemplating it because his family was located around Washington, D.C., and his wife really wanted to move back north. He was not anxious to have another new partner, but Dakota didn't need training and would be great to work with. She knew the ropes and had quite an impressive arrest record under her belt. She could hold her own with all of the guys and was a genuinely likeable person. He would have to speak with the Captain about having her for a partner, if Marty made the move.

Dakota, still wide awake was also thinking about her partner leaving. She wondered who she would get saddled with, hopefully not a newbie. She hated having to train

180

someone. She didn't really have the patience for it. All of a sudden she heard a noise, very slight but still audible in the quiet house. The lights had all been turned off except for a lamp in the living room. She could see the dim glow of the lamp faintly lighting up the walls outside the bedroom door, which was slightly ajar. Very softly she gave the wall a light tap, and heard a soft tap in return. That indicated to her that Stormy had heard the noise also. Now she was alert, her weapon held in a firing position. She didn't want to shoot but would if she had to.

Stormy had heard the noise and then the light tap on the wall. He knew she had heard it also and was letting him know. He stood ever so quietly and gently pulled the closet door almost closed, leaving just enough of a gap to see in the bedroom. From his angle he didn't see the light go out, but his senses were now heightened. He kept his eyes on the bedroom door, waiting for someone to enter, his gun trained in the direction of the door. If it was Rolando, he was taking his time, being very cautious. Time seemed to stand still as he waited. He hoped Dakota was alert and wouldn't let her guard down. He was sure she was waiting like a tiger in the brush, waiting to pounce on its prey. Then he heard it, a slight bump on the baseboard in the hall, as if someone was hugging the wall, slowly feeling their way and accidentally bumping something in the dark.

****

Rolando had driven down the street and didn't see anything that looked out of place. Johnnie had his Explorer parked in the driveway – at least he figured it was his. He still didn't take a chance. He parked a block away in the driveway of a house, turning off his lights as he pulled in. The house was dark, as it should be at this time of the morning, so he felt secure parking there. It wouldn't matter – he wouldn't be parked there very long. He was going to make quick work out of this killing. He knew that Johnnie was married, and he didn't want to harm the woman. If she got in the way, he would hit her with the stun gun, bind her and place her out of the way.

He got out of the car, quietly closing the door, not locking it. If by chance he was chased again, he didn't want to be fumbling with keys. He walked slowly, staying out of the glow of the street lights, scanning both sides of the street. He still didn't see anything out of order, no cars that looked out of place, just nothing. He made the decision to enter the house and crossed the street directly for it. He had his hand on his gun, which was clipped to his waistband, ready to pull it if he had to. Suddenly he was at the side of the garage, in the deep shadows, invisible to anyone that should pass by.

Rolando stood as still as a statue for several minutes, waiting, listening, and carefully watching the street. When he determined he was alone, he turned his attention to the side door of the garage, similar to the one at the judge's house. He hadn't been able to get here earlier and fix the door to his advantage, so he would have to use his knife to work the lock open. Because of the darkness and having to be so quiet, it took him several minutes before he was able to get the door open. Pulling it ever so softly, hoping it wouldn't squeak, he entered the garage. He didn't bother completely closing the door. He walked to the kitchen door. Some people thought that if the garage doors were locked they didn't have to worry about the kitchen door, so Rolando gripped the door knob and slowly turned it, only mildly surprised when it opened. He cracked it just enough to step into the kitchen before closing it, gently but not gently enough. There was a click as the latch closed, softly echoing in the kitchen. Rolando froze, standing in place for a full minute, hoping the noise hadn't been heard by Johnnie or his wife, or a pet he hadn't thought about before now.

When he was sure no one had heard the click of the door latch he crept slowly to the living room where a table lamp was lit. He reached down and pulled the plug, not wanting to turn the switch on the lamp in case it also made a noise. Before the light went out he saw the hallway leading to the bedrooms. He made his way across the living room, slowly, even though there was plush carpet on the floor. The carpet extended into the hallway, for which he was grateful. It would help keep his footfalls muted. He put his hand on one wall and stealthily moved down the hallway towards the two bedrooms. He had no idea which bedroom Johnnie would be in, so he made a choice to go in the first one he came to. Just feet away from the door his shoe bumped into the baseboard, not a loud noise, but just the same, a noise. He stopped, standing silently for a minute, listening for any sound of someone getting up. When he figured it was okay, he resumed his pace to the door.

In front of the door he saw that it was ajar, which was great for him. He wouldn't have to worry about it being locked or worse, making a noise when he opened it. Gently he pushed the door open and entered the room, pulling out his taser at the same time. He approached the bed and saw two shapes under the covers. At that instant he realized that he had been set up – the shapes on the bed were staged. In a split second he turned his head and saw someone coming out of the walk-in closet. Something in their hand extended towards him. He knew instantly that it was a gun and lunged towards the person.

****

Stormy was on pins and needles, watching the door slowly open. Then he watched as someone walked over to the bed, a weapon in their hand, aiming at the shapes under the bed covers. He began to push the door open when the person by the bed turned and saw him. The person lunged at him, at the same time bringing his arm around and aiming something at him.

Stormy yelled, "POLICE, DROP YOUR WEAPON!" And then he was hit with over 50,000 volts of electricity. He immediately dropped to the floor, his weapon falling from his useless hand, no control over his body. He could only lay there and watch as the person stood over him. He was expecting to be shot as he lay there, and there was nothing he could do about it. Instead, the person he now recognized as Rolando, despite the lightened hair and moustache, turned and ran to the door.

As he exited into the hallway, he slammed into Dakota, knocking her to the floor. Thinking fast and knowing that Stormy would be up and after him before he could get to his car, he took out his gun and deliberately aiming at Dakota, fired a round into her leg. Stormy wouldn't chase him now – he'd be too busy helping the detective he had just shot. Rolando knew she was a detective because he had seen her before in the Detective Bureau. She was obviously helping Stormy now.

As Stormy was beginning to come around, he heard the gunshot and then someone moaning. Staggering to his feet, he picked up his weapon from the floor and stumbled to the hallway, not knowing if Dakota had shot Rolando or if she had been shot. Just outside the door he saw her, lying on the floor, blood flowing from her pants leg, writhing in pain. He heard the front door slam shut and knew that Rolando had fled the house.

There was no decision to be made. He had to take care of Dakota. He didn't know if she had been shot in the femoral artery or not, so he whipped off his belt and wrapped it around her leg above the gunshot wound. He tightened it.

Keying his radio, he yelled out, "10-00," which was the signal for officer down. He told them to send an ambulance and to hurry. He didn't have to request additional units, every officer on the road would be responding because of the officer-down signal.

****

Rolando was furious! First it was Leo and now Stormy! He couldn't get a break! They were managing to stay one step ahead of him every time now. He had fled the house after shooting the detective in her leg. He hadn't really wanted to shoot her, but he had to slow

Stormy down, giving him a chance to get away.

As he drove from the area he could once again hear sirens wailing off in the distance. When he would see one coming, he would quickly pull into a driveway or business and turn off his lights, waiting for them to pass. Finally, he was out of Hialeah and heading for Southwest 8th Street.

He needed to get out of sight quickly because he knew that another BOLO would be issued soon, and to all adjacent cities. If they found him on the street there was no telling what they would do. After all, he had seriously injured two police officers, and they wouldn't act too kindly to that.

Soon he was at the rooming house and parked his car in the same spot as before. He jogged to the apartment building and was soon safely inside his room. After pounding the wall with his fist in frustration, he calmed down and stretched out on his bed. He had a lot of thinking to do. And he had to consider using his ace in the hole.

Chapter 15

STORMY PACED BACK AND FORTH in the hospital waiting room. The doctors had been working on Dakota for over an hour now, and he was worried. No one had come out to tell him anything. Captain Paradis had arrived on the scene as they were loading Dakota in the ambulance. Stormy had quickly briefed him on what had transpired, and the Captain told him to go with the ambulance to the hospital and he would take charge of the scene. During the ride, he called Leo and filled him in. Leo asked if he should come to the hospital, but Stormy told him there was nothing he could do at this time. Leo told him he would be in his office if he needed him for anything.

Stormy stopped at the water cooler and was halfway through filling a cup when he saw the doctor in scrubs walking down the hallway towards him. He couldn't read his expression, so he dropped the cup in the trash can and started walking towards the doctor.

"How is she, Doctor?" he asked anxiously.

"She is doing fine," he replied. "The bullet passed through her inner thigh, the fleshy part and didn't hit any major arteries or bone. Other than being pretty sore and limping for a few days, she should recover just fine."

"Thank God, I was worried that it was far worse than that, with all the blood she lost," Stormy said.

"We gave her a transfusion, about two pints of blood, so she'll be fine now," the doctor said.

"She's asking to see you," he said. "It's okay, but don't stay too long. She needs rest now."

"Thanks, Doc, I'll make it short," Stormy said.

Stormy went back into the emergency room and was told that Dakota had been taken to a room on the second floor. After getting the room number, he headed for the bank of elevators, taking one to the second floor. When he walked into her room, he was surprised to see that she was sitting up and on the phone. She quickly hung the phone up and smiled at him.

"I really screwed things up, didn't I?" she asked.

"Not at all, he was just too fast for us. I'm just glad you're alright," Stormy said. "Tell me what you remember." he said.

"I was sitting in the chair and saw the glow of the lamp go out and knew someone was in the house. That's when I tapped the wall to alert you. Then in a minute, or maybe two or three minutes, I heard another noise right outside the door. I waited for him to enter my room, but then I heard you shout at him and knew that he had taken your room instead. I jumped up and ran to the hallway with the intentions of getting the drop on him in your room. I guess he was running out at the same time I was, and we collided in the darkness. I went down to the floor and the next thing I saw was him pulling out a gun and aiming at it at me. I thought I was a goner for sure, but for some reason he shot me in the leg instead."

"Do you think his aim was off, or do you think he deliberately aimed at your leg?" asked Stormy.

"Oh, I was looking right up at him and watched him aim his gun straight at my leg," she said.

"At least he's not trying to *kill* cops yet, only injure them. Maybe he has a conscience after all," Stormy said.

After leaving the hospital, Stormy headed for Miami to meet with Leo. When he arrived the street in front of the building was a mass of reporters with television vans parked up and down the street. Not wanting to deal with overly zealous reporters right now, he entered the parking area in the rear and quickly entered the building. He knew they had a job to do, but he was in no mood to talk with them now. Besides, it was Leo's show, and he was probably putting together a press conference at this minute.

When he exited the elevator, he saw a beehive of activity – detectives going over maps and on computers and Leo talking with Major Aramas. They spotted him walk in and motioned him over.

"I see you were able to make your way through the throng of reporters out front," Leo said.

"I used the back door, avoiding contact with them," Stormy replied.

"I'm sorry about Dakota getting shot," Major Aramas said, with genuine sympathy.

"She'll be fine. The bullet didn't hit anything major," Stormy said, "and thanks for your concern."

"Can you walk us through what went down last night?" asked Leo.

Stormy relayed to them everything from the time they

had parked Dakota's vehicle in the driveway to the visit to the hospital. He expressed his frustration that Rolando had got the drop on him and had gotten away.

"There's one other thing, too," Stormy said.

"What's that?" asked Major Aramas.

"Rolando has dyed his hair and now sports a moustache, so his look is completely different from the photo on the BOLO."

"That may make it harder to spot him now," replied Leo.

"He may just go underground being so close to getting caught, twice now," the Major said.

"Somehow I don't think he's going to. He should have when Leo almost caught him, but he didn't," Stormy said, "It's like he will let nothing stop him from getting to the other jurors."

"At least they're safe now, out of their homes and at locations unknown to Rolando," Leo said, "or do you think we need to post men at the locations where they are?"

"I'll check with the other agencies and see if they can spare some manpower to help us," Major Aramas said.

"Stormy and I will go over everything again and see if we can come up with something," Leo said, as the Major headed to his office.

****

Rolando was starving. He hadn't eaten for a day now and was hesitant to leave the room. But, he had to have food, so he put on a ball cap and left his room. He knew there was a Latin cafe just down the block, so he figured he would make a quick jaunt there, grab some to go food and bring it back to his room.

When he walked out of his room another person was coming out of the room across from his, an older Cuban man, who only gave him a passing glance at first. As he looked at the man, they nodded, and Rolando let him go first, following behind. When they left the building, the Cuban man turned and watched as Rolando walked down the street. He hesitated at first, but then he turned and followed the man, feeling sure he knew him.

When Rolando went into the cafe, the Cuban man, Pablo, walked on past, stopping at the street corner. He stepped back against the building on the corner and leaned against it, looking as if he were waiting for a bus or someone. When Rolando came out of the cafe he glanced at Pablo and saw him looking at him. Worried that he may have been recognized, he turned and walked swiftly back to his room. At the entrance to the building, he glanced back and saw that the man was still leaning against the building. Maybe he was just imagining things. Or was he? He couldn't be sure, so he'd have to keep a closer eye on him.

In his room, Rolando had an idea. He quickly looked around the room for something sharp. He found a thin nail sticking in the wall, probably used once to hold a picture, and pulled it out. He went outside the door, and seeing no one around, he took his gun and using the butt he hammered a small hole in the wooden door, just about eye level. This place was so cheap there wasn't a peep hole in the doors, but now he had one.

He stood for several minutes before he was rewarded with Pablo stepping into view. Pablo opened his door and for a second he stared at Rolando's door. Rolando thought for a minute he was caught looking at him but dismissed the thought when Pablo closed his door. Still, he couldn't get over the ominous feeling that he had been recognized.

Rolando thought for a minute about what to do – leave or stay? On impulse, he softly opened his door and walked over to Pablo's door, pressing his ear against it to see if he could hear anything. What he heard sent chills down his spine. *What were the odds?* he thought.

****

While Stormy and Leo were going over the press release, Stormy's cell rang. Leo laughed at the ringtone, which caused every detective in the room to look up. Seeing that it was Pablo calling, he excused himself and walked over to the elevator door for privacy.

"Hello, Pablo," he answered.

"Stormy, have I got something for you," Pablo said excitedly.

"What is it?"

"I think the cop you're looking for is here," Pablo said.

"Here?" asked Stormy.

"Yes, right here in my building. In fact he's in a room across from mine," Pablo said.

"Are you sure, Pablo, really sure?" Stormy asked with mounting excitement.

"Even with the blond hair and moustache, I recognized him, even followed him to a cafe," Pablo said.

"Pablo, stay in your room and don't make contact with him. He's killed several people already and will not hesitate to kill you if he feels you may have recognized him," Stormy pleaded.

"I'll stay in my room, but I don't think he knows I saw him," Pablo said.

"Okay, just stay in the room. We're on our way," Stormy said, breaking the connection.

"Leo, let's go!" Stormy shouted, startling the others in the room.

Without hesitation Leo ran to the elevator where Stormy was holding the door open. On the ride down to the lobby Stormy told him they would take his car. Going out the back door, they quickly jumped in and drove out the gate.

"I'm assuming you know where Rolando is," Leo stated.

"Yep, and we don't have time to assemble a SWAT team. We're taking him down ourselves," Stormy said with finality.

****

As Rolando held his ear pressed against Pablo's door, he couldn't believe what he was hearing. He clearly heard the man inside say Stormy's name. When he heard the rest of the conversation, he knew that the man inside was none other than Pablo, Stormy's secret informant.

Going back into his room, Rolando packed what few things he had in an overnight bag and went back out of the room. Stopping in the hallway, he decided to take care of something first. Placing the overnight bag on the floor, he walked over to Pablo's door and with his foot raised, he kicked the door in. Pablo had just hung up the phone and was startled when he heard the door crash. He saw Rolando standing there, a cold smile on his face. Then Rolando walked over to Pablo and introduced himself.

"Hello, Pablo. I'm Rolando," he said coldly. "You've been a very nosy man."

Rolando grabbed Pablo, pushed him to the floor and told him to stay there. Then he walked over to the couch and grabbed a cushion. He returned to Pablo and told him, "I'm sorry, but you shouldn't have gotten involved."

He took the cushion and held it on the back of Pablo's head. Pablo began praying out loud, knowing he was about to die. Rolando took out his gun and placed it against the cushion to muffle the shot and then pulled the trigger. Although muffled the gunshot still rang out in the small room. Pablo slumped over on the floor, blood slowly forming a dark pool around his head, his eyes closed. Rolando tossed the cushion back on the couch and left the room. Evidently no one heard the shot or the door being kicked in because there was no one in the hallway. The entire episode had only taken less than a minute.

Rolando left the building and jogged to his car. He was on the run once again and still hungry, not having a chance to eat the food he had just purchased.

****

Stormy drove like a man possessed, the loud roar of the Charger's powerful engine causing some cars to move out of the way. Leo hung on for dear life. With his siren warbling and the blue lights in his grill flashing, he passed cars, ran red lights and at one point when traffic was backed up, he drove down the sidewalk. Leo said nothing.

It seemed as if it took forever for them to reach Pablo's building, but actually only about fifteen minutes had passed. Screeching to a halt in front of the apartment building, Stormy jumped out, followed by Leo, their weapons drawn. They ran into the building, but Stormy suddenly realized he had no idea which apartment was Pablo's. They passed a woman coming out the front door and quickly asked her if she knew what apartment Pablo lived in. Luckily for them she had an infatuation with Pablo and knew exactly which room he was in. She looked fearfully at the weapons in their hands but saw the badges on their belts and knew better than to get in the way.

Running up the stairs they quickly made it to the second floor. Looking at the door numbers they ran down the hall, suddenly seeing the splintered door standing ajar. It was Pablo's room. Stormy became filled with trepidation as to what he was about to see.

Entering the room Stormy saw Pablo, face down on the floor, a pool of blood forming a halo around his head.

"NOOO," he screamed.

He ran over to Pablo and knelt down to take his pulse. Finding none, he stood, shaking in anger, the fury etched on his face. Leo was on his radio calling for EMS as Stormy raised his gun and ran from the room, straight across the hall. He used his shoulder as a battering ram and splintered the door frame. He could see that no one was in the room, but Pablo had told him that Rolando was directly across the hall from him. Looking around the room, he saw that there was nothing there. Rolando had eluded him once again, and he was getting really pissed off.

EMS arrived at the front of the building within three minutes, the siren still dying down as the emergency personnel ran up the stairs.

Stormy stood in the doorway, anguish written on his face as he watched the medics work on Pablo. Suddenly he heard one of the medics say to the other, "I have a pulse, faint but it's there." Stormy felt a huge sigh of relief, but Pablo was still critical. He stood back while they put Pablo on a gurney and carried him down the stairs. He felt Leo's presence behind him and then his hand on his shoulder.

"He may make it, Stormy."

"It's my fault. I shouldn't have put him in this situation," Stormy said.

"Nonsense. How could you have known Rolando would move here?"

"I just feel as if I should have done something, anything," Stormy said.

"Snap out of it. There was nothing you could do, and we have to find that maniac. So let's go," Leo said.

As they were heading to their car, Stormy's phone rang. Glancing at the screen he saw that it was an unknown number and a chill ran down his spine. Somehow he knew it was Rolando calling.

"Stormy, my friend," Rolando said.

"Don't call me your friend, you piece of crap,"

Stormy retorted.

"Now let's not get nasty," replied Rolando.

"Why did you have to shoot him?" asked Stormy, the rage evident in his voice.

"Because he was nosy, and I don't like nosy people," Rolando said, with a humorless laugh.

"You're insane. You don't just go around shooting people for being nosy."

"I understand you've shot a few people in your time, Stormy," Rolando replied, again laughing.

"Don't even begin to compare my actions with what you've done," Stormy said.

"Well, I just wanted to say hi, so I'll be going now," Rolando replied.

"I'm coming for you, Rolando, and I swear to you, the next time there'll be a different outcome."

Before Stormy could say anything else the phone went dead.

The ambulance pulled from the curb, siren wailing, and headed for the hospital. Stormy got in his car along with Leo and followed it. He wanted to be with Pablo since he had no one else in Miami.

"I'm assuming that was Rolando on the phone," Leo said as they pulled out into traffic.

"It was, and it's possible he was out here watching as we arrived," Stormy said.

"Don't you think we should search the area?" asked Leo.

"We'd be wasting our time. He's long gone by now," Stormy replied, "He only called to taunt us."

"Yeah, you're probably right."

When they arrived at the hospital the stretcher bearing Pablo had already been wheeled into the trauma center where doctors were working fast and furiously on Pablo. When a person with a head injury as severe as Pablo's arrived they were usually given top priority, especially a gunshot wound. Stormy could only wait, just as he had earlier with Dakota. Just knowing she was going to be okay gave him a big sense of relief. She was a good partner and a great detective. Now Rolando had made it personal by harming two people he cared about. Leo asked if he wanted something to drink from the cafeteria. Stormy declined and advised him he would wait here, in case the doctor came out.

After about two hours, several cups of water and endless magazines that he couldn't even remember looking at, a doctor in his scrubs walked into the waiting room and called for Detective Storm. Stormy stood and motioned to the doctor as he walked towards him. The doctor had a solemn look on his face, so Stormy prepared for the worst. Leo walked up to join him as the doctor began talking.

"Detective Storm, first let me say how sorry I am about your friend. He's suffered a severe gunshot wound to the back of his head. The bullet passed clean through so there are no fragments in the brain. Luckily for him it was diverted by the skull and only passed through a small area, exiting just above the ear. His hearing in the right ear may be impaired, and there is considerable swelling on the brain. We're going to medically induce him into a coma, so we can remove a part of the skull above the ear. This will keep the swelling from compounding the injury.

It's a very serious injury, and he's not out of the woods yet. There's a fifty percent chance of recovery. That means there is also a fifty percent chance he may not make it. We can only wait. There's nothing you can do at this time. Do you have any questions?" asked the doctor.

"No questions. I just want to be notified of any change, good or bad."

"We'll inform you as soon as there is any news," the doctor said.

Stormy and Leo walked out of the hospital. Stormy had a grim look on his face. "I know it may sound like empty words, but I promise you, Rolando *will* pay for the harm he's brought to Dakota and Pablo," Stormy vowed.

"That doesn't sound like empty words, Stormy, but I will have your back. We'll find him. He can't run forever," Leo replied.

Leo's phone rang, and Stormy listened at the one-sided conversation. After Leo hung up, he told Stormy, "That was Major Aramas. He wants us back in his office as soon as possible. He took care of the news release and had the PIO handle the media. Now he wants us there because he's forming a task force, dedicated solely to finding and apprehending Rolando. Captain Paradis has agreed to send over two of his detectives to assist."

Chapter 16

T HE SQUAD ROOM WAS FILLED with detectives, some from Hialeah, some from Metro-Dade, but most from Miami. Major Aramas took to the podium and the hubbub of noise subsided as he began speaking.

"Gentlemen, each and every one of you are in this room because you have been selected to be part of an extremely important Task Force. When I asked your lieutenants and sergeants to send me their best, you were selected. I want to thank Metro-Dade and Hialeah for participating, and believe me, your assistance is needed.

"For those of you who don't know the full story, it's simple. We have a rogue cop who has killed several people, wounded a Hialeah detective and gravely injured one of our own. His latest shooting was a civilian "friend," of Detective Storm. He's in the hospital in critical condition from an execution-style shot to the head. Felix Gunter, one of ours, was seriously injured, but I'm happy to report that the doctors give him a good chance of a full recovery, although it will be a long healing process. Stormy tells me that Dakota Summers, his partner, is on the mend and should be out of the hospital within a few days.

"This man is extremely dangerous and should be considered armed at all times. I will not take a chance of losing any of my men, nor those in this room. Therefore, I'm making the call to bring him in, dead or alive."

There was an instant buzzing of voices as the detectives reacted to this statement.

"I'm not finished yet. All ten men in this room are now under the command of Lieutenant Dedrick and will report to him and only him. The purpose of the formation of this Task Force is to brainstorm, put your ideas to work and track down this rogue cop. The killing has to stop! Anything that is needed to bring this manhunt to a successful conclusion will be provided. Anything! I want to reiterate, this is not open hunting season on Rolando Fuentes. Every attempt will be made to bring him in alive to answer for his crimes. Deadly force will only be used if necessary. Do I make myself clear?"

Every man in the room said yes, and the Major left the room. Lieutenant Dedrick made his way to the podium and after holding his hand up for silence began to speak.

"Alright men, listen up," he said. "We will divide up into two-man teams. This room will become our command center unless we face a situation where we have to go mobile. Each team will be given a packet containing all of the information we have on Rolando Fuentes. His last known address was where he shot his last victim, on Southwest 8th Street. Somehow I don't think he'll go back to that address, so we need to find out where he is *now*. He knows we're after him and I would like to say he's running scared, but somehow I don't think he's scared at all. That makes him dangerous! Stay on your toes and for

God's sake, don't be a hero. If you find out where he is, I'm ordering you to call for backup before making a move on him. Any phase of your information that may lead to him is to be brought to my attention at once. Now, split up, choose your partners and let's get to work."

It was unspoken that Leo and Stormy would be partners. They watched as the rest of the men in the room paired up. The two Hialeah detectives naturally aliened with each other as did the Metro-Dade detectives. Since Stormy and Leo had been on the case from the beginning, two other teams began gravitating towards them, the questions already forming in their minds.

For the next ninety minutes Stormy and Leo fielded questions, mostly about Rolando and why he was committing these murders, how was he armed and what kind of vehicle was he driving. They were impressed with the revelation of how the meaning of the numbers was discovered and what they meant. It was clear that Stormy and Leo were going to be more of a liaison to the others than Lieutenant Dedrick, only because they had the most knowledge about the case. When Stormy told them about the phone call from Rolando immediately after the shooting of Pablo, they realized just how cold, callous and indifferent to human life Rolando was.

Stormy told them, "If any of you have C.I.'s, use them. Put every ear you can trust to the ground, and sooner or later we'll find him. He can't hide forever with such a massive manhunt going on. As the Lieutenant said before, don't try to be a hero. This guy will not hesitate to take you out. With that final piece of advice imparted, Stormy and Leo left the building.

****

Now that his photo was being televised on every television channel and plastered on the front page of the *Miami Herald* and other newspapers, Rolando was starting to feel trapped. He knew he would have to change his appearance once again since Stormy and Dakota had seen his present disguise. So far there had been no artist renderings on television of his new disguise, but that could change anytime now.

Rolando had driven aimlessly for the past two hours and soon he was in Broward County. He stopped at a gas station just off I-95 to fill up. When he finished, he went inside to pay. He purchased a pack of disposable razors and went into the restroom where he commenced to shave off the moustache. So far that was the only thing he could do for now. Later he would have to change his hair color again, but first he had to find a place to hide out.

He got back on I-95 and drove north, and for no reason got off on Taft Street in Hollywood. He continued east until he reached US 1, on the beach. He turned north, and when he reached Sherman Street, he spotted a rooming house with a vacancy sign out.

He parked the car and walked into the front door. He was greeted by an elderly woman who appeared to be in her eighties at least. Squinting over her glasses, she smiled and asked if he would like a room. Rolando couldn't believe his luck. The lady appeared to have a vision problem, so she probably wouldn't recognize him at all. He asked if he could get a room for a week. He paid cash and signed the register as "Jack Storm."

After chatting with the lady for a few minutes he excused himself and went to the car and retrieved the overnight bag he had packed before fleeing Southwest 8th Street. His intentions were to lay low for awhile, maybe a week, and hope things would calm down some. He would only go out at night and would eat his meals in his room.

That evening he walked down to a local grocery store and picked up a few items, including some hair dye. This time it was medium brown, and he would add a goatee. When he was almost back to the rooming house, he noticed a man standing in the yard of the house next door, smoking a cigar. The man nodded at him as he blew a smoke ring, and he gave a slight nod back. Once in his room he started grinning and couldn't stop. In his research he had obtained photos of all of his victims, always wanting to make sure he had the right person. The man he had seen smoking the cigar was none other than Johnnie Hurst, the elusive jury foreman!

****

"Okay, where do we begin?" Leo asked.

"I don't have a clue. We've had his charge cards tagged, and there's been no activity on them at all. He doesn't stay on the phone long enough to trace the call, and I'm sure he's using burn phones now since there's no answer on his personal cell," Stormy said.

"I'm famished. Let's get something to ear," replied Leo.

They ended up in Hialeah, so Stormy drove down south of 103rd Street to Chico's Cuban Restaurant. They both ordered *arroz con pollo* and after finishing the meal followed it up with a cup of espresso. While they slowly sipped the strong beverage, they discussed the case. They really had nothing to go on, not a clue as to where Rolando was at now. The BOLO's hadn't produced any leads yet, and there wasn't a speck of information on the street according to the informants.

"I'm taking the rest of the day off. I'm too beat to think straight," Stormy said.

"I'm with you. I could use some rest myself," replied Leo.

Stormy drove back to Miami and dropped Leo off. Then he headed to Miami Beach. He hadn't talked with Marie in awhile now, and she was probably getting miffed. She said she understood, but for how long? He could take a nap at her place, and they could go out to eat later in the evening. On his drive to the beach he called the hospital and was told that Pablo was still critical but hanging on. He arrived at Marie's building and pulled through the gate. He saw that her car was in her assigned parking space. He parked in the visitor's space and entered the building, stopping at the call box. After he punched her button, she quickly answered and told him to come on up. She met him at the door even though he had a key and gave him a big hug and kiss.

"I was beginning to think you had forgotten about me," she said with a mock pout.

"Forget *you*? That's not going to ever happen. You can't imagine what the last twenty-four hours have been like!"

Marie insisted he talk about it, even though she never

Earl Underwood

cared for the gruesome details of his work. She listened. When he was done, she just shook her head, not understanding how someone, especially a police officer, could be so cruel. She had never been exposed to that side of humanity, except what she saw in the news. To her it was another world, and she was not a part of it. Stormy knew how she felt about his work and often wondered if she would be able to accept and handle it after they were married.

"You want something to eat or drink?" she asked.

"Leo and I ate something a couple of hours ago, but maybe later. I know you haven't eaten," he replied.

They sat and watched the early news edition on television, listening to the recaps of the ongoing search for Rolando. Stormy finally had enough of it and turned the television off.

"We don't need to watch that. Let's just talk about us," he said, turning to Marie with a smile.

They just sat, enjoying being with each other. Marie talked about her work a little, but sensing that it was boring to Stormy, she soon changed the subject. She suddenly stood and told Stormy to change clothes, that she wanted to go out and get a drink before dinner. Soon they were ready and left the building, driving to a quiet little lounge on the beach. The house band was fairly decent so they nursed their drinks and enjoyed the music until around nine. They left the lounge and found a steakhouse nearby. After their meal they returned to Marie's apartment. She asked Stormy if he was staying the night. He turned, picked her up in his arms and walked to the bedroom.

"I guess that's a yes," she said, a blush appearing on her face.

Stormy just smiled, closed the door and turned off the lights. Within five minutes the only sound in the room was moans of ecstasy.

Chapter 17

ROLANDO HAD A DILEMMA on his hands. He wanted to go next door and take care of Johnnie, but he couldn't. He was sure that Stormy and Leo had made the arrangements for where Johnnie and his wife were staying. They would have moved the remaining jurors for their safety until he was caught. If he killed Johnnie and the body was found, he would have to leave again. They would be all over the area looking for him. There had to be a way, he just needed to think it through first. He couldn't afford to make a mistake now – the heat was getting heavy. On the other hand, were they watching the juror's new locations now? Had he been spotted? Now he was getting worried, wondering if his door was going to come crashing in at any time, his room swarming with cops. Finally, after thinking about it, he turned out his light and left the house through the rear door. He had to see if he could spot any surveillance in the area before he could sleep.

He walked behind the houses, and when he was a block away he turned and walked to the sidewalk. There were several people around, some walking their dogs, some just talking, like neighbors do. He avoided them, not wanting to start a conversation. He had some scouting to do and didn't want to be disturbed. As casual as he could he looked up and down the street for unmarked police cars or people that looked out of place. Seeing nothing that alarmed him, he began to feel more at ease, even walking down the street a little for a better look. He was good at spotting stakeouts, and nothing he saw indicated that there was one on this street. That didn't mean there wasn't someone in the house, just waiting for him to show, like the one in Hialeah. That was too close and was totally unexpected. He would be a lot more cautious when he went to take Johnnie out. But first he had to figure out *how* he was going to do it.

Rolando ducked back between the houses at the end of the street and walked back the way he had come, entering the house by the rear door. No one saw him, and soon he was in his room.

Lying on his bed, his mind raced, trying to find a solution, a way to carry out the execution of Johnnie. He had planned to stay here at least a week until things cooled down, but he would possibly have to move again. He still had plenty of money so that was not a problem. Just finding the right place without detection was the problem. He was still doing some heavy thinking when he fell asleep, still fully clothed.

The next morning he woke up and looking at his watch saw that it was eight o'clock. He showered and changed clothes before heading out the door to get some breakfast. He would use a drive-thru at a fast food restaurant and either eat in the car or come back here. He didn't want to eat inside a restaurant out of fear that someone would recognize him. He opted to take the food back to his room and eat.

Sitting on his bed, he ate the fast food breakfast, not really enjoying it, because he was still in his thinking mode. Frustrated, he finally decided that he would have to do it here and move on when he was done. The window in his room actually afforded him a view of the front of the house where Johnnie was staying. While he was looking out, he saw Johnnie's wife, or at least he assumed it was his wife, leave the house. She got into the gray Volvo parked in the driveway and backed out. Once on the street, she turned and headed in the direction of Sheridan Street.

Rolando couldn't believe his luck! It was possible she was going shopping, and now was the time for him to make his move. Quickly he packed what few clothes he had and slipped his 9-mm into his rear waistband. He was taking no chances on being surprised again. He stashed the roll of duct tape and knife into his front pocket. He put the taser in his back pocket. It caused a bulge because he didn't have on his jogging suit now, just a pair of jeans. No matter, he only had to cross the yard, and he could hold his hand over the pocket if he saw someone.

Picking up his bag, he left the room, hoping that the elderly lady wouldn't be out. If she was, he would tell her he was going to do some laundry. He opened his car door and tossed the bag in the back seat and looked at the house where Johnnie was staying.

Casually strolling up the walkway to the house, he kept watching the street, in case he saw the Volvo returning. He had to work fast. He didn't know how much time he had before the wife returned. With his hand on the taser in his back pocket, he tapped on the front door. Looking through the glass he could see Johnnie arise from a table where he was eating breakfast. When he opened the door, thinking his wife had returned for something, he was surprised to see a stranger standing there. Then he recognized the man from the night before when he was outside smoking his cigar. His wife didn't allow smoking inside the house.

"Can I help you?" he asked.

"I really hate to bother you this early, but my car won't start and I'm already late for work," Rolando began. "I was wondering if I could use your phone to call Triple A. My battery died in my cell."

"Sure, come on in. Would you like a cup of coffee while you wait?" Johnnie asked.

"That would be great. You don't know how much I appreciate your help," Rolando said, entering the front room.

Before Johnnie could show him the phone, it rang. Johnnie answered, and Rolando stood waiting.

"Hello...Oh, hi, Detective Storm, how are you?

When Rolando heard the name Storm, he was startled. He stepped a little closer behind Johnnie, who had turned his back to talk.

"Yes, everything is fine here. How long before you think we can go back home?...Oh, sure you can stop by. I'm just waiting for my wife to return from the bakery...Okay, I'll come out and talk with you, but you can come on in if you like and have some coffee. When my wife returns, we'll have some Danish to go with it," he laughed.

Johnnie hung up the phone and turned to Rolando, almost bumping into him. "That was a detective friend of mine," he explained. "He and his partner are just around the corner and wanted to stop by for a minute. Just go on and use the phone. I'll be back in a moment," he said.

Rolando couldn't believe it. He watched as Johnnie walked out the front door. He saw Stormy's Charger pull into the driveway. When he saw Johnnie walk out to the car, he looked for the back door. He had to get out of there, not only because Stormy was there but he had heard Johnnie say that his wife would be returning any time now.

Slipping out the back door he stood out of sight until he heard the Charger start up. Peeking around the corner of the house, he watched as Stormy drove down the street. He quickly ran to his car, closed the door quietly, started the engine and backed out into the street. He drove away in the opposite direction Stormy had driven.

****

Stormy met with Leo at his office, and they decided to check up on the jurors who had been temporarily relocated. They wanted to assure them that they would soon be able to go back to their houses, although they couldn't provide them with a timeline.

They were on I-95 northbound near the Hollywood exit when Stormy realized that he should call first. Using the number Johnnie had provided, he took out his cell and dialed it. Johnnie answered, and Stormy told him that they were in the area and would like to stop by and say hi. Johnnie said that everything was okay and that he would meet them outside. He offered them coffee, but Stormy said they weren't staying but a minute or so.

When they pulled into the driveway, they saw Johnnie coming out of the door. Stormy thought he saw someone else in the house but wasn't sure. Johnnie's car was gone, but he had told them that his wife had gone to the bakery. Stormy knew she would start bugging them about going home, and he didn't have a definitive answer for her as to when that could happen. So he planned to make the visit very short.

After some pleasantries and being assured he and his wife were doing fine, Stormy bade goodbye to Johnnie and left the house. When they had reached the stop sign at the end of the street, Stormy made a u-turn in the intersection and headed back towards Johnnie's house.

"What are you doing?" asked Leo.

"I thought I saw someone in the house when Johnnie came out. And then, as we were backing out of the driveway, I'm almost positive I saw someone peeking around the edge of his house at us. I just want to put my mind at ease, that's all," Stormy said.

"Oh, okay, I thought you had changed your mind about the Danish and coffee," he laughed.

When they reached the front of Johnnie's house they saw him standing in the front yard, scratching his head. Pulling to the curb Stormy rolled down his window and asked,

"Are you alright, Johnnie?"

"I'm fine. I was just wondering where that young man

went," he said.

"What young man are you talking about?" Stormy asked, suddenly getting a funny feeling.

"Oh, the young fellow that lives next door to me. He came over to use my phone. His car wouldn't start, so he needed to call Triple A. He was in the house when you were here a few minutes ago, but when I went back in he was gone. I guess he went out the back door."

Stormy looked at Leo, both thinking the same thing, *Rolando!* When Stormy had driven to the end of the street and turned around, no one had come in that direction. So if it *was* Rolando, he must have driven in the other direction, towards I-95.

"Quickly, Johnnie. Give me a description of him," Stormy said.

"He was probably in his mid-twenties, brown hair, goatee and mustache. Why?"

"Do you know what kind of car he had, maybe the color, too?" asked Stormy.

"It was an older Chevy, maybe an Impala, green...no, dark green," Johnnie replied.

"When your wife gets back, I want you and her to immediately head for the police station in Hollywood. Don't stop for anyone until you get there and wait for my call. Do you understand?"

"Yes, but why? Who was that guy?" asked Johnnie.

"He may have been the one we told you about, the reason you're here and not at home. Do as I ask please. We have to go after him now."

Stormy sped off down the street, knowing he would have to move fast, also knowing he would have to guess correctly whether the car went east or west on Sheridan Street. If he went west, he was heading for I-95, and there was a good chance they could catch him. If he went east, there was no telling what side streets he would be turning on. When Stormy reached Sheridan Street he took a chance and headed west, towards I-95.

Within minutes he was on I-95 and headed south. He turned on his blues and hit the accelerator, skillfully merging into the heavy morning rush hour traffic. Weaving in and out, some cars having the foresight to move over, he began picking up speed. Leo scanned the traffic ahead, trying to get a glimpse of the Chevy.

****

Rolando was furious, the blood pounding in his head. *It seems like everywhere I turn Stormy's there. I'm sure they didn't know I was at Johnnie's house. There's no way they could have known. It must have been pure coincidence that they showed up this morning.* Another close call but at least now he knew where Johnnie and his wife were living.

He wondered, *What did Johnnie think when he came back into the house and found me gone? He probably thought I had made the phone call and left the back way, not wanting to disturb him out front –* at least that's what he hoped Johnnie thought.

Rolando was driving with the flow of traffic, not wanting to get stopped by a trooper, not now of all times. He had to get back to Miami, lose himself and blend in with the thousands of nameless faces in the area. He decided to pick up a little speed. He looked into his sideview mirror before doing so. Cresting an overpass about a half mile behind him he saw a car with blue lights flashing from the grill, coming on fast.

It can't be! he thought. *For some reason Stormy must have gone back to the house, and Johnnie gave him a description of me and my car. That's the only possible explanation. Or, it could just be an officer responding to a call.*

He couldn't take the chance, so he eased over to the right and took the exit ramp. At the bottom he drove straight across the intersecting street and pulled over on the grass by the ramp that would take him back onto I-95. Watching closely, he soon saw the gray Charger speed past. He realized at once that it was Stormy's car.

I was right – they had evidently gone back to Johnnie's, and now they were after me.

Giving Stormy time to get about a mile further down the road, he then pulled back onto the ramp and headed southbound on I-95 again. He couldn't see Stormy's car ahead of him, but he stayed in the right lane, just in case he had to get off again. He decided to turn off on the Palmetto Expressway and head to Kendall instead of going directly to Miami. He was taking no chances of Stormy spotting him.

Another day, Johnnie, another day!

****

Stormy and Leo drove as fast as the traffic would allow. When they neared Miami, the gridlock began, traffic

216

barely creeping along. They still hadn't spotted Rolando's car and weren't sure he had even come this way. He could have taken Sheridan Street towards the beach. It was a fifty-fifty toss up, and they may have chosen the wrong direction.

Leo had radioed the other detectives on the Task Force, on a dedicated channel, the description of the car. He had advised them to take up locations at as many exits from I-95 in Miami as they could cover.

Soon Stormy was at the end of the road. After exiting, they spotted one of Leo's guys parked by the intersecting street. They pulled over next to him and were advised that no car fitting the description had come their way. After a radio check with the other units, they all stated the same thing. Rolando had slipped through their grasp once again.

Chapter 18

ROLANDO REACHED THE KENDALL AREA and exited onto Kendall Drive. He turned east and continued to drive, having nowhere in particular to go. He needed to think, and his first thought was changing cars. He turned down some side streets and soon saw what he was looking for, a car in someone's driveway with a for-sale sign on the window.

He drove back to Kendall Drive and found a shopping center. He pulled in and parked the car among hundreds of others. It would be awhile before a roving police officer or mall security finally ran a tag check on the abandoned car. Although it wasn't registered in his name, it wouldn't take long for Stormy to find out about the car. He was sure that the description would be on every officer's BOLO sheet by now.

He walked back to the street where he had seen the car for sale. By the time he got to the house he was beginning to sweat. The overnight bag he had retrieved from his car was getting heavy. The house was further away than he had thought.

He rang the doorbell, and almost immediately the door opened. A man in his thirties answered the door and said, "No soliciting in this neighborhood pal!" He had looked at the bag Rolando was carrying and assumed he was selling something.

Rolando replied, "Oh, I'm not soliciting. I'm interested in the car you have for sale."

"I'm sorry, I just thought…"

"No problem, a natural mistake. How much for the car?" Rolando asked.

"I'm asking two thousand but will take an offer if you're interested," the man replied.

Rolando looked at the car – a black Ford, at least eight years old and in rough shape. It was worth nowhere near the asking price, so Rolando played the role and offered twelve hundred. The man thought for a minute and said if he would pay thirteen hundred he had a deal.

Rolando pretended to think it over, asked to hear the engine and was given the keys. He started the car, and it seemed to run smoothly, no miss in the engine, no warning lights on the dash glaring at him. The interior was decent, and it wasn't as rough as he first thought, just dirty on the outside. He agreed to the price, telling the man he would go directly to the nearest tag office and complete the title transfer. The man hesitated at first, not really wanting to have to get dressed and go to the tag agency.

Rolando smiled at him and said, "Really, you don't want to go out in this heat, and I promise I'll take care of it. Besides, you'll have the money, in cash, and I can get started on my trip to the Keys," Rolando said, displaying his most sincere smile. After he counted out the thirteen hundred dollars in one hundred dollar bills, the man thanked him and went back into his house. Rolando was beginning to wonder if the car was even his.

He opened the back door and tossed in his overnight bag. Getting in the front seat he made a big show of looking in the glove box, revving the engine and trying out the wipers, just in case the man was watching. He tried to act as normal as possible. Backing out of the driveway, he continued on down the street, circling the block before heading back to Kendall Drive. The car ran better than he expected, so he felt a little better about getting ripped off on the price. It wasn't really worth any more than eight or nine hundred dollars.

Heading east on Kendall Drive, he glanced at the gas gauge and saw that it was nearly empty. Spotting a Race Trac service station, he pulled in and went inside to pay for twenty dollars worth of gas. Once back on the road he turned on the air conditioner and felt it barely blowing out any cold air. It would have to do for now, so he kept driving, heading east to the Miami area. As he drove in the congested traffic, his mind was racing, trying to figure out where he could find a place to hide out. Then it hit him, he remembered that about a mile east of his houseboat there was a huge freighter, abandoned and waiting for the necessary permits to tow it out to sea. The plans, which had played out on the news for weeks, were to tow it out five miles into the ocean and sink it, creating an artificial reef. As far as he knew, the permits hadn't been issued yet. The holdup was an environmentalist group that had filed an injunction.

Taking a left on Southwest 27th Avenue, he drove north to Southwest 8th Street and then proceeded east until he reached South Miami Avenue. Turning north he drove only a few blocks before he crossed the river. Working his way back west, he soon arrived at Southwest North River Drive, his destination.

Parking his car in front of a rundown bar, he sat and looked at the ship. It was big, ugly and beginning to rust. There was a chain-link fence around the lot in front, the gate locked. He noticed the sign in red and white lettering on the gate warning that it was private property and to stay out. *That could work to my advantage,* he thought. *No one around and a locked gate, how much better could it be.* Now he had to figure out where he could park his car without it being stolen or vandalized. Looking at the bar he had an idea.

Inside the dimly lit bar there were only a couple of old timers, sitting and sipping their beers. The bartender was kind of rugged looking, unshaven and looking bored to tears. Rolando took a stool at the bar, as far from the other two men as he could get. He didn't need for them to start a conversation. He didn't have the time. The bartender strolled down to where he was seated, looking at him with an unreadable expression.

"*Cerveza, Senor?*" He asked.

"Yes, please, and make it very cold," Rolando replied in English, not wanting to get into a long-winded conversation in Spanish with him.

"I never see you here before," said the bartender, in broken English, placing the cold beer in front of him.

"I have a little problem, and maybe you can help me," Rolando started.

"What is the problem?"

"I just went through a divorce and my wife…ex-wife now, was awarded my car as part of the settlement. I need the car for work and don't want her to find it. If I could park it here for a few days, I would be willing to pay you a little something for the trouble," Rolando said.

"I don't need *la policia* bothering me," replied the bartender.

"No...no...they won't be. It's not like that."

"How will you get to work?" he asked.

"I'll probably take a taxi," replied Rolando.

The bartender started wiping down the bar top while he thought. Rolando kept quiet and sipped the beer, waiting patiently. Finally, the bartender came back to him, setting another beer down.

"You pay me twenty dollars a day," he said.

"Hey, I'm a working man, how about ten?" Rolando asked.

"Fifteen, I'm a working man, too," he said.

Rolando smiled and shook the man's hand, in essence consummating the agreement. As he stood, he pulled out forty-five dollars and handed it to the bartender, telling him that was for the first three days. Then he placed a ten-dollar bill on the counter, payment for the two beers and a generous tip. The bartender smiled and nodded, then turned and walked back to the register.

Rolando left the bar and got back into the car. Driving a block further west he came to an Ace Hardware store. Going inside he purchased a small pair of bolt cutters, a Coleman lantern and some fuel. He paid cash and left the store. He drove further, looking for a Wal-mart or K-mart. After driving for a few miles he found one, parked in the lot and went inside. He purchased a blanket, pillow and sleeping bag.

It was now past noon, and he was getting hungry. So he looked for a place to grab some lunch. He spotted a small Cuban cafeteria and went inside, ordering a Cuban sandwich with an iced tea to wash it down. Seeing a rack with several free papers and the *Miami Herald* he took a few of the free ones and paid for the newspaper. Now he needed to find a park, one with lots of shade, and wait for darkness. The reading material would help him kill the time until he was ready to enter the freighter.

Chapter 19

STORMY HAD JUST FINISHED LUNCH with Leo when his phone rang. He answered, and suddenly his ears perked up. It was the doctor calling to advise him that Pablo was awake, the swelling subsiding enough that he was brought out of the coma. He was told that Pablo *would* make it, but it would be a long haul and that he would lose the hearing in his right ear. Other than that he would be up and around in about two weeks. Asking if he could see him, he was told that he could, but only for short periods of time. Pablo would tire out very quickly and needed the rest, so he could only speak with him for ten minutes every few hours.

Stormy told Leo about Pablo's recovery and asked if he wanted to take a ride with him to the hospital. It didn't take long before they were at the hospital, parked and inside the reception area. They were told that the doctor had left instructions for only one visitor at a time to come up, so Stormy left Leo in the waiting room. During the ride up the elevator to the Intensive Care Unit, Stormy felt relief that it wasn't worse than it was.

When he saw Pablo, he hardly recognized him. His head was wrapped in gauze, his face swollen and intravenous tubes hooked to his body. There was the steady beep of the monitoring equipment echoing in the room. He actually looked like death warmed over.

Pablo slowly opened his eyes when he heard Stormy walk into the room. Stormy waited until Pablo's eyes were focused before saying anything.

"You had a close call my friend," Stormy said.

"Yes...I...I...I remember. He shot me," Pablo said through his hoarse voice.

"How did he get in your room?" asked Stormy.

"He...he...kicked in the door while I was on the phone with you."

It was obvious that Pablo wasn't coherent enough to talk now, so Rolando told him to get some rest and that he would be back. Pablo weakly reached out his hand, and Stormy took it. They just looked at each other for a minute before Pablo's eyes closed, and he fell asleep. Gently disengaging his hand Stormy, silently left the room and went back downstairs to the lobby.

"How is he?" Leo asked.

"The doctor said he was recovering, but he looked like hell to me," Stormy replied.

"Getting shot in the head would tend to do that to one," Leo said. "What now?"

"I have a feeling that Rolando feels more comfortable in the Miami area, and I believe that's where we'll find him. So, let's go take a look," Stormy said as he began walking to the door.

For the next two and a half hours they just drove up and down the streets in South Miami, scanning every face, hoping to see Rolando. Finally, their efforts futile, they decided to call it a day. Stormy dropped Leo off at Miami P.D. and headed for North Miami Beach to see Marie.

When he reached the Condo, he saw that Marie was already home. Entering the building, he buzzed her apartment and then went to the elevator, riding to her floor. Inside the apartment Marie had started preparing dinner, in anticipation that Stormy would be coming back tonight.

"Something smells good," he said.

"I decided that we would eat in tonight," she replied. "Take off your shoes and relax. I'll bring you a drink."

Stormy sipped the cold beer while he watched the evening news. The only mention of Rolando was in reference to the ongoing search for him. He heard Marie call out to him that dinner was ready, so he flipped off the television and went to the table.

Marie had prepared spaghetti, a salad and hot garlic rolls. She had even made his favorite cold beverage – green tea. He didn't know just how hungry he was until he smelled the aroma of the meat sauce and garlic rolls. Neither spoke much during the meal, both enjoying their time together, just an occasional look and smile. When the meal was finished, he helped Marie with the dishes, over her protests, and then made the coffee as she loaded the dishwasher.

Sitting on the couch together, they sipped the scalding coffee and made small talk. He asked about her day, and she spent several minutes relating to him how her day went. When it was his turn, he told her about the incident in Hollywood and the chase down I-95. When he stopped talking she asked him what was wrong.

"You remember my confidential informant, Pablo?" he asked.

"Yes, I remember him. What about him?"

"He was shot by Rolando yesterday," he replied.

"Oh, my God. Is he okay?" she asked.

"It was touch and go for a while, but it looks as if he'll make it."

"How did it happen, and how did he know who and where Pablo was?"

"Just an unlucky break it seems. Evidently Rolando rented a room in the same building as Pablo, directly across the hall, not knowing he was there. I'm assuming he overheard Pablo talking with me on the phone, just prior to getting shot, and put two and two together. He shot him in the head, like a dog," Stormy said.

"Don't beat yourself up over it. It was an unlucky break for Pablo," she said.

"I still feel responsible," he said.

"You can't feel that way. You had no way of knowing and neither did Pablo."

"I know. I just feel so frustrated, having been so close twice now, and letting him get away."

"You'll get him. I know you will," she said, giving him a hug.

"I hope it's soon. God only knows how many more people are going to suffer because of him."

****

Darkness had fallen, and there were about a half dozen cars parked at the bar when Rolando returned from the park. He had read all the papers and even taken a short nap. It had been the most peaceful he had been in several weeks.

He parked his car near the rear of the bar, and seeing no one around, he took the materials he had bought and his overnight bag and locked the car. He walked around the rear of the bar and headed across the street to the chain-link fence. A vacant lot adjacent to the fence seemed the prime area for him to make his entry, so he headed there. There were only two lights near the freighter – one a street lamp on the road and the other a single bulb in what appeared to be a storage shed near the front of the gate. He scanned the entire area for cameras but saw none. The freighter sat moored on the river, barely rising with the current, empty and ghostly. The ship itself was pretty much all in shadows, the light on the shed not emitting enough wattage to light it up.

Rolando walked to the edge of the river, following the fence line. When he got to the end, he took out the bolt cutters. He took one last look and didn't see anyone around, although it would have been hard to spot him in the darkness. He cut away at the fence until he had cut an area about five feet up from the ground. Peeling the fence back, he stuck his bag inside, and then he scrambled through. Carefully he placed the cut fence back in place. It wouldn't do for anyone to see it gaped open.

Taking his possessions, he trotted over to the big ship, staying in the shadows. He kneeled down and scanned the area for a night watchman or anyone else in sight. Seeing no one he arose and began looking for the gangway to get up onto the ship. Soon he found it, but there was a chain barring entry and a lock on the door. He stepped over the chain and using the bolt cutters, he cut the lock off. It took some extra effort to open the door because it was sticking or caught on something.

Apparently, no one had been in here for quite some time. Dust covered the floor, and cobwebs were in abundance just inside the doorway. He brushed the cobwebs down and took slow, careful steps into the ship. Complete darkness engulfing him. He took out the Coleman lantern and after pushing the door closed, turned it on, illuminating the interior.

It appeared the entrance he had taken was through the cargo hold, which was cavernous. He could hear his breathing in the deep silence. He searched for stairs that would lead topside. Holding the light in front of him, he soon espied metal stairs on the far side of the hold. He began carefully walking towards them, his steps echoing in the empty bay. All at once he heard a scurrying noise. Looking at the floor, he saw several dozen rats, some as large as his shoe, their beady eyes glowing red in the light, squealing and running away. They were probably water rats, and he hoped they were only in the cargo hold. He didn't want to worry about them biting him as he slept.

When he reached the stairs, he began climbing up, hoping the door up top was not bolted. Reaching the top of the stairs, he saw the door and pushed down on the handle. He was relieved when it sprung open. He was glad to be out of that cargo hold! The rats, the stifling heat, and the musky smell were more than he was willing to deal with.

Stepping into the hallway, he could see another door that led to the outside deck, on the river side of the ship. Just inside that door was another door, which he pushed open. It turned out to be living quarters for some of the long-departed crew. There were bunk beds, a table and two chairs inside. He had no intention of sleeping on the bed, but after further thought decided it wouldn't be a bad idea, in case there were rats up here, too.

The beds were bunk style and he would take the top. After placing his sleeping bag on the top bunk, he walked through the door leading to the outside deck. He pushed it open and quickly turned off his lamp, not wanting anyone to see the glow and call the police. There was a soft breeze blowing off the water so he propped the door open and left the inside door open also, to better cope with the heat.

It was nearing ten o'clock, and Rolando was dead tired. It had been a long and exhausting day, and he was ready for some sleep. He checked the floors of the room and couldn't see any rat droppings. That was a good sign, and he felt better about sleeping here. But he still was planning to sleep on the top bunk, just in case.

He rolled out the sleeping bag he had purchased earlier, fluffed up a pillow and put his gun under it. Climbing to the top bunk he stretched out and let his thoughts run rampant.

He was getting tired of Stormy screwing up his plans. Now he had to seriously think about leaving town for awhile. He could always come back in a few months and finish up what he had started. That's what he would do.

But there was one thing he needed to do now – punish Stormy for foiling the rest of his mission. He hadn't liked Stormy from the day he was paired with him, so now he was going to use his ace in the hole.

Chapter 20

ROLANDO WAS IN A GRUMPY MOOD. He hadn't slept very well on the freighter. The thought of the rats and the heat inside the cabin were enough to keep him on edge. He slept fitfully, tossing and turning all night, waking occasionally when he would hear a noise. He was now parked across the street from the condo where Marie, Stormy's fiancée, resided. He had arisen early, stopping for a sausage and biscuit and a cup of coffee before driving on to North Miami Beach. He planned to follow her and find out where her office was located. He had big plans for her. She just didn't know it yet.

It was seven-thirty, and she hadn't left the building yet. He could see her car still parked in her parking space. While he sipped the lukewarm coffee, he kept an eye out for any patrol cars. He saw only one pass while he sat there. The street was coming alive now with all sorts of people getting into their cars, heading for work or other pleasures. There were several walking down the sidewalk, never even giving him a passing look.

He had just turned his attention back to the condo when he saw her coming out of the building. She got into her car, and he watched as the backup lights came on. She backed out of the parking space and drove out through the gate, giving the guard a cheery wave. He started up his car, and as soon as she was on the street, he pulled out. He followed at a distance. Soon she turned onto the causeway and headed for the mainland. Keeping several cars between him and her, he kept her in sight, watching as she exited onto I-95 South. Traffic was beginning to get heavy, so he sped up and was only one car behind her now. She put on her turn signals and got off at the downtown exit. He continued following her until she reached Brickell Avenue where she turned into a high-rise office complex. He spotted an empty parking space on the street and quickly pulled in.

Rolando walked across the street to the office complex and into the lobby. While he waited for her to come in from the parking garage, he pretended to study the directory. He only hoped there wasn't a rear entrance she would use and bypass the lobby. In the reflection of the glass on the directory he saw her coming around the corner of the elevator bank. He walked over and stood behind several other people waiting for the same elevator. When it arrived, everyone entered, and Rolando worked his way to the back. Marie was standing in front of him, softly laughing and talking with another woman who had gotten on with them. The woman got out on the sixth floor, smiling and telling Marie that she would see her at lunch. The elevator continued with its swift upward climb, stopping at the fifteenth floor, where Marie got off. Rolando stayed in the elevator, and at the next stop he got off, taking another one back down to the lobby.

Now he knew where her office was and the floor it

was on. It never hurt to do one's homework! Now he had to figure out how and where he would snatch her, without getting caught. He couldn't just walk up to her, he was sure Stormy had told her everything. Besides, he was all over the news, and it would be hard for her not to know who he was now. It would take some careful planning, but he was confident he could pull it off.

Tomorrow would be Friday, and unless he wanted to spend three more days in that rat infested stinking freighter, he would have to make his move sometime tomorrow.

Chapter 21

S TORMY WAS ALREADY ON HIS WAY to Miami C.I.D. when his cell rang. Leo was calling to let him know that there was another meeting with the Major and all of the Task Force scheduled for nine o'clock sharp. Stormy told him he was on his way and should be there by eight. As he crossed the causeway, he called the hospital to check on Pablo. He was put through to the nurse's station, and the nurse in charge answered.

"Good morning, this is Detective Storm and I was wondering if you could tell me how Pablo Gondar is doing," Stormy said.

"Good morning, Detective Storm, I just left his room, and he's sitting up and having his first meal since he was brought in. His condition continues to improve. That's all I can tell you for now," the head nurse said.

"That's great news. Thanks so much," Stormy replied. "Could you please tell him I'll be in to see him later today?"

"I'll give him the message, Detective."

"Thanks again. Have a nice day," Stormy said, hanging up the phone.

Stormy pulled into a 7-11 and grabbed a cup of coffee, loading it with vanilla creamer. He couldn't stand the powdered creamer Leo had in his office.

Parking in the rear, he entered the building, telling the desk sergeant good morning. When he was in the squad room, all of the Task Force and Leo were standing around, drinking their coffee. Noticing Stormy's cup, Leo smiled and asked, "Can't handle ours?"

"To be honest, I can't handle the creamer. The coffee is fine," Stormy replied.

At that moment Major Aramas walked in and over to the podium. Everyone in the room took their seats and waited for him to begin. As he started talking, Stormy's phone rang, startling everyone in the room.

"Sorry, Major. I'll take it outside," Stormy said with a slight touch of embarrassment. Normally in meetings such as this, he would have put the phone on vibrate, but he forgot.

Walking outside the room he glanced at the number. He didn't recognize it but answered anyway.

"Hello. Detective Storm"

"Good morning, Stormy," Rolando said.

Not totally shocked, Stormy gritted his teeth, knowing it would be of no use to try to trace the call. Rolando had proven he was no dummy and was probably using a burn phone. He wouldn't stay on the line long enough for a trace anyhow.

"What do you want, Rolando," he asked.

"I'll make it short and sweet for you," Rolando said. "I want to meet with you, and you alone, without Leo or any of the Task Force I know you guys have working on this. If you can't come alone don't bother."

"I'm dying to meet with you," Stormy replied. "Give me a time and place."

"I will, but not now. I'll call you later today and let you know. And remember – alone!"

The connection went dead. Rolando had hung up. He wanted Rolando so bad it hurt, so he decided to keep this conversation to himself for now. He went back into the meeting just as the Major was wrapping up. He only half listened, wondering, *Why does Rolando want to meet with me. He has to know that he'll be arrested. Unless it's a trap! Maybe Rolando wants to kill me like all the others. But why?* He had no choice. He would meet with him but would be prepared to take him down, and down meant one way or another.

When the meeting was finished Leo asked who the call was. Stormy told him it was the hospital letting him know that Pablo was doing better, even sitting up and having a meal. Leo gave him a funny look, as if he knew he was lying. But he said nothing further about it.

"While I was waiting for you I called Hollywood Police and checked on Johnnie," Leo said.

"Crap, I completely forgot about him," Stormy said. "Did he say what he was going to do?"

"Yeah, he has a daughter in Georgia and is already on his way there."

"Did you tell him to stay in touch, so we'll know he's alright?" Stormy asked.

"I did, and he promised he would."

"What did the Major have to say?" asked Stormy.

"Only that he was adding two more detectives to the Task Force and that he wanted us to find Rolando. He can't understand why we haven't gotten more leads."

"The only thing we can do for now is hit the streets again and check out that houseboat again. Maybe there's something there we missed," Stormy said, heading for the elevator.

They drove to the houseboat and after revisiting the crime scene still didn't find anything of value. For the next three hours they drove all over Miami, keeping their eyes peeled, seeing nothing. On Southwest 8th Street they got out on foot and showed the photo to dozens of people, no one had seen him, or if they had they didn't recognize him.

They stopped and grabbed a burger and continued to drive the streets, eating in the car. Just as they were turning onto Bird Road, Stormy's phone rang again. Stormy knew that Leo was smart enough to hear one side of a conversation and come close to putting it together. He could stop and get out of the car to talk, but that would only make Leo more suspicious. He answered the phone.

"Hello," he said.

"You know who this is, so I'll make it short and tell you when and where to meet me. You know the conditions, no cops, only you. By the way, someone wants to speak to you," Rolando said.

"Stormy...don't...,"

The connection was broken, but not before Stormy recognized Marie's voice.

****

Rolando had watched as Marie left her condo, heading

The Cold Smile

to her office. He followed her as he had before but didn't stay behind her for long. He passed her on the causeway and headed for her office. When he arrived, he entered the garage, taking the ticket from the post, allowing the gate to lift. Guests could have their ticket validated at whatever office they were going to. Tenants had a transponder on their car and the gate would rise as they drove up.

There were plenty of parking spaces, so he parked in the nearest one when he entered the garage. He backed in the spot and waited for Marie to show up. He didn't have to wait very long before he saw her pull into the garage. She continued past him going to a higher level to park. He pulled out and followed her, holding back a little until she parked. When he saw that she was pulling into a space, he pulled in next to her, keeping his head turned away from her.

Getting out of the car, Marie opened the rear door of her car and retrieved a briefcase. She closed the door, clicked her key fob, heard the locks engage and began walking around the car. As she passed behind Rolando's car she didn't notice him until out of the corner of her eye she saw him closing in on her. Before she could say or do anything he had used the taser on her. She made a cry of pain and dropped to the floor of the garage. Quickly he put his hands under her arms and half dragged her to the opened rear door of his car.

He picked her up and tossed her into the back seat. Grabbing a pair of handcuffs, he swiftly clamped them on her wrists. Taking a roll of duct tape out of his pocket, he quickly taped her mouth and wrapped her arms and legs securely. Earlier he had taken off the inside door handles in the back.

Closing the door, he got into the driver's seat and backed out of the space, heading out of the garage. The entire act had only taken a little over a minute. Looking in his rearview mirror, he saw her briefcase lying on the garage floor where she had gone down. Another car was coming up the ramp, so he left it, wanting to get out of the garage before someone saw it and figured out what had happened.

The effects of the taser were beginning to wear off and Marie was looking at him with fear-filled eyes. Moaning, she tried to sit up, but Rolando yelled back at her, telling her he would stun her again if she didn't lie still. Rolando continued to drive, heading towards the freighter, wondering how he was going to get her inside without someone seeing him. It wasn't even nine o'clock yet, and there would be too much traffic for him to pull it off. He had wanted to snatch her after she was leaving for the day, but there would have been too many people leaving at the same time, too many witnesses. He would have to find a place where he could keep her out of sight until darkness fell – a secluded place where he wouldn't be seen. He was going to have to get out of the city, somewhere in a rural area, and find a place to hide out until dark.

Soon he was near the freighter, and he remembered seeing a boatyard that had been boarded up about a mile past. He drove slowly by it and saw that there was no fence, just overgrown weeds and a large boat storage building. The huge doors were standing open, and there didn't seem to be anyone there. Taking a chance, he turned in and drove onto the property, driving into the empty building. When he figured the car was far enough inside to be hidden from view of the street he got out and looked around. The place was deserted, not a soul present. It was perfect, if no one showed up. He pulled the car into the far corner of the building. He could see through the door, enabling him to drive away if he saw someone coming in.

It was hot, but the open door allowed some air to circulate, making it bearable. He opened the back door of the car and taking the tape off of Marie's mouth, told her if she made any noise he would put it back on. He then took a bottle of water he had in the front seat and tried to give her some, which she refused.

"I know who you are," Marie said.

"I'm sure you do," responded Rolando.

"What do you want, and why are you doing this to me?" she asked.

"Look, Marie. I know you've been told bad things about me by your boyfriend, and they're all true. I don't want to hurt you so just behave, and you'll soon be free to go," Rolando said.

"You still haven't told me why I'm here, tied up and cuffed like a prisoner."

"I need to talk with Stormy, and the only way I can get him to see me without a hundred police officers around is...well, you know. He'll come alone if he knows I have you."

"You want to hurt him, don't you?" she asked.

"No. Why would I want to do that?" he asked with an icy smile on his face.

"You'll never get away with whatever you're planning. Just let me go and leave while you can," she said.

Laughing, Rolando stood and looked at Marie for a minute, then put the tape back over her mouth. Walking a few steps away he took his burn phone and dialed Stormy's number. In less than fifteen seconds, took the tape off her mouth and put the phone to her ear. When she started talking to Stormy, he only let her speak a couple of words before hanging up the phone.

Chapter 22

L EO WATCHED AS STORMY held the phone, the blood draining from his face, leaving him pale and shaken. Thinking it was bad news about Pablo, Leo laid his hand on Stormy's shoulder and said,

"I'm sorry, man. I know how much you cared about Pablo."

Turning to Leo, Stormy's face changed from shock to rage, the blood rushing back, the veins bulging in his neck.

"It wasn't Pablo, Leo. It was Rolando, and the bastard has Marie."

"What? Are you sure?" Leo asked, stunned.

"He put her on the phone, and she only spoke my name before he hung up," Stormy said.

"But how did he get her? Where is he?" Leo asked.

"I don't know, and he didn't say," Stormy said, panic beginning to creep into his voice.

"What did he want?"

"I'll tell you, but I'll have to trust you to keep it between us. Her *life* will depend on it," Stormy said. "You have to promise me!"

"I promise. What did he want?"

"Remember the phone call I received during the meeting earlier, where I had to leave the room?" asked Stormy.

"Yes. It was him, wasn't it?" Leo asked.

"It was him. I didn't want to say it in the room because he told me that he wanted to meet with me and that under no circumstances was I to bring you or any other cops with me."

"I thought it was more than you were telling me, and I understand your reason for not telling me then. You can't meet him alone. He'll kill you and Marie, and you do know that," Leo said.

"I have no intention of letting him kill me, nor Marie. If he harms one hair on her head, I'll tear him apart – piece by piece," Stormy said with pure venom in his voice.

"Well, I'm not letting you go to him alone. We have to work out a plan," Leo said.

"You don't understand. I have to do this alone. If he suspects for one minute that you're anywhere close, he'll kill her."

"Stormy, we've worked together closely for over a week now. I've come to trust you, and you have my total respect. You're a hell of a detective and if you worked for Miami, I would fight tooth and nail for you as a partner. That said, I'm not about to let you do this alone. We can do it together and finally bring Rolando down," Leo said.

"If we can come up with a plan that won't jeopardize Marie, we go together. If not, I go alone. Understood?" Stormy said.

"Understood. But we can't really plan anything until he calls and tells us where he is," Leo said.

"I don't believe he'll call until its dark. He'll use that to his advantage for sure," Stormy said.

"I agree. So now we have to wait until he calls."

They knew now that Rolando wasn't on the streets, and it would be a waste of time to keep driving and looking for him. The only thing they could do now was to wait for the remaining hours of daylight to pass, as agonizing as it would be. It was killing Stormy that he couldn't do more. He knew Marie was probably scared out of her wits. Rolando now had three strikes against him, shooting Dakota, shooting Pablo and now taking Marie hostage. He was going to pay and pay dearly. It had become very personal now.

He drove around aimlessly and wondered how it was going to play out. If Rolando was in a house, it would be easier for him to use Leo. It would probably be an abandoned house somewhere. In that case there would be no power and therefore no lights. It could work, Leo coming from another direction in the dark. It was frustrating not knowing where Rolando was, making plans for a rescue almost impossible to formulate.

They stopped and ate lunch, Stormy picking at his food, understandably not having much of an appetite. They continued to drive around Miami and Hialeah. Stormy stopped in Hialeah to gas up his car.

"I just came up with a plan to give us some extra time after he calls," Stormy said.

"And that is?" Leo asked.

"We'll park the car in the center of Miami and wait for his call. I'll tell him we're in Hollywood checking on someone. He'll know without me saying, that we're checking on Johnnie, so I think he'll buy it. We'll tell him that we need enough time to get to wherever he tells us he's at. The drive from Hollywood would take at least forty minutes. Allowing us fifteen minutes or so to get to his location, we'll have about twenty-five minutes to scope out the house for any weaknesses," Stormy said.

"Sounds great. We'll definitely need some time to scout the location and that would do it."

With that settled they drove to the central Miami area and parked in a shopping center to wait for nightfall and Rolando's call.

****

Rolando took the tape off of Marie's mouth and loosened her legs, allowing her to sit upright in the back seat. He warned her of what would happen if she made any attempt to get out of the car. He had some fruit and water, so he left it with her in the back seat. She could eat and drink, or not. He didn't really care.

He walked to the open door, staying off to the side to avoid anyone seeing him. As he neared the door, he saw a car turning in, slowly driving across the overgrown, weed-infested driveway. The car had a yellow light bar on top, and he knew immediately that it was a private security car, probably hired to keep check on the property. He took notice that there was only one person in the car.

Rolando was on the verge of panic but quickly composed himself and hurried back to his car. He told Marie to lie down on the seat and not to get up. She wanted to know why, and he told her to do as he asked or someone was getting hurt. Marie lay down on the seat at almost the same time the security car pulled into the building.

The car stopped just inside the door, the driver obviously surprised to see someone inside, much less a car. He kept his engine running and sat there for a minute before cautiously getting out of the car. With his hand on his gun grip, he called out to Rolando.

"This is private property. What are you doing here?"

"I'm sorry, sir. I got evicted from my house and needed somewhere to stay the night. I won't bother anything," Rolando said, with as much humility as he could portray in his voice.

"I'm sorry. You'll have to leave because the owners don't want anyone on the property, for liability purposes of course," the security officer said.

At about that time Marie raised her head, looking out the car window at him, and then ducking back down on the seat.

"Who do you have in the car?" he asked.

"Oh, that's my wife," Rolando said, smiling.

"I'm going to have to see some identification, for my report," the man said.

"No problem. I have it right here," Rolando said, reaching into his back pocket as he walked towards the security officer.

When he reached him Rolando handed him his open wallet, the man reaching out and taking it. He took a clipboard from the dash over the steering wheel and placed it on the hood of his car and began copying down the information. While the man's back was turned Rolando slowly took his taser from his waistband in the rear and shot the man in the back. He dropped like a rock to the floor, writhing in pain. While he was down, Rolando quickly used two plastic ties and bound his wrists together.

Marie had sat up, and she watched as Rolando walked over to the man and then saw him go down to the ground. When Rolando had finished binding the man's wrists, she yelled out to him, "Rolando, don't kill him! He's an innocent man just doing his job."

"I told you to keep quiet," Rolando said.

"I don't want you to hurt him," she pleaded, tears welling up in her eyes.

Rolando just stared at Marie for a minute, trying to make up his mind what to do. He couldn't just let the man go. He would call the police as quickly as he could. He turned and walking over to the man, who was beginning to come around, and taking him by his arms, dragged him further into the building. Then he got into the security car and drove it further inside and off to one side, out of sight of the highway. He lifted the man into the car and sat him in the front seat. Taking another plastic tie he fastened the man's hands to the steering wheel. Taking out a roll of duct tape he tore off a strip and placed it over the man's mouth.

"I plan to be out of here as soon as it gets dark. If you behave yourself, you'll live. If you don't…well, you know what I'll have to do," Rolando told the man. "Nod your head if you understand."

The man quickly nodded his head, fear evident in his eyes. He was supposed to be off tonight but was filling for another guy that called in sick. He could use the extra money, but it wasn't worth dying for. He would do whatever the man asked him to do to survive.

The security officer was a sixty-something year old man, probably working because he had to. Rolando didn't want to kill him, but if he had to, he would. He was too close to wrapping things up, and the security officer was a complication he didn't need.

The security officer watched as Rolando opened the hood and ripped out the wiring that went to the horn. Then the man opened the door and taped his legs together. Rolando walked over and picked up his wallet that had fallen to the ground when he had stunned the security officer. Taking a look outside the door he could see that darkness was finally creeping in. It would soon be time to take Marie to the freighter.

It was now dark enough to make his move. He walked over to the security man and ripped the tape off of his mouth.

"I'm taking the tape off so you can breathe better. After I'm gone you can yell all you want, although I don't think anyone will hear you this far from the road. I'm sure your relief officer will wonder why you're not in and follow the route you guys take and, eventually find you. Consider yourself lucky you're still alive," Rolando said.

Walking back to his car, Rolando opened the back door and put tape on Marie's mouth. This was going to be the tricky part, getting her onto the ship. He would have to take the tape off her legs so she could walk. Even as strong as he was he couldn't carry her through the small opening in the fence and then into the ship. Then there was the stairs to consider. He had no choice but to let her walk when he got to the ship.

After making sure she was lying down he started the car and drove out of the building, not turning his headlights on until he reached the street. Turning onto the street, he headed for the freighter. He knew he couldn't park at the bar. It would be too great a risk walking a bound woman across the highway. He would drive onto the vacant lot and park near the opening he had cut in the fence.

When he arrived he saw that the bar had more cars parked outside than he had seen before. No one was outside, and traffic was light. So he pulled into the vacant lot, and reaching the cut fence, he turned off his headlights. His car was a dark color, so it should be fairly hidden from the road in the darkness, at least he hoped so. Telling Marie to stay down, he got out of the car, and retrieving his bag, he pushed open the fence and tossed it inside. Then he opened the rear door and helped Marie sit up. He didn't take the tape off her mouth. He knew she would scream out for help if she saw anyone. After undoing her legs, he helped her stand, giving her a minute for the stiffness in her legs to loosen up.

He guided her by her arm and lifting the cut fence he gently pushed her through the opening. Once he was inside he pulled the fence back in place. He left his car where it was on purpose, knowing Stormy would home in on it. He wanted to guide him in a way that he could watch from the deck of the ship, hidden in the darkness. It was one way to be sure he had come alone. He didn't think Stormy would take the chance of Marie getting harmed by bringing someone along with him.

He kept his hand on Marie's arm, guiding her in the

dark to the door of the cargo hold. When they reached, it he lifted her over the chain and opened the door. Reaching inside on the floor he picked up the Coleman lantern he had placed on his way out. Closing the door, he led Marie further inside, making sure she didn't fall. It was dark outside, but it was pitch black inside the cargo hold. He turned on the lantern, and once again dozens and dozens of rats, their eyes glowing red, scampered away, running to the darkest corners.

When Marie saw the rats running, she froze. Her one big fear in life was rats and snakes. She was terrified that one of them would get on her and she wouldn't move. Finally, Rolando grabbed her by the arm and roughly forced her to walk across the vast floor towards the stairs. All of a sudden, a rat ran across her foot, brushing against her leg, causing her to freeze again in terror. Rolando laughed and picked her up and carried her across the remainder of the room. He put her down when he reached the stairs.

With her hands bound with the plastic ties it was going to be difficult for her to climb the steep stairs. Rolando told her to take her and time that he would be right behind her in case she stumbled or fell. It was slow going. Marie took each step with deliberate care, leaning against the bulkhead to keep her balance at times. Finally they reached the top and stepped through the door.

Rolando shined the light into the crew's quarters where he had slept the night before. He motioned to her to go inside . When she balked, he pushed her into the room. Sitting her on the lower bunk, he taped her legs again and also her hands to the iron posts of the bunk bed.

Stepping out on the outside deck, he took out his burn phone and dialed Stormy's number.

Chapter 23

THE SHOPPING CENTER WAS BEGINNING to close down for the night. The parking lot was emptying fast as shoppers went home and some employees began to leave. Leo had been dozing for the last hour, and Stormy was finding it hard to stay awake also. He hoped Rolando wasn't playing him and had no intentions of calling. He discarded that thought. Rolando wanted to have it out with him, and he was looking forward to it.

The phone rang, the ringtone sounding extra loud in the quiet car, causing Leo to jerk awake. Stormy let it ring a couple of times and then answered.

"I'm here," he answered.

"I knew you would be," Rolando replied.

"Let's quit playing games. Tell me where to meet you," Stormy said, anger showing in his voice.

"Are you alone like I asked?"

"Yes, I'm alone. Let me speak to Marie," Stormy said.

"I think you've talked to her enough," Rolando laughed.

"I said quit playing games. Let me speak to her, or you can go to hell," Stormy said.

"You'll play my games and like it, because I have

something you want!" Rolando said, his voice now rising in anger. "And this is not a game. Your girlfriend's life is in your hands. I'm holding the cards now, and you will do as I say or *I'll hang up* and you'll never find me or her! Do we understand each other?"

"Alright, alright, just calm down and tell me where to go," Stormy said, realizing he was pushing too hard.

"That's better. Pay attention because I'm only going to say it once. If I see anyone other than you, she's dead. I want you to leave your gun in the car. You're going to strip down to your underwear when you get out of the car, so that I can see you're unarmed. Once I blink a light you can put on your pants and shoes only. Do you understand?" Rolando asked.

"Yes, I understand, but I still want to speak to her and make sure she's still okay, or isn't she?"

"Okay, I'll let her say hi to you, but that's it. Hang on a minute."

Rolando walked back into the crew's quarters and took the tape off Marie's mouth.

"I have your boyfriend on the phone, and he's worried about you. Tell him you're just peachy, please," Rolando said with a smirk on his face. He held the phone to Marie's mouth and waited.

"Stormy, I'm okay...but."

"Now, now, that's enough," Rolando said, taking the phone away from her.

"There you are, Mr. Detective. Satisfied?" he asked.

"Okay, now tell me where to meet you."

"Where are you now?" asked Rolando.

"I'm in Hollywood talking with someone, but as soon

as you called I started heading back to Miami."

"You're lying. I can feel it. Why do you want to lie to me?" Rolando asked.

"I'm not lying, I had to relocate Johnnie, you know, the one you were going to kill until I showed up at his house," Stormy said, hoping he was going to buy it.

Rolando was silent for a minute thinking, *He's probably telling the truth. He would want to relocate Johnnie since I know where he lives.*

"Alright, how long will it take you to get to the Miami River from there?" Rolando asked.

Stormy pretended to be figuring how much time he needed and then answered.

"At least fifty minutes, give or take."

"You have forty, no more, or she's dead," Rolando responded. "And remember, come alone!"

"I'm alone and already on the way, now tell me where on the Miami River?"

Rolando told him where to come, describing the bar across the street and the freighter with the fence around the lot. He told him to drive down the vacant lot and to not shine his lights on the ship. He then told him to tap the horn once and leave the lights on, facing the river. Then he was to get out of the car, strip in front of the headlights and turn his pants pockets inside out.

"After you put your pants back on, look at the fence and you'll see a cut in it. Go through it and follow the waterline of the ship until you get to the door that leads into the cargo hold. Go inside and feel your way across the bay until you reach the stairs. I expect you to come in the door at the top with your hands clasped behind you head. Do you understand?" Rolando asked.

"I'm on my way. I'll be there in forty minutes or less. Count on it!" Stormy said, hanging up the phone.

Turning to Leo he told him where they were going. Leo told him that it was only about ten minutes to the freighter, that he knew where it was. Stormy pulled out of the parking lot of the shopping center and headed towards the river, driving like a man possessed. He used his blues to get around traffic. About a mile from the freighter, he turned them off.

About a block from the freighter he pulled to the side of the road. He and Leo got out and jogged down the side of the road towards the freighter, making sure they were off the road enough to stay out of the glow of headlights coming from cars traveling the street. They had to get near the ship and find a way for Leo to get on without Rolando seeing him.

When they were as close as they dared get to the freighter, they knelt down and studied the ship, looking for an entry point for Leo.

"Were you ever in the circus?" Stormy asked Leo.

"What in the world are you talking about?" Leo asked.

"See that huge chain that is tying the bow to the bank?" Stormy asked.

"Yeah. Wait a minute. You want me to shinny up that chain to get on-board?" he asked.

"You got it, and don't look down."

Leo looked at the chain for a few minutes and, shaking his head, said, "I think I can do it. I just don't know how much noise I'll be making. It looks taut so there shouldn't be any play in it...I don't know, but I think it'll work," Leo said.

"It's our only option, so you have to go for it," Stormy said.

"Okay, times running out, you get back to the car and once I see your headlights by the fence I'll make my move to start climbing. I hope it's not too wet from the night air.

"I think he'll be on the top deck, so make your way up there. And for God's sake, be careful. Oh yeah, there's one other thing, Leo?" Stormy said.

"Yeah, what is it?"

"If you have to shoot, don't try to wing him – just take him out!"

Stormy jogged back to his car, leaving Leo kneeling in the bushes near the freighter. He didn't relish the thought of entering the ship without his weapon, but Rolando had been a step ahead of him on that front. Stripping down was a brilliant idea, he could see from the ship whether Stormy was armed or not.

Looking at his watch he saw that he was approaching the forty-minute mark. He started the car and pulled back onto the street, heading to the vacant lot adjacent to the freighter.

He saw the freighter and the fence in front. He turned in and doing as he was told kept the headlights aimed at the river, not on the ship. He spotted a dark car parked outside the fence, and assumed it was Rolando's. He pulled up between it and the fence, not hindering the view from the freighter. He had no intentions of doing anything different from what Rolando had told him to do. He wasn't going to jeopardize Marie's life by getting cute.

But he wasn't stupid! He wasn't going in unarmed. He had securely taped his weapon on the inside of his pants near the back pocket. He had worried that it would come loose when he took off the pants, but it held.

Tapping the car horn once he left the headlights on and got out of the car. He looked at the freighter, but it was so dark he couldn't see anything but the outline of the ship. Stepping in front of the car, fully illuminated in the glow of the headlights, he slowly undressed, taking his shirt off, then his pants. He made a show of holding the pants up and turning the pockets out, demonstrating the lack of a weapon inside the pants. He put his pants on and walked over to the fence. He found the cut in the fence and pushed it back enough to slide through. Walking quickly, he followed the waterline of the ship and soon came to the chain across the boardwalk leading to the cargo hold. He stepped over the chain and prepared to open the door.

****

Leo stood almost invisible in the shadow of the freighter. He was only a few feet from the huge chain that held the ship in place. They were hoping that Rolando would be watching Stormy so vigilantly that he wouldn't think of looking to the other end of the ship. As soon as he saw Stormy pull up and walk to the front of the car, he began working his way to the seawall where the chain was secured.

He climbed up onto the damp seawall, making sure he had good footing. He looked at the chain and his eyes followed it all the way to the hole in the bow where it fed out. He calculated that he would have to shinny about forty to fifty feet before he could get a decent handhold to climb on-board. He reached out and felt the chain links to determine how wet they were. He was pleasantly surprised that they were barely damp, but he would still have to be sure of his grip. The links were large enough that he was able to put the toe of his shoe inside, although he wouldn't be climbing it like a ladder. He took a good grip and began his ascent, slowly, making sure he had a good strong hold on the chain. Slowly he inched his way up, his belly down on top of the chain.

When he was only about ten feet up the dampness on the chain increased, causing him concern. Disaster almost struck when he made his next move. His toe hold was so wet the leather bottoms of his shoe slipped out of the link. The next thing he knew he was on the bottom of the chain, hanging on for dear life. The fall wouldn't hurt him but the noise would be enough to make Rolando come and check it out. One flashlight beam on him, and he would be a sitting duck.

Leo held his breath while he barely hung on. He knew he would have to climb the rest of the way hanging onto the bottom. It was going to be a test of his strength, and he prayed he would be up to the task. He abandoned the toe holds and wrapped his legs around the chain, beginning to slowly climb upwards, one link at a time. He couldn't afford to rush – one mistake and it was over.

The muscles in his shoulders began to burn from the strain. His hands were very wet now and his grip tenuous at best. He glanced over to where he had last seen Stormy and saw that the headlights were still on, but Stormy was not in view.

It seemed to take forever to reach the handrail on the bow but it actually was only about ten minutes. Carefully reaching out, he grasped the handrail, paused to make sure he had a good hold and then let his legs drop from the chain. Dangling over the side and hanging onto the rail like a man possessed, he was barely able to pull himself up and over onto the deck of the ship. The climb had taken all of his strength, and he was exhausted. But he couldn't rest for long. He dropped down and propped his back against the bulkhead, quickly pulling his weapon out of the holster. He stayed in that position for a full minute, catching his breath, listening for any sign that Rolando was coming his way.

He couldn't hear anything but the water from the river gently slapping against the bottom of the ship and a few cars passing by on the street. Slowly and quietly he stood and began stealthily working his way to the stern of the freighter.

Chapter 24

S TORMY STEPPED OVER the low slung chain in front of the door to the cargo bay. Inching his way to the door, he was mindful of booby traps – he wouldn't put it past Rolando. Slowly pushing the door open, he was faced with the inky blackness of the interior. He hadn't brought a flashlight and would have to find the stairs leading topside completely blind. It was a moonless night, and the open door didn't allow what little light there was to penetrate the darkness of the cargo bay.

He paused inside the doorway, listening for any sound that would point him in the right direction. There was none. He decided that instead of walking blindly in the darkness he would skirt the bulkhead walls, feeling his way until he found the stairway.

Before he started he dropped his pants and retrieved the gun taped to the inside of his back pocket. As he pulled the tape off, the gun slid down the pants' leg, falling to the floor. The noise echoed in the vast empty chamber, causing him to freeze in place for a minute before reaching down and feeling for the gun. The floor was littered with trash and rat droppings, and he quickly wiped his hands on his pants.

With his gun in his right hand he used his left to feel for the wall. Leo suddenly came to mind. He hoped Leo had been able to climb the chain and get on-board without incident. It was a precarious climb and would take a lot of stamina, not to mention strength. Slowly he began to inch his way around the bulkhead, the walls damp to his touch. He couldn't have known that he was going the long way around to the stairs. Suddenly he heard a squeal and something wiggling under his foot. He had stepped on a large rat, probably its foot or tail, because it was still alive. Lifting his foot he allowed it to scurry away. He wasn't afraid of rats and mice, but he would have felt better if he could have seen them. Now, instead of lifting his feet, he would have to slide them instead. Between the noise of his gun hitting the floor and the squealing of the rat, he had no doubt that Rolando heard it too and was waiting for him.

****

Leo had boarded the ship on the land-based side and was pondering which side he should proceed on. His reasoning was Rolando would probably be on the land side so he would be able to see anyone trying to board the ship. His reasoning turned out to be wrong.

Slowly he crept down the deck in the darkness, staying away from the rail, keeping in the shadows. He would stop every few steps, intently listening for any sound that would indicate he was getting close to Rolando. He passed several doors and detected no lights or voices coming from within. He kept walking, ever so stealthily, beginning to see the stern of the freighter outlined in the

262

faint glow of Stormy's headlights.

When he reached the end he was puzzled, *Where was Rolando?* Sidling across the stern, he approached the river side of the ship and began to edge his way back towards the bow.

About halfway down the deck he detected a faint glow of light, softly spilling out of an open door. He inched a few feet closer to the open door, stopping short of it. He kneeled down as he saw someone step out onto the deck. It was Rolando, and as he stepped out he looked away from Leo, down the deck towards the bow. Then he turned and looked towards the stern, in the Leo's direction.

****

It seemed to take forever for Stormy to work his way around the cargo bay. It was very slow going, having to feel his way in the total darkness and avoid the rats that scurried ahead of him. Thankfully none of them had attempted to climb his leg, or worse, bite him. He had passed a couple of closed doors and figured they were entries to the engine room.

Finally he bumped into an object protruding from the wall. Feeling with his hands, he determined it was the stairway. He put his hand on the rail and felt his way to the first step. He paused, considering how he was going to make his approach, *More than likely Rolando will be waiting on the other side of the door at the top of the stairs.* In fact that's exactly where he would be, that's why he had him come in through the cargo bay. Rolando was steering him in the direction he wanted and where *he* would have the biggest advantage.

Stormy stood at the bottom of the stairs, pondering as to how he would proceed. He knew that if he rushed the door, Rolando would begin shooting, more than likely killing him before he could get through the door. If he took his time and slowly opened it, Rolando would still have the advantage. He would just wait for him to enter and still have the drop on him. At this point Rolando was in control of the game, and Stormy couldn't see any other way to get to the upper deck, other than through that one door at the top of the stairs.

Slipping his gun behind his back and into his waistband, he slowly started climbing the stairs, trying to keep his footfalls soft. He wanted to get to the top undetected and see if he could hear any sounds coming from the other side of the door. His main fear was that Rolando had already killed Marie. *But, why would he? Just to get even with me for discovering he was the killer? It doesn't seem likely that Rolando would be egotistical enough to think he could take me alive and then kill Marie in front of me. That isn't going to happen if I could help it.*

Stormy was only three steps from the top when his foot sent several tin cans scattering. The cans clattered down the steps, one at a time and fell into the empty cargo bay. The noise was deafening. His heart began racing. He was expecting the door to fly open at any second and bullets begin slamming into his body.

****

Rolando started to walk in Leo's direction, not spotting him yet in the darkness. He was heading to the stern to look to see if anyone had come to investigate why there were cars parked below, one with the headlights on. As he took his first step he heard the clanging sounds of the tin can trap he had set for Stormy.

Rolando never realized how close he had come to dying at that moment. Leo had slowly raised his gun and began slowly squeezing the trigger as Rolando walked towards him. Leo heard the sound of the cans falling also and watched as Rolando stopped short and whirled around, heading back to the open door. Leo took his finger off the trigger and stood up, letting out the breath he had been holding. He correctly assumed that Rolando had placed an obstacle to announce Stormy's arrival. *That means Stormy is almost there!*

During the few minutes he and Stormy had earlier to make a plan, they decided that the most important thing was getting Marie out safely. It wouldn't do for him to step into the room where Rolando had just gone and start firing his gun. There was no way to know where in the room Marie was, if she was even in the room. Stormy had told him to wait outside until he had entered the room, so that's what he would do, for now.

Chapter 25

ROLANDO HAD MADE SURE he would be alerted to Stormy's arrival. He had found the empty number two cans in the galley down the hall. The idea had come to him in a flash, and he had carefully placed them on the stairs a few steps down from the door.

When he was out on the deck and headed for the ship's stern, he heard the cans clattering down the stairs and knew Stormy was near the door. He turned and rushed back into the room, pulling his gun and positioning himself several feet from the door Stormy was going to enter. Marie still had the tape on her mouth, so she couldn't warn Stormy. Rolando watched as the door slowly open, and as one foot stepped into the hallway.

"That's far enough," Rolando said to Stormy. "Raise your hands and come on in."

"Alright, my hands are in the air. I'm coming in," Stormy replied.

Rolando kept his gun trained on the doorway and watched as Stormy stepped into the hallway, his hands above his head.

"The door on your left, go in it," Rolando said, motioning with his gun.

Stormy walked to the open door and, looking in, saw Marie bound to the bunk beds, tape on her mouth.

"Are you okay?" he asked her.

She couldn't answer but quickly nodded her head. Stormy walked over and put his arms around her, feeling her trembling, seeing the fear and then the relief in her eyes.

"It's okay, honey. I'm here. Everything will be alright," Stormy told her.

"You really believe that, Stormy?" asked Rolando.

"Okay, you have me here, now let her go," Stormy said, not taking his eyes off Rolando.

"Oh, that's not the way it's going to work," Rolando said. "Turn around, get down on your knees and put your hands behind your back."

Stormy was in a panic now. If he turned around Rolando would see the gun in the waistband. He didn't know if Rolando was going to shoot him when he turned around or not.

"Are you such a coward that you have to shoot me in the back?" Stormy asked.

"Don't get macho on me, Detective. I could shoot you now if I wanted," Rolando said. "Just do as I say or I *will* shoot you, in the *leg*. Is that what you want?"

As Stormy resigned himself to obeying Rolando a noise came from outside the door, on the deck.

Leo had listened to the entire conversation and knew he had to take action. He started for the door, his gun up and ready. He had only taken two steps and was almost to the door when he suddenly tripped over an object lying on the deck. In his rush he hadn't seen the object in the

267

darkness. When he fell to the deck, his gun flew from his hand as he tried to break his fall. The gun was just out of his reach, and he began scrambling on his knees to retrieve it.

Rolando heard the noise and whirled around, aiming at the door. *Stormy has brought someone after all and he will pay for it, after I finish off whoever is outside, and it's probably Leo!* Kneeling down, he kept his aim on the door, waiting for someone to show.

Suddenly Leo was in the door, down on his knees also. He was aiming his gun into the room, but the lighting was too dim for him to see anyone at first. Before he could make out Rolando and get off a shot, he saw the flash of a gun and felt the bullet hit him. The pain was excruciating, a hot burning sensation, and the impact caused him to drop his gun as he fell to the deck.

Stormy saw his chance and lunged for Rolando, who was still in a kneeling position. Stormy realized that Leo had been shot, and in a blind rage he dove onto Rolando's back. Rolando held onto his gun and tried to get it around where he could get a shot off, but Stormy was too strong. They struggled on the floor of the cabin and Rolando, in desperation, fought like a madman. He managed to slam Stormy on the side of his head with his weapon, stunning him for a moment.

Jumping up, he ran out onto the deck and headed for the bow of the ship. He didn't know if there were more cops on-board or not, but he was taking no chances.

Stormy saw stars for a second and attempted to grab Rolando by his legs as he jumped up. As soon as he saw him run out the door, he got up and gave chase, at the same time pulling his gun from the waistband of his pants. As he stepped onto the outer deck he took a fast look at Leo and saw that he wasn't moving.

Abandoning his chase for the moment, he went back inside the cabin and using the sights on his weapon, sawed the plastic ties that bound Marie's hands. Taking the tape off her mouth, he told her to tend to Leo while he went after Rolando.

"Let him go, Stormy," she said in panic. "He'll shoot you."

"He had his chance, and now it's my turn," Stormy said. "I'll be fine. Just see what you can do for Leo," he said, running out on the deck.

When he got outside, he quickly knelt down and looked both ways. Rolando wasn't in sight, but he had seen him turn towards the bow. So he carefully began walking that way. There wasn't much cover on the deck because almost everything had been cleared when the ship was stripped for burial at sea. As he crept towards the bow, he hugged the wall, hoping Rolando wouldn't think he was coming this quickly.

Rolando was fleeing for his life. He didn't think Stormy would be coming after him before he took care of Leo. He had seen Leo go down when he shot him and figured he was dead. That would make Stormy a dangerous man, and he had to get off this ship. He was right about one thing, it did make Stormy a dangerous man. But he was wrong about him not coming after him.

When Rolando reached the bow of the ship, he couldn't see a way down. The only way he knew was back in the hallway, down the stairs and out the cargo bay. He couldn't go that way. Stormy was in the room or on his way out. He stepped forward and looked down over the bow, gauging how far down it was if he were to jump into the river. He could barely make out the murky water of the river. He definitely couldn't see if there was any kind of obstacle below that he would land on if he jumped.

In his indecision he turned around to find another option and saw Stormy standing only eight feet from him, his gun pointed at him.

"Drop the weapon," Stormy demanded. "I don't want to shoot you, but I will. And believe me, I'll take pleasure in doing it."

"I've come too far to let you take me in," Rolando said, the panic now gone, his voice almost a whisper, as he slowly began to raise his gun.

"Don't do it, Rolando," Stormy warned.

With a cold smile on his face Rolando swiftly raised his gun and fired a shot at Stormy, the bullet so close Stormy felt it whiz barely inches past his head. At the same time, Stormy, who had already taken aim at center-mass on Rolando, fired one shot, hitting him in the chest.

Rolando stood for a second, a stunned look on his face, a dark circle of blood slowly beginning to widen on his shirt. Exhibiting a slight smile of puzzlement to Stormy, he stumbled backwards and fell over the bow rail, plunging into the Miami River fifty feet below.

Stormy ran to the rail and looked over. He saw the splash as Rolando hit the water and then watched as he sank beneath the dark waters. He waited for several minutes for his body to surface, but Rolando never came back up. He must have gotten caught on some clutter in the bottom of the river. If he wasn't dead from the gunshot, the fall would most certainly have killed him.

Remembering Leo and Marie, Stormy ran back down the deck. When he reached the door, he saw Marie cradling Leo's head in her lap. She had taken her blouse off and wrapped it around his wound in an attempt to stop the bleeding. She sat there in her bra, the night air causing her to shiver. More than likely the shivering was due to shock more than the night air. She had been kidnapped, watched Leo get shot and didn't know if Stormy was coming back.

When he got to her, he knelt down and checked Leo's pulse. He felt a faint heartbeat and breathed a sigh of relief. He had to get Leo to a hospital, and quickly. Rummaging in Leo's pockets he found his cell phone. He had left his in the car because he had to empty out his pockets for Rolando. Leo had insisted on taking his but agreed to turn it off. He didn't want it to ring at the wrong time and alert Rolando.

Stormy quickly turned on the phone and dialed 9-1-1, telling the dispatcher a police officer had been shot and to send an ambulance. He gave her the location where they were and told her to hurry. As the dispatcher tried to get more information he hung up. Then he called Miami C.I.D. and surprisingly someone from the Task Force was in the office this time of night. He quickly explained that Leo had been shot and that Rolando was dead, or at least he thought so. He gave him the location and told him to hurry. The detective told him to hang on, and he would alert the other Task Force teams and they would be there in fifteen minutes.

Within thirty minutes Leo had been loaded into an ambulance and a blanket given to Marie to cover up. The vacant lot was covered with police cars, so many blue lights flashing it lit up the entire ship in an eerie glow. Major Aramas had been called, and he in turn had put in a call to Captain Paradis. They both arrived at nearly the same time.

Stormy spent nearly an hour relating everything from the call Rolando had made to him during the meeting to the moment he had shot him. When he was finished, he asked if he could go to the hospital where Leo had been taken. He was told to go, but to also go home afterwards and clean up. They wanted him at the office in Miami for debriefing as soon as he could get there. There were still plenty of unanswered questions, and at this time only he could provide them.

Taking Marie by the waist he walked her down the stairs and into the cargo bay. C.S.I. had set up portable flood lights in the bay and up top, in order to process the scene. The rats had fled the ship, or found another hiding place. They borrowed an extra C.S.I. shirt from one of the techs for Marie to put on and then got into Stormy's car and headed for the hospital.

After Stormy and Marie had left, Major Aramas put in a call to Metro-Dade, requesting their Marine Patrol send out a boat to search for Rolando's body. He had taken charge of the crime scene because the fallout was going to be huge. The media would be irate that they hadn't been "in the loop," and the Major would have a lot of explaining to do to his Chief. He wasn't worried – everything had been by the book, except for Stormy and Leo coming to the freighter without the Task Force being involved. Of course the Florida Department of Law Enforcement would have to investigate Stormy's shooting, but he didn't see a problem there either. His main concern now was that one of his detectives had been shot, and he didn't know if he was going to make it or not.

Chapter 26

A S STORMY SPED TO THE HOSPITAL, Marie sat quietly in her seat, the shock beginning to wear off. They
didn't talk much but held hands as he drove. He wanted
so desperately to hold her, to comfort her, but the console
between them prohibited it.

Soon they arrived at the hospital and Stormy left his
blues on and parked in the driveway at the emergency
room. He ran around and opened Marie's door, helping
her out of the car. They walked into the emergency room,
and a nurse took Marie back for observation. Stormy
followed, refusing the order to wait outside. The hospital
staff had been expecting her and Stormy because the
Major had called ahead and alerted them.

While the emergency room nurses checked Marie
over, Stormy sought out someone to give him an update
on Leo. The head nurse was just coming through another
door, and Stormy made a beeline towards her.

"I'm Detective Storm, and they just brought in my
partner, Leo Sharp, for a gunshot wound," he said. "Can
you tell me how he is?"

"They just took him in for emergency surgery, Detective Storm. If you'll have a seat, I'll let you know as soon

as I learn anything," she said. "But, it may be awhile, his injury is very serious."

"Thank you. I'll be here until he comes out," Stormy said.

Stormy walked back to the partitioned off area where Marie was being examined. The curtain was pulled shut so he leaned against the wall and waited. She had seemed to be okay, but it wouldn't hurt for her to get checked out.

While he waited his thoughts went to the shootout on the freighter. *I would have taken Rolando alive, but he didn't give me much of a choice. When Rolando fired at me, my instincts took over – self preservation comes first. I thought I wanted to take him alive, but I guess deep down inside I wanted to kill him for hurting so many people, especially those close to me. Pablo didn't deserve to get shot the way he had, down on his knees execution-style. Dakota was only doing her job, and Rolando could have just run away instead of shooting her. She was already down on the floor. Then there's Felix Gunter, Leo's partner. He's in serious condition from a crushed skull at the hands of Rolando. Now Leo! I pray that Leo will survive his injuries. I've come to like and respect Leo, and we work so well together, almost as well as me and Gil.*

Stormy was jolted from his thoughts when he heard the curtain slide open. The doctor who had been examining Marie walked out, a chart in his hand. As he was making a note, Stormy asked him, "Is she okay, Doctor?"

"She's fine, just a little dehydrated, some cuts on her wrists from being bound, but other than that, there's nothing else wrong with her," the doctor replied. "You can go in and be with her if you like," he said, walking away.

Stormy walked into the cubicle. Marie was sitting on the edge of the bed, sipping some water from a straw in a plastic cup. When she saw him enter, she smiled and put down the cup. He stepped up to her and sat on the edge of the bed, putting his arms around her, holding her close. She began to softly cry, clutching at his shirt. He let her get it all out before he said anything. Finally she released him and reached for a tissue on the table, dabbing her eyes.

"How is Leo?" she asked Stormy.

"He's still in surgery," Stormy replied.

"God, honey, I hope he'll be okay," she said, tears beginning to well up again.

"He's tough, sweetie. Don't worry about him. He'll make it," Stormy said.

"It was so awful, that guy Rolando grabbing me, shooting poor Leo…"

"Don't think about it now, just relax and …"

"Did you catch him?" she asked, interrupting Stormy.

"They're looking for his body now," Stormy said.

"Is he dead?"

"I tried to get him to surrender, but he fired his gun at me, and I had to shoot him. He fell overboard into the river," Stormy told her.

"Oh, my God, that's awful. Are you hurt? Did he shoot *you*?" she asked, panic in her voice.

"No, honey. I'm fine, not a scratch on me," he replied.

"He was going to kill us both, wasn't he?" she asked.

"We don't know that for sure, honey, so let's not talk

about it now, okay?" Stormy said.

"Okay, but I'm so hungry. Do you think they have some crackers or something at the desk?" she asked.

"I'll go to the cafeteria and get you something. Lie down and rest until I get back, okay?"

"Okay, but nothing greasy," she said, lying down on the bed.

Stormy went to the cafeteria and bought two turkey sandwiches and two cups of tea for both of them. He hadn't realized it until now, but he was ravenous himself. When he returned to the cubicle, he found Marie sleeping. He sat her sandwich and tea on a table and went out to the nurse's station to see if there was any news on Leo's condition. He had been in surgery for over two hours now. He was told that there was no news yet, but he would be the first to know.

Stormy paced the hallway, eating his sandwich and washing it down with the tea. As he was throwing his trash into a bin, he saw a doctor walk into the room, scrubs and a surgical mask hanging below his chin. Quickly he walked over to him and asked if he was the one that operated on Leo.

"Yes, it took some extensive work but we were able to get the bullet and fragments out. He lost a lot of blood, so he was given transfusions. He's out of surgery now and doing well, considering the damage the bullet did," the doctor said.

"What's his prognosis?" asked Stormy.

"He'll recover fully, but he'll need some rehab on his shoulder," the doctor said.

"When can I see him?"

"Not until in the morning. He's still in recovery and being monitored. He's not fully awake yet, and I don't expect him to be for quite awhile."

"Thanks, Doctor. I really appreciate all you've done for him."

"No thanks needed, and you look as if you could use some rest yourself," he said.

"I know, and I'm going to do just that. Thanks again," Stormy said, turning and heading back to Marie.

When he entered the cubicle, Marie was still asleep, the sandwich untouched. A nurse walked in and asked if he was family. He told her he was her fiancé, that her family hadn't been notified yet. She told him that she had given Marie a sedative earlier and that's why she was so sound asleep. She advised him to let her stay overnight, just to be on the safe side. Stormy agreed, and giving Marie a light kiss on the lips, he left the hospital.

It was almost dawn when he arrived home. He could hardly keep his eyes open. Without taking a shower, he fell across his bed and was instantly asleep.

He awakened at noon and was still half asleep. But he got up and took a shower. As he came back into his bedroom, his phone rang – Marie was calling.

"Hey, sleepy head, time to come and get me out of here," she said.

"I was just getting dressed. I'll be there in thirty or forty minutes. Love you, honey," Stormy replied.

After hanging the phone up, he finished dressing, grabbed a glass of orange juice from the fridge and headed out the door. When he arrived at the hospital, Marie was up and eagerly waiting for him. He needed to get to

Miami C.I.D. but first he was taking Marie home. She needed to shower and change clothes. They would go pick up her car later in the day when Stormy had completed his debriefing.

****

Three weeks passed, and things were getting back to normal, or as normal as they could under the circumstances. Metro-Dade had dragged the river for four days, and no sign of Rolando's body was found. Eventually the recovery effort was called off, the consensus was that his body had either washed out to sea or was pinned down somewhere on the bottom of the murky river.

The remaining jurors who had been relocated for their safety were allowed to return home, to their delight.

Felix was out of the hospital now, but still recovering at home. It would be months before he would be able to return to work. There was even talk that he would take a disability retirement.

Leo was back at work. The rehab worked wonders on his shoulder, and other than a little soreness, he was feeling fine.

Dakota returned to work on light duty, but was being released for full duty status within the week. Her partner, Marty Reynolds, had closed on his new house. He had been offered a job with a large security firm in Coral Gables at a six-figure salary. After considerable deliberation, he decided to accept this position rather than going with the Secret Service. Stormy asked Captain Paradis for Dakota as his new partner, and the request was granted.

The security officer Rolando had left bound at the

abandoned boat house was found safe the following morning by his relief, after retracing his route.

Hector was returned to Raiford to finish out the rest of his sentence, with an additional five years tacked on for the escape. His wife was released from jail after Stormy and Leo declined to press charges.

Stormy and Leo were given the Miami Police Department's Award for Valor for closing the case on the murders.

The date for Stormy and Marie's wedding was set for the following July, and Leo was to be the co-best men, alongside Gil, Stormy's former partner.

True to his promise, Stormy sent Grant Snow a photograph of Marie holding out her hand displaying the diamond ring.

Pablo was released from the hospital ten days after he was admitted. He had lost the hearing in his one ear but was thankful to be alive. Pablo was also given an award, in a private ceremony, in order to keep his identity secret. He continued to be Stormy's informant and would also be at the wedding, in disguise of course.

****

One month after Pablo was released from the hospital, he called Stormy and told him he needed to meet with him as soon as possible. Stormy was curious but didn't ask any questions over the phone. They agreed to meet the following day for lunch, Stormy's treat. Stormy could hear the urgency in Pablo's voice but didn't have a clue as to what he wanted.

The next day at noon, he met with Pablo at Chico's in Hialeah for lunch. They ordered their usual meal and avoided talking shop until they had finished. Pablo ordered a large Cuban coffee to go, and they left the restaurant after Stormy paid the bill. Getting into Stormy's car, they drove to Miami Lakes, at Pablo's request, and pulled into a park. He wanted to be away from any prying ears when he talked with Stormy. Getting out of the car, they walked over to a picnic table under some trees and sat down. Pablo opened his coffee. Stormy's curiosity was totally piqued now.

"Stormy, we've been through a lot together," Pablo started, "and I've given you a lot of valuable information."

"Yes, we have and what you've given me has been invaluable," Stormy replied. "Is this some sort of good-bye?" he asked, dreading the answer.

"Oh, no, I'm not going anywhere. I just want to tell you I've obtained probably the most important piece of information I have ever given you," Pablo said.

"You have my attention, *amigo*," Stormy replied, alert now.

Pablo began talking, and Stormy listened with rapt attention. His eyebrows rose higher with each word, and then the hair stood up on the back of his neck.

"When Rolando fell from the ship after being shot, he landed flat on his back in the river. He broke a few ribs and was knocked unconscious for a few seconds. When he surfaced, he was up against the waterline of the ship. The curvature of the hull had hidden him from view from above. In severe pain he slowly swam around the boat and when he was out of sight of where you were standing on the deck, he swam across the river to the opposite bank. He crawled up and lay there for an hour or more before he was able to get up. He walked for another thirty minutes through an old neighborhood before collapsing on the sidewalk, unable to go any further.

"At the same time he collapsed, an older man, Manuel Soto, was driving past on his way home from work and saw him fall. He stopped and asked Rolando if he was okay, that he would drive him to the hospital if he wanted. Rolando declined, but Manuel wouldn't leave him laying there. Helping him into his car, he took him to his home where he offered him some dry clothing. They were close to the same size, so the pants and shirt fit well.

After giving him some hot liquids, Manuel offered to let him stay at his home until he felt better. Manuel is a personal friend of mine. He is also from Mariel. He has a criminal record but has been straight for many years now. His wife passed away two years ago, and he now lives alone.

"Without telling Manuel who he was, Rolando did tell him the police were after him. Manuel, having been in the same situation years ago, offered to let him stay until he healed and could travel.

"Rolando stayed with Manuel for two weeks. He had been wearing a t-shirt type bullet-proof vest when you shot him. The vest had a flaw, and the bullet happened to hit directly on the flaw, allowing it to penetrate his chest, but only about an inch. Manuel was able to extract the bullet with a pair of long tweezers, and he bandaged the wound. Then he bound Rolando's ribs with tape. Although painful they began to heal.

"Rolando needed to get out of town, so Manuel gave him a ride to the bus station. Rolando had a few thousand dollars left in his pocket and gave Manuel a thousand. He thanked Manuel and boarded the bus.

"It was only two days ago that I ran into Manuel on Southwest 8th Street. Catching up on old times, he told me the story about Rolando. I was astounded when I heard Rolando's name, but I didn't tell Manuel that Rolando was the one who had shot me, in case he was still in touch with Rolando. I asked him if he knew where Rolando had gone on the bus. Manuel told me he knew exactly where he had gone. In fact, he had recommended the city for Rolando to 'get lost' in."

Stormy sat back in disbelief, aware that Rolando's body had never been recovered. Now he knew why. Rolando was still alive!

"Pablo, I need you to give me the name of the city where he went," Stormy said.

"I don't know where he went," Pablo lied. "Manuel wouldn't tell me, and I didn't want to push him so much as to make him suspicious."

"You have to ask him again. We need to know," Stormy pleaded.

"I'll see if I can find him, and I'll get him to tell me," Pablo said, lying again.

Pablo had no intention of telling Stormy where Rolando had gone, he had his own agenda. It was personal to him also, having been shot and left for dead at Rolando's hand.

"As soon as you find out, call me immediately,"

Stormy said. "When you do, I'll contact Leo and let him know so we can make arrangements with the authorities where he's at for an arrest."

"It may take a few days, but I'll find Manuel and ask him again," Pablo said. "But give me a couple of days."

"Okay, I'll be waiting to hear from you."

Chapter 27

I T HAD BEEN OVER THREE MONTHS since he had fled Miami, taking a bus to New Orleans. Rolando was still furious over the debacle in Miami with Stormy and Leo. As far as he knew, they thought he was dead and that's the way he wanted it to stay. He had no plans to return to Miami, the last straw being when he almost died after Stormy shot him. Thank God he had the foresight to wear a bullet-proof vest, even though it didn't hold up as it should have. The flaw almost caused his demise.

Manuel had been a Godsend, tending his wounds, giving him a place to recover and letting him hide out from the police in his house. It was at Manuel's recommendation that he could get lost in New Orleans.

He would have to get a job soon - his money was running low. He still had the stolen credentials and was concerned about using them, but he would have to take a chance for now.

The three months he had been in New Orleans had been wonderful. He didn't have to worry about looking over his shoulder all the time, since he was supposedly a dead man. Yep, life was starting to look good for him, and now he was going to attend his very first Mardi Gras. His apartment was downtown, overlooking Bourbon Street, and he would have a front row seat for the festivities from his balcony.

He had kept in touch with Manuel via phone. He still used a burn phone – one could never be too cautious the way phones were so easily tracked now. He had invited Manuel up for Mardi Gras, telling him he could stay with him. He didn't give Manuel his address, but he did tell him about the great view he had from his place overlooking Bourbon Street. Manuel told him he would let him know, but he hadn't heard from him, so he assumed Manuel wouldn't be coming.

****

Consuelo Alvarez, sitting in first class, handed her empty wine glass to the stewardess. The flight was about to land at the Louis Armstrong New Orleans International Airport, and the buckle-up sign was on. She had left Miami almost two hours earlier and had been lucky to get a room at the Crowne Plaza. During Mardi Gras there usually weren't many rooms available for miles around. Her former lover happened to be the hotel manager for the Crowne in Miami, and he had pulled some strings. She told him she had never been to Mardi Gras and wanted to see it for herself. Thinking it could give him a chance to get back with her, he made the call and was able to book her a room, probably at the expense of someone getting bumped.

After she got off the plane, carrying only one piece of luggage, she walked down Concourse C until she reached the hub. Walking outside, she hailed a taxi and asked him to take her to the Crowne Plaza.

Consuelo had been one of the few female prisoners released during the Mariel boatlift. She had been imprisoned for killing her abusive husband when she was only sixteen. She was still a striking woman at her age now and knew it. She had used it to her advantage more than once. She had processed out in Key West alongside Pablo, and they struck up a friendship, nothing more. But it had endured all these years. Consuelo settled in Miami and after a few years of menial labor, she knew there had to be a better way to earn a living.

Using the skills she learned in prison while in Cuba and her determination to succeed, she became a paid assassin. She had killed her husband, and even though he deserved it, she had never felt emotion or remorse. For a long time it bothered her that she felt no remorse but soon grew to accept it. Her first contract almost turned out to be her last. Luckily she had managed to overcome her victim and finish the job. From that point on, she only grew better and more deadly at her tradecraft. Now, she was in demand and could pick and choose her jobs. Her fee, which was expensive, enabled her to live an above average lifestyle, but she didn't overdo it. The less attention she attracted the better.

Pablo had come to her and told her about Rolando and how he had nearly killed him, execution-style. He told her he had no money to pay her but would be at her disposal whenever she needed him as a form of payment. She had laughed that rich throaty laugh he had loved from the day they met. She told him that she would take care of his problem. There was no need for payment since they had been good friends for far so long.

Pablo had paid a visit to Manuel and in general conversation learned that Rolando was staying on Bourbon Street. But Manuel didn't know the apartment. This information Pablo had relayed to Consuelo, and she said it didn't matter – she would find the address. Pablo had arranged to obtain a photograph of Rolando from Stormy, no questions asked. He gave the photo to Consuelo and a rough physical description.

Although there was a sea of humanity flooding the streets downtown, she spotted Rolando on the second day. He was sitting on a balcony overlooking Bourbon Street, just where she had been told.

That night she returned and stood among the throngs of people flooding the street. She waited for him to come out onto his balcony. A light was on in the apartment, and she felt it was only a matter of time before he came out. She had a small backpack on, the safest way to carry personal items in the crowd. She stood by a lamppost, sipping a margarita. The open container law was a wonderful thing. She warded off several inebriated men attempting to make conversation with her.

Glancing up at the balcony, she saw him come out, a beer in hand. She kept looking up at him until he spotted her watching him. Acting coy and smiling demurely at him, she motioned with her finger, beckoning him to come down and have a drink with her. Rolando smiled back at her and held his hand up, motioning that he would be down in a minute.

When he came out onto the sidewalk, she was waiting

for him on his side of the street. He was a little taller than Pablo had said, but he *was* a good-looking man.

"You looked so lonely up there, I figured you needed some company," she said.

"Actually I enjoy sitting and watching the crowd," Rolando said.

"Well, the view is much better down here," she said, forcing a little blush.

"Now that I'm here, I can see that you're right."

"Let's go get a drink and party some," Consuelo said.

"Actually, I have a better idea," Rolando said, smiling, obviously other things in mind.

"And what would that be?" she asked, giving a little chuckle.

"We could go up to my room and have our own party," he said.

"I don't party with strangers," she laughed.

"I'm Rolando, now I'm not a stranger," he replied, also laughing.

"I'm Consuelo," she said, holding out her hand.

"Pleased to meet you. Now let's go have some fun," he said.

Taking her by the waist, he led her inside the building and up the stairs to his apartment. She took her backpack off and laid it on the floor by the bed. He asked if she wanted something more to drink, and she said a beer would be nice. Pulling two bottles of ice cold beer from the fridge, he took her out onto the balcony where they spent an hour watching the raucous crowd. There were girls flashing guys, almost everyone with a drink in their hand, and the noise so deafening they could hardly hear each other speak. Finally Rolando suggested they go inside and get more comfortable.

As Rolando started to kiss her, she told him to wait a minute while she went to the bathroom and freshened up. Grinning he told her to hurry. She picked up her backpack and went into the bathroom and closed the door. Placing the backpack on the closed toilet seat, she took out a small leather case and opened it. It contained a syringe and a vial of insulin, packed in dry ice. She took the syringe and drew fifty units of insulin from the vial.

Carefully placing everything back in the backpack she undressed, slipped on a short negligee and ran water in the sink for a minute before going back into the room. Rolando was undressed and lying on the bed, a sheet covering the lower half of his torso. Consuelo sat the backpack on the floor, by the bed.

"Come here, good looking," he said.

Taking off the negligee she posed for a minute and then climbed in the bed with Rolando. He wanted to start making love at once, but she held him off, telling him that she didn't want to rush things, that they had all night. While he was kissing her and running his hands over her body, she made the moans and groans he would appreciate. She slowly reached down by the side of the bed and slipped her hand inside the open backpack. Gripping the syringe, she kept his face turned away while she lay on his chest, murmuring sweet nothings.

Consuelo knew what she was doing, having performed it many times before. She started nibbling on Rolando's body, his neck and nipping him with small bites. It was during one of the bites that she inserted the syringe into his buttocks and injected the fifty units of insulin. Rolando felt the slight pinch of the needle but disregarded it, thinking she was still playing rough with him.

Suddenly Rolando started feeling shaky and disoriented and sweat began to break out. Pushing Consuelo off of him, he sat up and told her that he didn't feel too good. She told him it was probably the excitement and the beer and that they would wait for a few minutes for it to wear off. The longer he waited, the more confused and disoriented Rolando became. His blood sugar was dropping at an alarming rate.

When she knew his time was close, she leaned over him and whispered in his ear, "Pablo sends his regards."

Within a minute Rolando lapsed into a diabetic coma, one he would never come out of.

Consuelo dressed quickly, wiped down anything she may have touched and left the room. Making sure there was no one in the hallway, she went down the stairs and joined the street party, slowly working her way to the main street. When she reached it, she caught a taxi back to her hotel. The next morning she was on a flight home – First Class of course – and never thought anything more of her trip. To her, Rolando was a job, and a job well done!

****

The next day the weekly rent was due, and the landlord knocked on Rolando's door. He entered the room after the door opened slightly when he knocked. He saw Rolando, naked, lying on the bed, apparently dead.

The medical examiner never saw the tiny pinprick on his buttocks. He couldn't determine the cause of death, so he ruled it a heart attack. The New Orleans Police conducted an investigation to find out who he was. The name on his identification was checked, and it came back to a dead man in Miami. Raising their suspicion, they ran his fingerprints through the National Database, and his true identity was revealed.

The name Rolando Fuentes was familiar to the detectives of the New Orleans Police Department since they had been following the news a few months ago. They contacted the Miami Police Department and told them what they had.

Leo called Stormy and told him. Leo was astonished that Rolando had been alive and living in New Orleans all this time. The local media ran the story on the front page, but after a few days Rolando became a footnote.

****

A week later Stormy received a phone call from Pablo. When he answered the phone, Pablo asked him, "Did you see the news about Rolando?"

"Yes. Tell me you didn't have anything to do with it," Stormy said.

"Let's just say, this ones on me!" Pablo responded.

AUTHOR

EARL UNDERWOOD WAS BORN AND RAISED in a small town in North Carolina. In 1961, at the age of 20, he and his family moved to Miami, Florida. He served in the United States Army Corps of Engineers from 1964 to 1966 and did a tour of duty in Viet Nam.

Upon returning home, he married Linda Susan Albert and pursued a career in law enforcement. He retired after serving the public for many years. Most of his police career was that of a homicide detective where he received many awards.

After retirement he relocated to Grand Island in Central Florida with his family. Earl enjoys spending time with his four children, Shaunie, Scott, Michael, and Dejah, and his four grandchildren, Victoria, Erica, Zachary, and Mikaella. Family is the most important thing to Earl and his wife Sue.

Earl came out of retirement and served another fourteen years in law enforcement in Central Florida before finally retiring for good in 2003 with a total of almost 32 years. He now spends his time golfing, painting and pursuing his life-long passion of writing.

Earl may be contacted at Underwood914@yahoo.com.

Other Books by Earl Underwood

Austin Steele Space Adventures

Austin Steele's New Life on Xova (**2013**)
The Scourge of Alpha Centauri (**2015**)

Detective Jack Storm Mysteries

The Cold Smile (**2014**)
Sting of the Scorpion (**2016**)

Autobiography

This Is My Story and I'm Sticking to It (**2012**)

The above books are published by Shoppe Foreman
Publishing. For more information go to
www.ShoppeForeman.com/Underwood.
To purchase a book in softcover or e-book
go to www.Amazon.com.

Made in the USA
Columbia, SC
01 May 2020